Sensing that I was on the brink of uncovering a great secret, I asked how the Countess brought about lactation out of season, but the Big-Titted One shook her head.

'I do not know, but some here suggest there is a poison in the bites she regularly delivers to our breasts.'

I was horrified.

'The bites?'

For answer she merely nodded downwards at her own ample globes, and I stooped to examine them. Tenderly though I lifted and parted them, she shivered and whimpered with pain, and I realised they were even fuller of milk than they appeared. I paused, feeling an excited pulse starting in my throat as I looked up from my examination and said, 'You are very swollen. Would you care for me to draw a little off and relieve the congestion?'

By the same author:

DISCIPLINED SKIN
BEAST
PALE PLEASURES
SIX OF THE BEST

VAMP

Wendy Swanscombe

Nexus

This book is a work of fiction.
In real life, make sure you practise safe, sane and consensual sex.

First published in 2003 by
Nexus
Thames Wharf Studios
Rainville Road
London W6 9HA

www.nexus-books.co.uk

Typeset by TW Typesetting, Plymouth, Devon

Printed and bound by
Clays Ltd, St Ives PLC

ISBN 0 352 33848 2

Contents

Not distant far from thence a murmuring sound
Of waters issu'd from a Cave and spread
Into a liquid Plain, then stood unmov'd
Pure as th' expanse of Heav'n; I thither went
With unexperienc't thought, and laid me downe
On the green bank, to look into the cleer
Smooth Lake, that to me seemd another Skie.
As I bent down to look, just opposite,
A Shape within the watry gleam appeard
Bending to look on me, I started back,
It started back, but pleas'd I soon returnd,
Pleas'd it returnd as soon with answering looks
Of sympathie and love; there I had fixt
Mine eyes till now, and pin'd with vain desire,
Had not a voice thus warnd me, What thou seest,
What there thou seest fair Creature is thy self,
With thee it came and goes: but follow me,
And I will bring thee where no shadow staies
Thy coming, and thy soft imbraces, hee
Whose image thou art, him thou shalt enjoy
Inseparablie thine, to him shalt beare
Multitudes like thy self, and thence be call'd
Mother of human Race: what could I doe,
But follow strait, invisibly thus led?
Till I espi'd thee, fair indeed and tall,
Under a Platan, yet methought less faire,
Less winning soft, less amiablie milde,
Then that smooth watry image . . .

John Milton, *Paradise Lost* (1667), Book IV.

The girl went on her knees, and bent over me, simply gloating. There was a deliberate voluptuous-ness which was both thrilling and repulsive, and as she arched her neck she actually licked her lips like an animal, till I could see in the moonlight the moisture shining on the scarlet lips and on the red tongue as it lapped the white sharp teeth.

Bram Stoker, *Dracula* (1897), chapter 3.

Llangoffan
A rare Welsh cheese made from unpasteurised Jersey cows' milk, rich, soft and creamy with a golden yellow crust.

Sandy Carr, *The Simon and Schuster Pocket Guide to Cheese* (1981).

Authoress's note: Readers will find unfamiliar words and phrases (identified on first appearance with an asterisk) defined in a glossary at the rear of the book.

1

Joanna Harker's Journal

3 May. Calais. Left Munich at 8.35 p.m., on 1 May, arriving at Paris early next afternoon. After a short delay while my luggage was hunted out for me I hired a *trăsură* and rode to my hotel. I had forgotten how eerie the solitary hooves of a horse can sound in a day-deserted city, muffled though these were by the triplex curtains I had drawn against the sun, and I must admit that I shivered a little at the thought of the bare, light-drenched streets invisible around me, clean and uncloaked as a skeleton as the trotting echoes volleyed and revolleyed over them. The mood was transitory, however, for I had to resort to my dictionary to discover what I might call a *trăsură* on arrival in Transmarynia. One word is 'carriage', but another is 'fly' and how Mina will laugh when I tell her of it, particularly when she hears that the word started my stomach rumbling, for it means the same as *muscă** and I had not eaten for many hours.

When I arrived at the hotel the day porter, whose dark-rimmed eyes and yawning bespoke a recent as-sumption of her shift, told me that I could have an early breakfast in my room, but I decided to wait the extra hour and dine in the hotel's restaurant, of which I had had great report. It exceeded my expectations for, though the food was no better than I had expected, that

1

is to say, of nigh-on unsurpassable excellence, it provided me with a good portent for the journey that still lies before me, across the sea to Transmarynia.

In a word, one of the wines on offer was a native Transmarynian, but two years over. Mina will forgive me, I am sure, when I describe how my cunt tingled as the wine-list was put into my hand and my eyes fell upon the description of the vintage and the no-less-than-six litres of finest quality yielded in each of the two years of availability. I had to sample some, despite the expense, and, after I had finished a plate of *coléoptères frits au beurre de lait Parisienne**, I ordered it wheeled to me. In France they do not uncork until the wine has arrived at table, but the chalice is bare beneath the white silk flounces of the wrapping and threads of warm musk nevertheless trickle forth as the wine is wheeled into place before – the French wine-barrows all have the newfangled treadles* upon them – being adjusted to the satisfaction of the menopote*. My waitress pumped to the exact height I desired, her lips twitching for a moment at my evident eagerness. The little hydraulic squeaks brought forth by her shining shoe from the treadle were counterpointed by squeaks from the wine-barrows of other diners, and for a few moments a melody seemed incipient – one of those fugues from that Johanna Sebastienne Bach whose genius Mina's German friend Helena has so often urged upon us.

A thread of spittle spilled down my chin as the pumping was complete and the waitress wheeled the barrow the final inch towards me, presenting the white curls of the wrapping almost to my face. I paused to wipe the thread of spittle away with my fresh wine-napkin, savouring the smooth silk against my skin, teasing myself with my own delay, then, fingers trembling, began to fold back the wrapping, drawing the outpouring musk of the chalice deep into my lungs on a single prolonged in-breath and allowing my ears to fill with the soft whisper of opening cloth. The giant nub of the cork appeared between the white flounces and there it was: my first Transmarynian wine. I fear that my first words confirmed the waitress in her diagnosis of my unsophistication – my eagerness as the wine was treadled to height; my thread of spittle; my trembling fingers – for I gaped with surprise and asked, 'She is shaved?'

'*Elle est blonde, mademoiselle,*' the waitress murmured. 'I uncork?'

I nodded, speechless with surprise-turned-excitement, and the nimble fingers of the waitress reached in, took firm grip of the cork and withdrew it with a moist osculatory pop. My first Transmarynian cunt, and a blonde one! The first trickles of blood were creeping between the glistening chelce* cunt-lips, moving down over the *mons Veneris*, running like fingers through the light dusting of pale hair that I had mistaken at first blush for bare skin. And I *was* blushing, glowing with excitement and lust as I gazed upon the sight of this blonde hair, though my stomach curdled a little with the uncanniness of it. It seemed almost a disease, an unnatural bleaching, a mutant albinism against nature and, though I had, of course, read of the condition and of how frequently – comparatively speaking – it is encountered among the Transmarynians, to encounter it here, so unexpectedly, with my head still befuddled from lack of sleep and length of journeying, seized hold of my senses and my intellect in a way I have not known since the earliest nights of my love for Mina. She will forgive me for saying so, I know, for my love is such that I could not bear to conceal anything that is in my heart from her, though I know it may cause her pain.

The waitress murmured something to me and I gaped foolishly at her, noting the ironic curve of her lips and the flicker of a thin eyebrow at the flush on my face.

'*C'est tout, mademoiselle?*'

3

'Uh, yes. It's all.'

She bowed and, murmuring, 'I 'ope mademoiselle 'ave a good menses', withdrew, raising the cork to her nose as she did so with a sniff of carefully calculated volume and *ennui*. Her insolence heightened my excitement, for delicious images of punishing her flashed in on me as I returned my gaze to the leaking cunt before me. The leaking *blonde* cunt. The threads of blood were almost at the *circumcingulum** now, which was a pale metal I recognised after a moment as that new stuff, aluminium. Typical French ostentation. The thought made me smile a little and I reached forward to wipe up the first bead of blood that collected on the *circumcingulum*, wishing the waitress were back to see how steady my finger was. I raised it to my nostrils, closing my eyes, taking the first slow breath, analysing its components, separating tang from musk, decomposing the chord of ammonia, salt and iron as though I were unpicking the threads of a small patch of embroidery or plucking apart the petals of a rose, but then allowing them to fall back together and beat upon my nostrils with a single sour/sweet fist.

Then I allowed my oozing mouth to fall open, dropped the blood-bearing finger between my glistening lips and pressed the bead of menses to my tongue. The squeak of a treadle had begun at the table just behind me – three wines were murmuring, one even crying out for a moment, bird-like, under the tongues and lips of advanced diners – but I was flung beyond all this on a wave of foaming joy: the bead of menses bloomed on my tongue as though the moon had thrust aside a black curtain of cloud and stood forth in all her naked white glory, bleaching aside the very stars. But this was a cupreous moon, a sanguineous orb, blazing with bloody rays, scooping me for a moment outside time and space so that for a moment – Mina forgive me! – I could not have named the one dearest to me in all the world or

4

even recalled the contours of her face and pantherine lustre of her hair.

For a moment only, and then I was back, shivering a little as I pressed the fresh blood-rose of this experience into the white pages of memory. The rose would be crushed between them, flattened from three-dimensionality, paled from rich blood-sowl*, its musk drained and thinned, so that when in future I opened the pages of my memory-book I should find almost nothing of what the reality had been, only a fragile husk. Perhaps it was better so. I leaned forward and greedily, with famished gulosity, began to drink direct from my first Transmarynian cunt. My first *blonde* Transmarynian cunt. I lapped; I sucked; I gnawed, feeling the rich tissues of her inverted cunt-lips fill with excited blood, tumescing to the lip-praise I lavished upon them, the lip-service I paid, and a shifting spot of heat seemed to glow on my chin, marking the thorn of the clitoris that I knew had sprouted between the inverted upper folds of her cunt-chalice. When, finally, I had lapped her cunt clean, I kissed her clitoris delicately in passing, cruelly denying her the release of the orgasm I had begun to tease from the swollen folds of her cunt-lips. Then I lowered my lips and lapping tongue to the half-dried streaks of menstrual blood clotting her silken blonde pubes, leading down, down, to the ring of half-clotted blood in the *circumcingulum*.

But when I had drained this, licking left and right over cool, tasteless aluminium, I raised my head again to her neglected clitoris and sucked slowly, rewarding it for the rich taste that was still filling my mouth and throat and the glow of iron health in my gut. Her clit-thorn had softened; now it grew hard again, aching out at me, and I heard her whimper as I set to work with my teeth, nibbling on her, then sucking hard to soothe, then nibbling again. My nose nudged her open cunt, dilated with delight, and her blood-musk filled my head.

5

She began to squeak, little splinters of expelled breath thrust into my ears, and I felt the muscles of her thighs tightening as orgasm rose into her, or rather fell, from the gorgeous instrument, the bleeding cunt on which I played. An antepenultimate suck, antepenultimate nibble, penultimate suck, penultimate nibble, ultimate suck, ultimate nibble, her squeaks mounting as though she were straining to pierce the cloth that veiled her face and upper body, and then she came, surrendering her orgasm to me as she had surrendered her menses, and I almost tasted, almost chewed the cunt-joy flooding out of her. Her thighs quivered and jerked, spastic with pleasure, and with a final kiss I lifted my face from her, licking for final traces of menstrual blood on my lips and chin as I surveyed the sprawling platter of cunt and inner-thigh now presented to me, licked clean and glistening with spittle.

I signalled for the wine-waitress, who I knew had sardonically observed my sanguicunnilinctus* from a discreet distance. She came forwards, eyebrows arched.

'Mademoiselle?'

'She has fainted.'

'I congratulate mademoiselle.'

'I wish her punished for it.'

'But of course, mademoiselle.'

'Then bring me the punishment list.'

'At once, mademoiselle.'

I wiped at my face with my wine-napkin, noting that the Transmarynian was reawakening. Her thighs trembled, the still-swollen lips of her cunt quivering juicily as fresh blood began to leak between them, almost enough to bring me back and licking at her, but my own cunt was seething too stickily for me to delay. I wanted the privacy of my room, but first I needed the satisfaction of knowing what awaited her, so that I could lay it with my orgasm at the altar of my devotion to Mina. Yes, I wanted to know what awaited her. And what awaited the waitress who slipped sleekly to my side, holding out the discreet black folder of the punishment list. I opened it and scanned the columns, pursing my lips, licking them a little.

'Mademoiselle will order now?'

Mademoiselle sniffed, drawing in a fresh draught of blood-leaking cunt, and nodded slowly.

'I wish her flagellated.'

'*Oui. Flagellée. Avec des . . .?*'

'I think . . . nettles.'

'*Avec des orties brûlantes. Très bon.* And for aftaire?'

'I think . . . electrified nipples.'

'*Oui, une electrification des . . . Ah, non, mademoiselle. C'est impossible.* It is not permeeted for the techniques to be mixed in a single session upon a single individual and –'

I waved my hand dismissively, pushed back my chair and turned towards her a little more to observe the effects of my words.

'It is not for her. *C'est pour toi.*'

Surprise drove those ironic eyebrows – unironic now – up her alabaster forehead.

'*P-pour moi, mademoiselle?*'

'*Mais oui. Certainemente.*'

She blinked, recovering her composure.

'Mademoiselle will 'ave 'er joke. It is not permeeted for employees of –'

I already had my fingers on the Countess's telegram in an inner pocket of my travelling jacket. Now I drew it forth and waved it gently. She stopped speaking and stared at it.

'You will read this,' I said.

She nodded shortly, taking the telegram as I handed it to her. I watched her face, almost able to read the gradations of disbelief, shock, then resignation as each word passed into her head.

Please note that I am a majority shareholder in the Hotel d'Azure in Paris and promise you that any dissatisfaction you experience there will be compensated to the uttermost from the body and nerves of those who are responsible. Show this to the manageress on your arrival and tell her that I answer for her zeal with my fortune. COUNTESS CARADUL.

4 May. Great disappointment on the crossing, for I had nothing but the briefest glimpse of the entrance to the Tunnel as the train rushed between its walls, and Mina had specially asked me to record my impressions. I remember how excited she was by the final nights of the drilling, when the teams working from opposite sides of the Transmarynian Channel were within feet of meeting and all Europe was about to ring with the names of the engineers. Hannah, whose head was then stuffed with the disgusting theories of that Viennese quack Sigmunda Freud, teased Mina that she was excited by a *deeper* symbolism in the event: that the tunnel represented a vagina and the drilling teams and soon-to-come trains a series of – but no, I will not set the word down, for I remember how the nausea rushed into your face, dear Mina, at the very mention of it, and how even Hannah, for once, realised that she had gone too far.

I was almost resolved now to invent a sighting of the Tunnel entrance but I cannot say what was not so, and Mina will have to be content with the handtinted postcard I purchased in Calais, which I will post, if I have the chance, before I arrive at the Countess's castle. I have the card before me as I write and regret almost as keenly as you, dear Mina, that I could not have examined the entrance at close quarters: the outer and inner rims of chelce, sculpted marble arching upwards to meet at a small platform where a chelce-painted guard's hut sits, the carefully tended plot of fragrant lavender that waves above and around the hut on the swelling mound of heaped spoil, and the pipemouth beneath the hut that discharges rainwater in a long stream into the drain between the twin tracks below.

Still, no matter, for on my return I will take the time to attend one of the guided tours and Mina shall have her first-hand account. I smile as I write those words, for I wonder now whether to give her a first-hand account of my final hour in the Hotel D'Azure, when the insolent waitress experienced *me* at first-hand (ha!). No, it is better in a letter than in a journal destined to be read at some remove. In a letter I know Mina will be wanking over the description within the week and, if I take a copy myself and give her an hour in which to wank and a minute on which to come, we can achieve simultaneous orgasm despite the leagues that separate us. Such a sweet thought. Perhaps – yes, the edges are suitable – I will ask her to use the postcard. But no, I should have thought of it earlier, then I could have purchased two and used one myself. Our fingers will be adequate and perhaps she will already have used the postcard by the time the letter reaches her. Yes, if I know my Mina, she will. The stamp will be sufficient to excite her if it is clearly postmarked *Kent*, for she helped me study Transmarynian before my journey and knows its near homonym as well as I. This reminds me of what I did in the hour of the crossing: a final review of my notes on the history and culture of Transmarynia. I shall enter some of them here, as they may refresh my memory when I talk over my travels with Mina.

In the population of Transmarynia there are two distinct nationalities: the Celtic, in the north and west, and the Saxon, in the south. Among the Saxons the land is known as *Anglia* and among the Celts as *Gwlad y llaeth*, which signifies 'Land of Milk', for the inhabitants of Transmarynia have long been famed for the curious ability many of them possess to lactate even before childbirth and even, if the tales are true, without pregnancy. Nor is this precocious lactation confined to the Celts, whom I suppose we must call the natives, for within a short time of the Saxons' arrival, if the chroniclers are to be trusted, they too began to lactate without pregnancy. Mina worried lest I should succumb myself, but I told her I would not be on Transmarynian soil long enough to respond to whatever influence it is in the water or air that explains this strange affliction – if affliction it can be called – now that the treacherous waters of the Transmarynian Channel are byp– no, *under*passed – and the Tunnel enables Transmarynia to export freely her rich girl-cheeses and yoghurts to the mainland. She is now growing rich and the Countess, who has long held shares in the dairy industry, is growing rich with her. Myself, like Mina, I do not care particularly for cheese or yoghurt, but I am looking forward particularly to sampling the wines of Transmarynia, which must, like those of all regions, be sampled at source. But even here Transmarynia is distinct, so it is said, from the rest of the world, for there are said to be Transmarynians who shed not sowl wine but white. I cannot explain the tales myself, unless there is some ignorant confusion with leucorrhoea or some symbolic identification of the Transmarynian cunt with the Transmarynian breasts. (*Mem.*, I must ask the Countess all about it.)

All this I reviewed as I sped beneath the stormy waters of the Channel, though the journey was not so dramatic as might be supposed. Indeed, not dramatic at all, for every minute is like the first and it is only if one visualises the weight of stone and water above one's head that one experiences a little excitement. The Tunnel *is* the ninth wonder of the world, but one recognises this with one's head, barely at all with one's heart. Perhaps I should not say this, for I know it will disappoint dear Mina, but I am resolved to conceal nothing of what I feel and frankly the crossing 'left me warm', as the Anglish expression has it. Surprisingly, my arrival in Oxford did not ameliorate my warmth. No mist, dear Mina! I had expected to step on to a platform swept by wraiths of funereal white and to see nothing of the landscape as the train emerged from the Tunnel and sped the miles to Oxford. On the contrary the air was perfectly clear and with the moon nearly full I clearly saw the beginnings of the great Transmarynian forest that stretches uninterrupted, save for the clearings of their towns and cities, to the sea lapping the shores of the far Celtic north and west. But by the forest I was disappointed again, for a forest viewed from the windows of a train, unless the train achieves some elevation, is merely a succession of close-ranked trees and I quickly fell asleep, waking I knew not how long later, though the moon had set, as the train slid into the station at Oxford (I had apparently slept right through the stop – no, two stops – at London).

On disentraining, absurdly proud of my mastery of the language, I ordered a 'fly' to take me to my lodgings, but I discovered that one was already waiting for me; the Countess had written to the innkeeperess with careful instructions for my arrival. Indeed, a meal was already waiting for me when I arrived, kept cool in covered dishes on a table that puzzled me a little: it was round and of dark, polished wood carved with runnels, shallow near the circumference but deepening as they ran inwards to end at a central hole. There were also odd iron brackets hanging at intervals around the edge of this table, but despite my curiosity I could not spare much attention to it, for three young maids were waiting with the innkeeperess, among whom, beside my second blonde, was my first sowlhead*. Imagine my excitement, dear Mina, when I discovered why exactly the innkeeperess, sparing no expense or trouble, had ordered her and the two others' attendance at the breaking of my fast. She, and they, were nothing less than solid, fleshly confirmation of those beautiful Celtic vocables *Gwlad y llaeth*: young women whose virgin breasts are full of sweet, cool milk. I was, as I say, uncertain of why they were standing at the table when the innkeeperess and her twaughter* bowed me into my chair, and I told her that I would need but one to attend me (I had fixed already on the slender sowlhead and could barely keep my eyes from her hair and 'milky' skin). The inn-keeperess, with a laugh in which I detected an odd note almost of fear, told me that they were not there to attend me but to provide part of my meal.

'The food has been waiting for some time, your ladyship,' she began in charmingly accented Romanian, 'and may be a little dried. They are here to moisten it for you. With milk.'

'But surely one would be enough to pour? And I see no jug on the table.'

'Ah, no, your ladyship. You mistake my meaning. They will provide the milk themselves. They are *milk-maids*, your ladyship, which is to signify –'

But I interrupted her with a laugh of my own (though mine was of sheer delight), and gazed upon the smooth faces of the three young women with a greedy smile before turning to look again at the innkeeperess.

'The milkmaids of Transmarynia are famed far beyond your shores, hostess, though there are many who do not credit them, or believe that any woman could lactate freely before parturition.'

The innkeeperess smiled herself, seeming to lose a little of her nervousness, and, nodding to the girls, said, 'The proof, as we say, is in the pulling. Gwendolyn here' – a darkly smouldering Juno – 'and Beth' – the slender sowlhead – 'and Anna' – the petite blonde – 'there's not one of them is above eighteen. Is that not so, girls?'

The three girls, stepping forward to press their hips to the edge of the table, chorused, 'Yes, mistress.' The twaughter now moved up behind them, reaching for-

12

ward and around their bodies to swing up the iron restraints attached to the edge of the table ('handcuffs'? I shall check in my dictionary) and slipping the unresisting hands of the three girls into them. The handcuffs (yes) snapped shut like hungry little iron mouths, and when all three were fastened to the table the twaughter began to unfasten their blouses. I had been watching the face of the innkeeperess, which had flickered nervously at each fastening snap, but the opening of the blouses dragged my attention swiftly away, as you can imagine, dear Mina. How I wish you had been there to share it with me! Cords slithered loose, whispering in the sudden silence, and one by one the blouses were tugged apart to reveal, still in half-shadow, the firm breasts within. Smiling, the twaughter reached around and through the open gap and, pair by pair, levered them up and out for my inspection. My mouth dried and pulses hammered in my throat as I gazed upon the three pairs, the six breasts, so ripe, so firm and pliant, with the chelce, puffy nipples from which beads of milk were already beginning to trickle. The innkeeperess reached out for darkhaired Gwendolyn, who was standing nearest her, took hold of the nearer breast and carefully squeezed a nipple. A jet of milk sprang forth, splashing on the shining wooden surface of the table, and Gwendolyn moaned softly with pain. The innkeeperess clucked with satisfaction and released the breast, before turning back to me.

'They have all gone unmilked these past few nights, ever since we got the Countess's final instructions, and they have waited your coming, as you can imagine, with some eagerness. Such a load is an agony to carry, as I know myself, for I began work in this very hostelry as a milkmaid myself, nigh on thirty years ago tonight.'

'So long?' I murmured flatteringly, though not so very insincerely, for the innkeeperess was a ripe, well-fleshed woman of what seemed to me no more than forty or forty-five summers, and I should have been very glad to see her own blouse unfastened and udders on display, that I might compare them with the udders of her twaughter, who might almost have been her true twin. Indeed, from the manner in which their four breasts quivered as the innkeeperess and her twaughter bent forwards over the table and began to lift the covers off the dishes that awaited me, I could see the elder woman's had lost little, if any, of their youthful firmness and amplitude. I was almost tempted to try how far the Countess's writ ran by asking the innkeeperess to unveil them to me that I might indeed conduct the comparison with those of her twaughter. But it would have been an abuse of my privileged position and doubtless have humiliated her in front of the milkmaids, so I decided to wait until I got her alone. Later in my room, perhaps, as an appetiser before I composed the letter to Mina in which I would describe the punishment of the insolent waitress in Paris and give careful instructions for the hour at which the description must be read and the minute at which Mina must achieve orgasm. Yes, later in my room; for now I had more than enough: three pairs of firm young breasts, swollen with the milk and pain of prolonged unmilking.

'There, my ladyship,' the innkeeperess said (I watched a final shudder in her tits as she straightened from the table, leaving one dish still lidded). 'We will leave you now, though do not hesitate to ring if you require service. My twaughter will be with you in a twinkling, as we say. I trust you will enjoy your meal.'

'And my proof?' I asked her with a smile.

'Your proof, my ladyship?'

'My proof in the pulling?'

'Oh, yes. Certainly, my ladyship. Your proof will be in the pulling. Pull them as cruelly as you like.' I noticed slender sowlhead Beth swallow apprehensively at this. 'They are sluts, all three, and I was delighted to receive

14

the Countess's letter and refuse them this week's milking. As we also say, the surest training is through paining. Pain them well, your ladyship.'

'I will, I promise you.'

She nodded silently and she and her twaughter bowed themselves out, closing the door softly as they went and leaving me alone in my room with the three handcuffed young milkmaids. My first action, as you can easily guess, was to rise from my seat and examine what was on offer. Were they truly virgin maids? Were they truly eighteen years of age, truly five years at least from the first possible nights of pregnancy? It seemed so: Gwendolyn blushed deeply but defiantly as I stooped a little and, still gazing at the eyes that gazed into mine, flipped the hem of her dress, slid my hand beneath and rummaged upwards between her smooth thighs for her knickers and the cunt concealed within. My fingers slipped under cloth; stroked; probed; and an undoubted maidenhead met their probing. Even the growth of her silken pubes was scanty.

Murmuring with gratified curiosity, I turned my attention and fingers to apprehensive Beth, whose eyes could not sustain my gaze as I stooped to flip her hem and probe her cunt. It was moister, more inflamed – my fingers seemed to know it before they even touched and began to stroke and probe, discovering a second undoubted maidenhead between swollen cunt-lips. Murmuring again, I withdrew my hand, its fingertips a little stickier now, and turned to Anna, the blonde. She too blushed deeply as I flipped her hem and probed her cunt, but her eyes did not fall or flicker from mine as I rummaged to discover – could I have doubted it? – a third and final undoubted maidenhead. A milkmaidenhead. The tales were confirmed in the most tangible fashion conceivable – or should I say inconceivable, dear Mina? – and the milk-swollen breasts that were mine to abuse as I pleased were truly those of virgin maids.

I returned to my seat, planted my backside upon it with a sigh of satisfaction and examined the dishes before me, stroking my chin and trying to decide with which to begin. The *fricassée* of damselfly? The purée of glartbottle*? The moth-wing salad? The selection of minced caterpillars and fried beetles? But why should I limit myself to one? I could eat as I pleased, and in any case I was going to drench every dish in milk. I looked up and examined the three faces on the other side of the small table, thinking hard, then lifted the finger from my chin and began an improvisation of the rhyme I had learned – so long ago it already seemed – in Romania. All three were startled to hear the first words of it, for I had spoken with the innkeeperess in Romanian (Beth, as I should have guessed, was least able to conceal her surprise).

'Eenie, meenie, minie, mit,' I said in Anglish, my pointing finger resting on each girl in turn, 'catch a milkmaid by her tit. If she squeals, relent not a bit. Eenie, meenie, minie, mit.'

And there was my finger, pointing gently in the direction of blonde Anna. I slipped back off my seat, walked around the table and closed up behind her, resting my mouth close to the delicately sculpted milk-coral of her ear.

'I won't be gentle with you, my dear,' I whispered in Anglish, and she shivered deliciously with fear. And with excitement, I think, though I closed my hands on her tits in what I think was almost the same instant and the blood was roaring so in my ears that I could scarcely tell one second from the next. I was clumsy at first, of course, both in directing the jets of milk over the table and in directing the jets of pain in my little milkmaid's body. She gasped and cried out as milk squirted and fell everywhere but where I wanted it to fall, but her voice was not tuned to the exquisite heights I wished to hear and I knew my kneading fingers had barely begun their

16

apprenticeship. I tried again, firing a long jet from her left tit, a long jet from her right, learning how to heft the firm and heavy bulk of the breast and control direction and arc. There: I was learning. I had aimed for a dish and landed a jet of milk neatly between the foreshortened circle of its rim. A fluke? No, for with my next shot I did it again and, although my third and fourth fell respectively short and wide, they did not do so by very much. But the jets were not so copious now and I realised that she was half- or three-quarters milked out. I released her nipples from between my index and middle fingers and allowed my fingertips to roam the hemispheres of her breasts, juggling them slightly, then holding them firmly, ready to read her reaction to the words I sent into her ear after a slow puff of breath.

'Thank you, my dear. But I will save a little for afters.'

I smiled as the relaxation that had been plainly tangible in her breasts was broken with the tension of knowledge, then released her breasts fully and stepped round to tall Gwendolyn, the biggest-breasted of the three and perhaps, from the moan that escaped her as my hands closed around her breasts and my milking fingers settled on her nipples, the most tender-titted too. I had to stand a little on tiptoe to put my mouth comfortably to her ear. I puffed breath, then spoke: 'Are you the tenderest-titted, my dear? No, do not answer. I shall see for myself.'

I squeezed both of her tits, sending twin jets of milk arcing across the table to splatter wide left and right of the dish I had been aiming for.

'Ah,' I said with satisfaction at her gasp of pain. 'I believe you are, my dear.'

I joggled her breasts fully under control and set to work, my cruel fingers jetting milk from her tits and gasps of pain from her mouth. The table shone with milk everywhere now, and it was gathering in the runnels and trickling towards the centre like the reversed rays of the moon. In the pauses I made to allow the pain to settle and heighten in the poor girl's abused breasts I could hear it dripping into the central hole with an oddly hollow, oddly exciting split ... split ... split ... Beneath my skirt I could feel my knickers positively glued to my cunt with juice, and I longed to close my palms on the tits I was milking and squeeze so that the milk spurted directly against them, soaking my hands and fingers for milk-masturbation. But no, I would carry a glassful up with me to my room instead, and milk-masturbate there while it was still warm from the breast. Gwendolyn's tits were now giving less of their bounty and I knew she too was half- or three-quarters milked out. Time for Beth, so up on tiptoes again I went, whispering, 'Thank you, my dear. But I will save a little for afters.'

Then I released her, allowing those glorious globes to take their own weight, and walked round to Beth, who shivered as I closed up behind her, my hands swinging forward to seize and direct her breasts. But pussy-juice had soaked its way under the hem of my knickers and was trickling down one of my thighs, and I paused to reach under my skirt and rub the fingers of my left hand in it, smearing it over the skin, transferring it to the other, as-yet-untrickled thigh. My cunt pulsed, pleading for attention, but I was as stern with it as I intended to be with Beth's tits, and lifted my hand free. Taking hold of her left tit in my left, un-pussy-juiced hand, I settled my mouth to Beth's milk-coral ear, tickled it with my breath, and spoke: 'Taste this, my dear. Lick them thoroughly.'

I lifted my pussy-juiced right hand to her mouth and felt my cunt squirm with frustration as her cool tongue licked it clean, flickering conscientiously at the web between each pair of fingers, then sucking hard at each

18

fingertip as I slipped it home into her moist little mouth. I puffed breath at her ear again.

'Thank you, my dear. But I wonder . . .'

I dropped my right hand to her right tit, took hold and began, discovering in the very first moment that the tenderest-titted of the trio had by no means been Gwendolyn. No, it was Beth, for she moaned as soon as I began to tighten my grip and shrieked and almost fainted – I felt her body slump backwards against mine for a moment – as I squeezed out the first jets of milk. I smiled, feeling my cunt squirm and bubble with excitement as I took firmer and crueller hold of her tits and began to squirt in earnest, allowing much of her milk to fall to the table-top and the collecting runnels. The split-split of milk falling into the central hole was almost continuous now and if it was collected for a purpose – as surely it was – I wished to ensure that there was a goodly supply.

How I wish that Mina had been there to share my tit-torturing with me, her small hands collaborating with mine in the milking of those tender hemispheres of milkmaid-flesh. How I wish the sowlhead had been a twin, so that her sister could have been fastened across the table from me, wrists cuffed to the tabletop, stripped, and with Mina stripped behind her, while I stood stripped behind my own sowlheaded twin. Then we could have fired jets of milk at each other, laughing gleefully through the moans and gasps of tit-pain, drenching each sowlhead with her sister's milk, soaking that milky skin with an echo of itself. Ah, the thought of it made me press my groin hard to the sowlhead's buttocks, grind against her as my hands worked to relieve her tits of their swollen load, spraying jet after jet of sweet fresh milk on to the shining dark surface of the table and the half-drowned dishes of food.

I had ground myself almost to orgasm when, with an effort, I forced myself to stop. Panting, I released her tits and stepped back. Her head was bowed and her shoulders shaking and, when I walked around the table to sit opposite the three and prepare to 'tuck in', I saw that she was sobbing freely, her tits shining with tear-splatters and shuddering juicily with her sobs. The other two had wept a little too from the pain of milking, for their faces glistened with half-dried tear-tracks. I squeezed my thighs together and shuffled my bottom, longing to masturbate, but I knew that the longer I delayed the more intense my first orgasm would be and I wished to save it for when (and while) I composed Mina's letter. But there were other pleasures to be had in the meantime. I drew the first dish towards me, picked up a fork and shovelled milk-splattered diving-beetle greedily into my mouth. Still chewing, I looked up at the sowlhead.

'Shut up, you slut,' I told her. Blinking, she raised her eyes and looked at me, her glart* eyes huge and swimming with tears, her coppery eyebrows raised timidly in interrogation. I chewed for a few seconds, savouring the contrast of the sweet milk and crisp, salty beetle, staring expressionless at her, then swallowed.

'Shut . . . up . . . you . . . slut,' I said, enunciating the words with exaggerated care. Her face tightened with self-pity and her sobs increased. I tutted with exasperation and forked more diving-beetle into my mouth, reaching for the dish of glartbottle purée, forking some of that into my mouth even as I chewed the diving-beetle. The milk seemed less happy in combination with glartbottle, as I confirmed when I swallowed the commingled mouthful and forked glartbottle alone into my mouth.

'Here,' I said, pushing my chair back and standing up. 'If you're going to *greet* –' the moment after I said it I remembered this was northern Anglish. 'If you're going to cry –' then I relaxed gladly into Romanian for the complicated apodosis '– at least don't let the salt go to waste.'

20

I put down my fork, picked up the dish of glartbottle purée, and strode around the table to the sowlhead.

'Cry into it,' I ordered her in Romanian, holding the dish out and in front of her. She shook her head, sniffing.

'*Maestră*, I do not understand,' she said haltingly in Romanian.

'Ignorant slut,' I told her, and switched into Anglish: 'Cry . . . into . . . it', adding in Romanian, 'But no *muci*, do you understand?' She was shaking her head again when the Juno – I had forgotten her name – translated into Anglish.

'No snot, Beth. The mistress wants you to cry into the glartbottle, but no snot.'

The sowlhead nodded this time and put her face forwards and down over the dish, allowing her tears to fall into it. But they were not falling so freely as they had a minute or two before.

'Harder, you silly slut,' I told her. I reached round with my free hand and gave one of her nipples a tweak. It was warm and spongy, oozing with milk, and she cried out with pain.

'Harder,' I said, giving her nipple another tweak. I let go of her tit, well satisfied, and licked my milky fingertips. She was crying hard into the dish now, her lachrymal ducts replenished by abuse of her lacteal. When I was satisfied I took the dish back around the table and forked another helping into my mouth. She was watching me fearfully, hoping she would not be required to weep more tears into the glartbottle, assisted with more tweaks on her tits.

'Satisfactory,' I said indistinctly through the mouthful, and spoke no more than the truth: the salt of the tears had overcome the slightly excessive sweetness imparted to the dish by the fresh tit-milk that had sprayed freely into it, jetting from the three fine pairs of tits on display across the table. I took another mouthful and reached out for a dish of fox-moth caterpillars, wondering idly what was beneath the dish left lidded by the innkeeperess and her twaughter. I forked caterpillars into my mouth, asking, 'Wh–?'

But I had to chew and swallow before I could continue. Here the milk had improved the flavour, counterpointing the sting of the caterpillars' hairs, which I knew would survive their passage through my body and provide some possibly painful and some possibly exciting irritation on the next two or three occasions on which I shat.

'What is under there, sluts?' I asked, gesturing with my fork at the covered dish before scooping up another mouthful of fox-moth caterpillar.

'We do not know, *maestră*,' said the Juno in Romanian. Gwendolyn. 'But I believe it is a – I forget the word, but "treat" we say in Ang–'

'Then speak Anglish, slut. I need to practise.'

'Very well, mistress,' she said in Anglish. 'It is a treat for you.'

'*Plăcere*,' I supplied. 'That is the word in Romanian.'

'Thank you, mistress. It is a treat. A *plăcere*.'

'Good. I will look forward to it. Now shut up, sluts, while I eat.'

I forked busily, chewing, watching the tits in front of me, not the faces. There was still plenty of milk there, still plenty for a game or two when I had finished eating. I could feel my knickers clinging hard to my cunt as I reached forward over the table for fresh dishes or slid finished ones back into place. Not much longer, I told it. Perhaps, if I asked the innkeeperess's permission, I could take two of them up to my room and see how they would perform fully stripped. Could milk be squirted with sufficient force to trigger orgasm in a cunt already brought to the brink of it? I should certainly like to see and perhaps certainly would see, if the innkeeperess were as anxious to keep – what is the expression? – to keep in the Countess's 'good books' as I had already deduced she was. I forked up a final mouthful from the dish of caterpillars. The sowlhead – Beth – was still snivelling, but not so hard as before.

'Tell me,' I said, scraping a last few hairs from the dish and slipping them into my mouth, 'have any of you sluts met the Countess?'

I looked up. The sowlhead's sniffs had stopped abruptly and her eyes were wide with what was unmistakably fear.

'Well?' I asked.

The Juno, Gwendolyn, swallowed before she answered, obviously choosing her words with care.

'*Nu, maestră,*' she began in Romanian, then shook her head and began again in Anglish. 'No, mistress. We – we none of us have met her. She does not come to the inn often.'

I frowned. Why did the mere mention of the Countess's name cause such consternation?

'You there, sowlheaded slut. Is this true? None of you have met the Countess?'

She shook her head, moistening her lips.

'No, mistress. None of us.'

Unlike the Juno, she was not a good liar. I stared at her for a moment, watching the first traces of a blush begin to glow in her pale skin, then looked sternly at the blonde.

'And you, you piss-haired slut, you say the same? None of you have met her?'

She shook her head too.

'No, mistress. None of us.'

She was not so good a liar as the Juno either, though she was better than the sowlhead.

'Very well.'

I put the empty dish back on the table and tapped my chest between my breasts, pausing for a second or two then belching contentedly, allowing the sowlhead to do what I had been waiting for her to do: sigh with apparent relief that I had accepted what they told me. I belched again.

'Very well. I will be meeting her in a night or two regardless. I can ask her myself. Now, we shall see what *treat* has been prepared for me. The final dish.'

I leaned forward in my chair, reaching out over the table for the final dish, its contents still concealed under a lid. As I lifted it towards me I frowned. Such a weight, and it seemed to be trembling in my hands. A live dish, obviously, but what could weigh so much? I put it on the table in front of me and lifted the lid away, feeling the dish quiver with the movement of the contents even as I did so. Imagine my surprise and delight at what I saw within: some of the largest and fattest stag-beetle pupae I have ever seen in my life, glowing rich mahogany in the lamplight. Or were they stag-beetle? I peered more closely, then reached in and picked one up, holding it in front of my face. The face stared blankly back at me, snouted like the sarcophagal mask of a theriomorphic pharaohess, but the thorax squirmed and twisted wildly, its tip poking and spiralling as though to sting.

'Hmmm,' I said appreciatively, as I opened my mouth and popped it in. Then, I bit down and the pupa cracked open on my tongue. 'Mmmm-mmmmm.'

It was delicious: the liquid interior gushed forth as I cracked the carapace, creamy, almost buttery, but with a delicious peppery undertaste. It was certainly not stag-beetle, but what was it? I chewed and swallowed.

'Delicious,' I said, reaching into the dish for another. 'What is it?'

The Juno shook her head.

'We do not know, mistress.'

'But perhaps,' the blonde added shyly, and slyly too, I could tell, 'perhaps Mistress Leonie will know.'

I put a second pupa into my mouth and slowly bit into it, staring at her. The glart eyes blinked nervously for a moment but did not fall from mine. I reached out for the little silver bell that had sat on the table during my meal and shook it briskly. The blonde essayed a timid smile. I chewed and swallowed the remains of the second pupa and picked up a third. As I opened my mouth and prepared to place it inside, the door rattled open and the innkeeperess's twaughter came in.

'Your ladyship?'

I paused.

'I have nothing clean to drink from, hostess, and particularly wished to take a glass of milk up with me to my quarters.'

'At once, your ladyship.'

She stepped back to the door and shouted something I did not catch, then turned back.

'I hope everything has been to your ladyship's satisfaction?'

'Hmm–mm,' I said, nodding as I chewed the third pupa. 'But –' I paused to swallow '– but I wondered what it was I am eating now.'

I wiggled a finger at the disk of pupae.

'They are good, your ladyship?'

'Excellent,' I said. 'As –' I popped a fourth into my mouth and continued indistinctly, feeling it move on my tongue '– as you can see.'

I bit into it.

'Then we are glad, your ladyship. And so, I am sure, is the Countess, for it was she who supplied them. They are the pupae of a tropical beetle cultivated by the Countess at her castle, where she has heated chambers for these purposes.'

I chewed, swallowed and nodded.

'I guessed as much. I did not think they could be native or wild-grown in a climate such as Transmarynia's.'

'Oh, no, your ladyship.'

The door swung open fully behind her and another young serving-maid, cheeks flushed and panting a little, came into the room carrying a silver jug and a tall glass. The innkeeperess's twaughter took them from her and turned back to me.

'From whom, your ladyship?'

'From . . .? Ah, I see your meaning.' I put a fifth pupa into my mouth and continued indistinctly, 'From all three, please.'

'Certainly, your ladyship.'

She put the glass on the table and moved with the jug towards the Juno.

'And will your ladyship care to stay for the churning?' she asked as she held the jug under the Juno's nearer breast and began with swift expert tugs to milk her into it. I bit into a sixth pupa, listening to the milk splatter against the bare bottom of the jug, my cunt squirming again as I watched the Juno's strong white teeth sink into her juicy lower lip. The innkeeperess's twaughter shifted the jug under the Juno's further tit and began to tug again. The innkeeperess's twaughter turned her head to look at me, eyebrows raised.

'Your ladyship will care to stay?'

I stared at her for a moment. The milk was falling into a quarter-full jug now, splashing and splattering.

'Will care to stay for what, hostess?'

'The churning, your ladyship. You will wish to watch?'

'I do not understand, hostess.'

'The table is a *churn-table*, as we say in Anglish, mistress. The milk that has run into the central hole now waits to be churned into butter. We will strip one of the maids and set her to work on it, just so soon –' she tugged a final jet of milk from the Juno's further tit and moved around the table to the sowlhead '– just so soon as I have milked them for you.'

The sowlhead's milk began to splash into the jug and I could hear little cries of pain stifled in her throat as the twaughter's slender fingers expertly tugged and squeezed.

'One of these sluts?' I said.

'Yes, your ladyship.'

'Then certainly I shall stay to watch the, ah, churning.'

'I am glad, your ladyship. Perhaps your ladyship would care to save a few pupae to use on the slut.'

I paused with my eighth pupa almost between my lips.

'The pupae?'

'They are highly energetic, are they not, your ladyship?'

Even as she said it the eighth nearly squirmed out of my fingers. I put it into my mouth and bit it in half.

'Hmm-hmmm,' I murmured, nodding. She began to milk the sowlhead's second tit into the jug. It was more than half-full now, I could tell.

'Then they will be highly suitable for use on the slut you have chosen, your ladyship. As you shall see.'

And then she milked in silence and I, after swallowing a ninth pupa, sat quietly and watched and waited, my cunt leaking freely into my knickers as the slender white fingers worked busily on the swollen chelce nipples, as the milk splashed into the jug and cries of pain jumped and throbbed in the sowlhead's and then the blonde's sweating throats. When the innkeeperess's twaughter had finished she carried the brimming jug back around the three sluts, picked up the glass where she had left it and brought jug and glass further around the table to me.

'A drink now, your ladyship?'

'Please,' I said. The innkeeperess's twaughter put the glass on the table and poured milk expertly into it. I sniffed happily. Warm girl-milk, fresh from the tit.

'If your ladyship pleases, while she drinks she can choose a slut for the churning. Here, your ladyship.'

I took the glass from her, closing my hand around its base to feel the faint warmth of the milk as it began to glow through the cool glass.

'I have chosen,' I said and took a long first drink. It was warm and sweet, sliding smoothly down my throat.

'Yes, your ladyship? And whom?'

I took the glass from my lips, knowing that a white streak clung to my upper lip, and waved the glass at the sowlhead.

'The sowlheaded slut. Can she strip for it?'

'She must strip for it, your ladyship. As you shall see.'

Indeed, as I saw. The innkeeperess's twaughter moved around the table opening the handcuffs that had held the three sluts in place since the beginning of my meal. Sending the dark Juno and the petite blonde off with crisp slaps at their firm bottoms, she stood the sowlhead near the door and ordered her to strip. I watched hungrily, sipping at my milk.

2

Letter, Joanna Harker to Mina Harker (never received by her)

Kent, 3 May.
My dearest Darling,
I have calculated that this letter should reach you within the week, in which case you must, as you love me, set it aside *now* and not pick it up again till the 10th of May, at exactly eleven o'clock, when you must have your knickers down, the fingers of your wanking hand pre-moistened with girl-butter (Transmarynian, for preference) and that accurate clock in the morning room positioned where you can easily see it.

There. Have you waited, my darling? Is it exactly eleven o'clock on the tenth? Yes, I know you have and it is, for you knew I would not ask except for your own pleasure, and mine. I have something to tell you that will excite you greatly, as it excited and will excite me. I could not share it with you at the time, much though I wished it, but I can share it with you through the medium of a letter, for I will, *Deâ volente*, be taking up my own copy of this at the same time on the same night, knickers off and the fingers of my wanking hand pre-moistened with fresh Transmarynian girl-butter. I will be watching the second

29

hand of the most accurate clock I have been able to commandeer, and as it reaches a minute past eleven I will strum gently at my pussy-lips for exactly twenty seconds. If you raise your eyes to our own dear clock the second hand should be approaching the same mark, and you must do the same as I before you continue to read.

There. Have you done it? Yes, I know you have, and I picture the fleshy-firm lips of your pussy beginning to swell and pout, with a gleam of that well-loved, well-licked juice between them. How I wish I could be there to minister to them personally with my lips and tongue, while you ministered to mine with yours! I would tell my tale to you between lappings, watching your pussy to see how it shifted and oozed to the rise and fall of my words. But my tale can be told in a letter in its own way, with its own pleasures. Look up at the clock again, my darling. Has the second hand reached the half-minute mark? If so, strum at your pussy again for twenty seconds and know that, for all the distance that separates us, I am doing the same.

There. Your breath is beginning to come faster now, I know, and I am ready to begin my tale. It is the 'tale of a tail', my dear, as the Transmarynians would have it. The tale of the beating of a bottom. Of two bottoms. 'Whose bottoms?' I hear you ask (and your pussy asks it too, its slit open and oozing musky interrogation). I will tell you. It was the bottom of a Transmarynian wine and an insolent young waitress at the Hôtel d'Azure in Paris. You know how the staff of a certain class of hotel loves calculated insolence to customers – remember that night in Vienna, when I almost wept with frustration at being provoked by, and denied the satisfaction of punishing, a slender young minx in a velvet black dress and stockings? Ah,

30

well – but look at the clock again, my darling. Is the third minute reached? Then wank again, for twenty seconds, and sniff your fingers deeply when you lift them away from your pussy. Remember that I am doing the same, all those miles away, and I will imagine that the pussy-scent on my fingers is yours, my darling, as I know you will imagine that the pussy-scent on yours is mine. Mirror-masturbation.

There. But where was I? Ah, yes, the Viennese minx, whose bottom went unpunished. I recalled her when I was served by one of her soul-sisters in Paris: another young minx, provoking a customer with calculated insolence, having judged it safe to do so. Shall I whisper that I encouraged her in this judge-ment? That I enticed her into the mouth of my trap, allowing her to stroke its velvet walls as she entered, little suspecting the steel jaws that lay beneath? Yes, I shall whisper it, and compare the whisper to the trickle of juice that I know has started down your inner thighs. Is the fourth minute coming up, my darling? And do you expect me to ask you to lower your hand again to your pussy? Then I disappoint you, for I do not ask it. Let thrice suffice, for now. Let your pussy seethe for a while, and those whisper-ing trickles of pussy-juice travel as far as they can down your thighs. While they trickle, I will continue with my tale. You remember the final telegram the Countess sent me, informing me that she held a majority holding in the Hôtel d'Azure and promising me compensation for any 'dissatisfaction' I experi-enced there? Well, this telegram was snug in my pocket all the while that young waitress was provok-ing me with her insolence, thinking her firm and pearly buttocks safe in her knickers, and the thought of it heightened the delight I took in drinking my first Transmarynian wine – and a blonde! When I had finished, I ordered the punishment list from my minx, for the wine-maid had fainted under the final attentions of my tongue and lips. I selected flagellation with nettles and then added a nipple electrifying. My waitress minx immediately informed me that this was forbidden, for the techniques could not be mixed upon a single woman in a single session; but I cut through her words with the curt rejoinder that the nipple electrifying was not for the wine-maid, but for *her*.

Imagine the look upon her face! In the next moment, however, she was telling me that waitresses were exempt – and then I produced the Countess's telegram. Imagine her face after *that*! Ah, if I was oozing at pussy after I had drunk the wine (and I was, my darling, I was), you can imagine (and will imagine, I know) that now I was positively drooling, and my knickers were thoroughly soaked. I had the manageress brought to my table (enjoying the looks of enquiry from my neighbours) and when she had read the telegram she was all eagerness to assist me in the consummation of my revenge on that minx of a waitress, whose face by now was a study in mingled consternation, fright and, struggle as she might to disguise it, excitement.

An hour later, I was being escorted to the Hôtel's finest punishment suite, where the wine-maid and waitress awaited my pleasure (and their own pain): the first strapped face-forwards and naked, thighs splayed, on a sturdy whipping-horse; the other spread-eagled on a rack, copper wires glistening from her nipples to the mechanism of an up-to-the-minute pedal-powered electrifier, which I had already told the manageress I wished to operate personally. Six bunches of nettles for the flagellation sat soaking in a tank of brine, and I lifted one and took it with me, dripping brine almost as copiously as I dripped pussy-juice, while I undertook my inspection of my victims, pinching the tender bottom of the wine-maid, before checking the wires on the waitress's nipples, and dribbling a little brine there to improve the contact. The pussies of both were beginning to ooze, as I had expected, and when I spoke to them, describing what lay ahead, I could hear the pain-lust in their voices as they protested their innocence and pleaded for mercy. Plainly the Countess, if she has any hand in the running of that hotel, has chosen wisely in its manageress, for she is just as plainly a shrewd judge of girl-flesh, and has appointed convinc-ed masochists to the staff.

And what did I say to them? What did I tell them lay ahead? First, that I would oversee the flagellation of the wine-maid's buttocks with nettles; next that I would personally operate the nipple-electrifier on the waitress; finally that I would turn her in the rack and deliver six sharp blows with a cane to those buttocks she had so foolishly thought inviolable. The hotel's flagellatrix was on hand – a short, broad-shouldered girl with a face of coarse sensuality – and when I was ready I nodded to her to take up the first bunch of nettles. I watched the buttocks of the wine-maid, then, when the nettles were ready in the hand of the flagellatrix, said in Transmarynian (though finishing in French), 'Take up your nettles, *flagellatrice*.' Imag-ine how my pussy squirmed and nipples peaked to see the quiver of surprise and anticipation that ran through the buttocks: surprise that I had spoken in Transmarynian; anticipation of the first blow. And it amused me, of course, to deliver an order unneeded, for the nettles were already in the flagellatrix's hand. I continued, 'Strike the first blow on the count of ten.' The buttocks quivered again, though less sharply, for they were tense with anticipation, and I had to watch closely to observe the effects of my count.

'*Un*,' I began in French. '*Deux. Trois. Quatre. Cinq. Six.*'

At six I smiled with sheer delight, for the buttocks had begun to shiver – positively to shiver – with fright, quite beyond the control of the wine-maid, who was plainly of the tenderest sensibility.

'*Sept*,' I continued, allowing a gloating note to creep into my voice – it was easy enough: I imagined the buttocks before me as a pair of rich pastries, overflowing with thick cream. '*Huit. Neuf.*'

Then I breathed in air to say '*Dix*', or so the wine-maid thought. But no! Instead, I tutted and shook my head, saying, 'Please forgive me, I should not have counted in French, but in Transmarynian. Let me begin again.'

And I did, from the very beginning: 'One. Two. Three. Four. Five. Six. Seven. Eight. Nine.'

Another pause for breath, then very softly, so that the little wine-maid had to strain to catch it (thus heightening the sensation of the nettles falling full upon her clenched and cringing buttocks) said, 'Ten.'

And now, my darling, imagine the soft swish of the nettles; the soft *thwack* of their impact on those tender white bottom-mounds; and the cry of pain as the sting of their impact begins to seethe through that silken skin. Have you imagined all that? Then if you have imagined it well and the clock has reached six past the hour, please reward yourself with a pussy-tweaking. And work at your nipples with your free hand. But not too long. I will trust you not to take yourself to orgasm. Not yet. I myself, all those miles away from you, will be working at my own pussy and nipples, but not to the point of orgasm. That must be delayed, and by being delayed be heightened.

There. Have you done? And sniffed your fingers again, imagining that they smell of my pussy as I, all

34

those miles away, have imagined that mine smell of yours? Good. It is going well. To proceed: after that first blow with the nettles I stepped forward to examine the buttocks of the wine-maid, running my fingers over the mottled patch of urtication, pressing my wrist there and to an unmarked spot lower down the fleshy swell to compare temperatures. Then I returned to my point of observation and nodded to the flagellatrix to continue, holding up my ten fingers six times, then five fingers of my right hand once. The flagellatrix nodded in confirmation, and began to deal out the five-strokes-to-the-minute of that initial flagellation, as I had signalled. Imagine the squeaks of the wine-maid, my darling, as the nettles began to beat out that rhythm on the milk-white mounds of her bottom. Imagine her squeaks slowly turning to gasps and her gasps to groans as the fire glowing in her buttocks heightens and begins to master her pussy, levering apart her pussy-lips and setting up an intolerable tingling in her clitoris. Imagine the glistening film of pussy-juice that creeps down the inner face of her splayed thighs. And if you have imagined it well and the clock has reached seven past, reward yourself with a pussy-tweaking as I, for the same reason and at the same time, reward myself with a pussy-tweaking all those miles away in Transmarynia.

There. We have done it. Tweaked and sniffed. Though I had the advantage, did I not, in my imagining. For I call up pure images of the hotel-punishment from recent memory, I do not weave them of past experience. You will forgive me for it, I know. To continue: when the wine-maid was positively sobbing with frustration at the denied greed of her pussyhorn* for orgasm, I ordered the flagellation paused and came forwards again to examine her buttocks. Ah! The heat in them was palpable now at a clear inch or more from their once-pearly curves. Yes, once pearly, for they were pearly no more, but deep sowl, darkening to vace*, as though blushing for shame at the state of her pussy, which lay gaping and oozing between her splayed thighs, spilling its juice in such thickness as you will never believe. I rubbed my fingers through it, murmuring with well-simulated disgust and distaste, then turned, holding up a dripping finger, to pass comment to the manageress.

'Look at this, madame,' I said. 'The filthy slut is leaking like a crushed peach. I have permission, of course, to continue with the punishment?'

'But of course,' returned the manageress, and I stepped back to my observation point and signalled to the flagellatrix to take up a fresh bunch of nettles and begin again at ten strokes to the minute. The sobs of the wine-maid had died away to murmurs, but now they woke to gasps as the nettles began to fall once more on her tortured buttocks, and she began to intersperse them with pleas for orgasm, begging us to finger her pussy for her or to untie one of her hands and allow her to minister to herself. All pleas were ignored: she would achieve orgasm by the path of pain, by being beaten with nettles until her overtaxed nerves could stand no more and overflowed spontaneously.

And what of the waitress? you are perhaps thinking. If not, then think it, I pray. She was still spread-eagled on her rack, nipples still trailing those glistening copper wires, but the glances that I spared her every so often revealed that the flagellation had worked on the nerves of more than the wine-maid and the official observers, myself amongst them. Yes, the flagellation had worked on her too, for her pussy was gaping between her thighs, which glistened as though in sympathy with her fellow *employée*. The second bunch of nettles was hanging moist and broken now in the strong hand of the flagellatrix, and I ordered it dropped to the floor and replaced before the strokes began again at twelve to the minute. Orgasm would not be long delayed, I judged, for the pain in the wine-maid's buttocks must be mounting to a peak now, blazing there volcanically, like twin *Vesuvii* in full eruption. I judged right, for which I shall reward myself, and you too, if the clock has now reached the quarter hour. So let pussy-tweaking commence, dear Mina, for those twenty seconds.

There. Tweaked and sniffed. But let us imagine this time not our mutual scents, but the scent of the pussy of that poor, pain-racked wine-maid, face-forwards on that sweat-soaked whipping-horse, buttocks raised and defenceless beneath the blows of those cruel, unending nettles. Let us imagine the scent of her pussy-juice, which positively squirted forth as her pussy writhed in finally provoked orgasm and her cries of anguished ecstasy filled the torture suite. I nodded to the flagellatrix and she ceased work, her dull, brutish eyes brightened now with the sights and sounds of the flagellation, as though she came truly alive only during the performance of her duties. As I can well believe is the case. But I had little time for speculation on the matter, for the nipple electrifying beckoned me but a few paces across the chamber. The electrifier was pedal-powered, as I have mentioned, and the operator had to set herself upon a little saddle and rest her hands on handlebars like those of a bicycle, with a small gauge set between them. As I set myself on the saddle and put my hands to these bars, I noted that the gauge ran left to right from 0 (where the arrow now rested) to 5, with an elegant *Dols* written beneath the numbers. I turned my head and called to the manageress.
    'Madame, your attendance for a moment, if you please.'

She came over to me and I nodded down at the gauge.

'What is this, madame?'

'*C'est un dolomètre*, maîtresse*. The unit of pain, in France, it is the *dol*.'

'But from nought to five only, madame?'

Her eyes met mine and she smiled cruelly.

'*L'échelle, c'est logarithmique.*'

My turn to smile cruelly, and to feel my pussy smile too, in its own moist way. The scale was logarithmic.

'*Et la base?*'

'*C'est dix, maîtresse.*'

I put my feet to the pedals and, without preamble, without warning, began to pedal. I was rewarded instantly with a shriek of pain from the waitress, whose body stiffened in its straps and commenced to quiver as the electricity generated by my turning feet streamed down the copper wires and into the fleshy buds of her nipples. I glanced down at the dolometer: it stood at 1·2. I began to pedal faster, provoking further cries from the waitress, whose body was almost bouncing in its straps. Specks of moisture landed on my face and I realised the violence of her movements was throwing off a spray of juice from her oozing pussy. I glanced down at the dolometer. 2·5 now, and climbing. To my left, where the wine-maid still lay strapped over the whipping-horse, I heard the moans of another orgasm, as her nettle-tortured nerves overflowed again. Imagine the mingling of their voices, my darling, as I pedalled and pedalled: the moans and murmurs of the wine-maid; the shrieks and pleas of the waitress, begging for the wires to be disconnected from her nipples. But I powered on, lifting the gauge to 3, where her cries were almost continuous and I was splattered with pussy-spray every few seconds.

But will you be disappointed to hear that the arrow of the dolometer peaked at 3·2, never pushing higher, into the algolagnic empyrean of 4 and 5? Please don't be, my darling, for 3·2 was exceedingly painful to that minx and, when, with legs and lungs aching, I climbed from that seat (the arrow taking some time to swing back through its arc to 0) and walked a little unsteadily to the rack of canes along one wall, I knew she had paid in full for her insolence.

Glance at the clock again, my darling. Has it reached twenty past? If so, pussy-tweak again as you read to the end of this paragraph, imagining me as I stood before the rack of canes, making my selection. They glistened like gold in the lamplight, like the thin pipes of a church organ fit to flute a fugue of fustigation, and they seemed to hang against the wall without support. As I made my selection, reached out and drew one from the wall, I realised the secret: there was a tug of resistance, for the handle was evidently weighted with iron and a magnetic strip had been set into the wall. I turned, swinging the cane, hearing the whimpers of the wine-maid as she approached her third spontaneous orgasm, her pussy gorged to over-flowing on the sensation in her nettle-tortured but-tocks, and I sewed the swish of the cane in amongst the notes of her voice.

There. Have you read that while you were pussy-tweaking, my love? Yes, I know it was so, and I know that I shall too, at the same time. Sniff your fingers again, my love, and imagine that my scent is upon them. Imagine that your fingers come fresh from tickling my pussy as I stood swinging that cane, preparing to punish the waitress on her bottom as she still trembled from the nipple-torture. Imagine me nodding curtly to one of the hotel staff, indicating that I wished the waitress swung in her rack so that her bottom faced me and my long, flexible cane. Imagine my murmur of delight as the buttocks swung to face me: so white, so perfect, so virginal, as though the Goddess had created them for me in that very instant. I stepped forwards, swinging my cane again, loosening the joints of my shoulder and elbow, carefully judging my distance, the angles of my feet and the distance between them. And now, as you read what follows, begin your pussy-tweaking again, but with a careful eye on the clock. You must come, as I intend to come, at twenty-seven minutes past the hour, and we must dedicate our orgasms to one another, sending our pleasure flashing between us, so that you experience my orgasm and I yours and our orgasm is doubled, or rather raised to the power of itself.

So, I am ready, and the buttocks lie bare and defenceless before me. The wine-maid is gasping out her third orgasm and wailing feebly in Transmarynian to be released, for her burning buttocks to be soothed with icy compresses and with the tongue of some companion whose name I now forget. For I was focusing my whole attention on the buttocks before me, deliberately excluding all other thoughts, all other sensations: all sounds and sights and smells. My arm swings back and I draw a single slow breath.

One. My arm has leaped forwards, carrying the cane crack against those pearly hemispheres and into the echoes of the crack travelling back from the unpanelled echo-wall of the torture suite comes the waitress's almost feline yelp of agony. The cane jumps free of the buttocks almost of its own accord and my pussy melts with delight, my nipples tingling and throbbing as I gaze upon the line of the first cane-stroke as it glows and gloats across the milky velvet of her buttocks. I take another deep breath and swing my cane back for the second time.

Two. The cane leaps forward and I know before it lands that my aim was perfect: I have landed the second stroke directly atop the first, lashing the full weight of the cane into nerves already singing with agony, and so redoubling that agony, or tripling it, as is clearly evinced in the increased volume and pitch of the yelp the waitress releases into the echoes of that second stroke. My pussy is oozing so copiously now that I feel as though it has melted altogether and I long to put a hand under my dress and tickle my pussyhorn, but to do so would be to delay the third stroke, and the third stroke will not wait. I take another deep breath and swing my cane back for the third time.

Three. The manageress, watching closely from her corner of the room, is unable to restrain a cry of '*Brava!*' and, as I recover from the slight stumble occasioned by the force and ferocity with which I have swung, I see what she is praising. The third stroke too has landed directly atop the line of the first, so that anyone coming fresh into the room might suppose I had beaten her only once, but for the deepness of the stroke and its angry colour. The waitress has not yelped this time: she has screamed, and I almost feel a twinge of sympathy for her. Never have I caned with such skill, and it was a sorry night for her when she crossed my path. I take another deep breath and swing my cane back for the fourth time.

Four. I have deliberately angled this stroke so that it overlaps the first (and second (and third)) at only one point, and intend to land the fifth stroke at a mirroring angle, before putting the sixth directly atop the groove of the first (and second (and third)) again. Her scream this time has lost something of its volume, as though the pain has peaked or as though she is lost in wonder that it does not peak. I take another deep breath and swing my cane back for the fifth time.

Five. Another crack of the cane and another scream. As I nod with satisfaction, noting that the fifth stroke is angled to mirror the fourth perfectly,

41

my eyes are attracted by the glistening sheets of juice on the inner surfaces of her thighs, and I realise that they have reached her calves now. This paining is causing her great pleasure, and I have an idea that will increase the latter even as she suffers from the final dose of the former. I turn to the manageress and outline my plan quietly in a few crisp sentences, my mind exhilarated and racing on the energy of domination. She nods and the wine-maid is unstrapped from the whipping-horse and given her instructions as I take another deep breath and swing my cane back for the sixth time.

And now, my darling, you must begin your final pussy-tweaking, as I, all those miles away, will be beginning mine. Read the following words slowly, extracting every sliver of meaning, conjuring up every sound, sight, and smell.

Six. Crack again and scream, and the manageress bursts out with a '*Bravisima!*', for I have put the sixth stroke so perfectly atop the first (and second (and third)) that any but the closest observer of those buttocks might swear they had been beaten only three times. The wine-maid, one hand rubbing frantically at her nettled bottom, the other at her gushing cunt, shuffles past me on her knees and I watch as she raises her head between the splayed thighs of her fellow *employée*, presses her tongue and lips to the gushing cunt waiting there and begins to suck and lap greedily at it. The waitress, her nipples still aching from the electricity passing through them, her bottom split and shrieking with the cane-strokes, succumbs almost immediately to a loud and prolonged orgasm, whose cries are echoed by the wine-maid as she achieves her fourth orgasm of the session, though this is purchased by her own efforts, with her fingers on her pussy. Feeling drained, the I-of-that-moment returns the cane to its rack while the I-of-this, her fingers blurring to a final frenzy on her sopping pussy, commemorates the orgasm-shriek of the two punishees with an orgasm-shriek of her own.

And there, my darling, I shall end, hoping that your eyes are blurred with the afterseethe of orgasm and can barely read these closing words. Take care, my dearest love, and when you lick your fingers clean, imagine my taste is there as I will imagine that your taste is on mine.

J.

Joanna Harker's Journal Continued

4 May. I had taken a fair copy of my letter to Mina and was sealing and addressing the letter itself when feet sounded softly on the stair and there was a timid knock on the door. 'Enter!' I called and the sowlheaded slut, blushing prettily, pushed the door open and peeped around it to inform me that the coach had been sighted on the hill-road and would be drawing up in the courtyard within the quarter-hour.

'Thank you, my dear,' I said, and asked, 'How are your tits this evening?'

She pouted unhappily.

'*Chinuit–*' she began. I interrupted her.

'Anglish, my dear!'

'They – they are sore, your ladyship.'

'Good. Pray inform mine hostess that I will be down directly.'

She nodded without speaking and I heard her light feet descending the stairs. I finished the final line of the address, dusted the wet ink, blew it dry and slipped it into my valise, meaning before I left to ask the innkeeperess to post it for me. Feet sounded outside again on the stairs and there came another knock on the door, still half-open from the sowlhead's message.

'Enter!'

Not the sowlheaded slut this time, I knew, for the feet had not been hers and the knock had had more confidence in it. But I would not have guessed in three attempts that it was the innkeeperess's twaughter, nor in thirty what her purpose was. She came into the room with a most serious expression on her face and holding something clasped in her right hand. A light silver chain hung from it, swinging as she ran towards me, eyes fixed on mine.

'Oh, your ladyship –' speaking in Romanian, her accent thickened by her evident emotion '– must you go?'

I was puzzled.

'Go?' I said.

'Yes, your ladyship. Must you go?'

'I am not going, I stay in Transmarynia, to be about the Countess's b–'

Her eyes widened as I spoke the name and she shook her head wildly.

'No, do not go to her! Stay far from her! Flee this night back to Romania for your life! For your very soul!'

'Hostess, I am afr–'

She shook her head again with a sob of frustration, seizing me by the arm.

'Do you not know what night this is, your ladyship?'

It was my turn to shake my head.

'It is the eve of St Georgina's Day. Do you not know that, when the clock strikes midday, all the malefic things in the world will have full sway?'

But she must have seen from the look on my face that her words meant nothing to me, for she broke off with another sob. Then her fingers tightened again on my arm and she asked, 'Then you will not delay your journey, even for a night?'

I shook my head.

44

'I am employed by the Countess and must be about her business.'

Again her eyes widened when I spoke the name.

'Ah, it is no good,' she said almost to herself, speaking now in Anglish. Then, resuming in Romanian, 'But at least, your ladyship, you will permit me to gift you this?'

She held up her clasped hand, opening it and letting what had lain concealed slip forth to dangle on the light silver chain before my eyes. It was a sacred emblem I had glimpsed around the neck of a maid the previous night and that believed, from the silver chains I had seen around their necks, was worn permanently by all the others employed in the inn (save for the three milk-maids, whose breasts had been bare). The innkeeperess and her twaughter wore it too, I believed, or at least wore something on light golden chains. And what was it, I hear you ask, dear Mina? It was a cross in the form of an X, though the upper legs were short and the lower long, as though it represented a pair of scissors or shears. I watched it tremble and twist as it hung from the twaughter's trembling hand, then forced a smile to my face. There was no answering smile in the twaughter's face as she stared earnestly into my eyes, saying, 'It is a criss, your ladyship. Will you take it?'

'But of course, hostess. If it means so much to you –'

Again she interrupted me.

'To me, it means a great deal. To you, it may mean everything. Wear it at all times, I beg you.'

I nodded without speaking and held out my hand for it. As she dropped it on to my palm and I closed my hand on it, she seized hold of my hand and kissed it. Drops of something warm splattered my wrist and I realised she had started crying. Then, as her sobs grew louder, she turned and fled from the room, leaving me staring after her in astonishment. Had I made such an impression on her the previous night, during the milk-churning? Even if I could flatter myself that I had, I could still see that the impression I had made was less important than the impression plainly made on her at some time by Countess Caradul. I slipped the criss, as I suppose I can call it, into my valise and even as I did so I heard the rumble of wheels in the courtyard. The coach had arrived.

I descended with my valise to discover two burly outdoor maids loading my luggage and the innkeeperess – of her twaughter there was no sign – in earnest conversation with the driver, who was shaking her head as though refusing some request. A number of other maids were talking in low voices outside the windows of the kitchen, which overlooked the courtyard, but as I stepped outside they fell suddenly silent and the inn-keeperess, after passing something I would not see to the driver, turned and saw me. She too, I saw to my surprise, had been crying, for her eyes were sowled and moist. She forced a smile to her lips and came towards me, holding out her hand.

'It is farewell, your ladyship, as we say, but I hope – and I pray – not goodbye. We shall see you again in a week?'

'If that is the Countess's will,' I said – I am afraid rather warmly, for I was growing a little tired of this perpetual mystery. Again as I spoke the Countess's name the eyes of my interlocutor widened.

'Yes,' the innkeeperess said. 'Then – then I will pray that it be the Countess's will.'

But it was said sadly, even hopelessly. The maids had resumed their low conversation now, whispering to-gether in a thick Anglish dialect in which I could barely catch one word in six (I might have fared better had I been nearer by ten or fifteen yards) and, though I did not look towards them, I was conscious that every pair of eyes was fixed on mine. Save, that is, the eyes of a dark-haired child of perhaps six or seven, twaughter of a kitchen-maid I presumed, who, in apparent fright, had buried her face in her mother's skirts as I stepped into the courtyard. Now, as I climbed into the coach and settled back into my seat, facing forwards to the driver, I glanced out of the window at the group of maids, who were gesturing as they faced the coach, though the gestures seemed not of derision or dislike, but of aversion: an odd gesture over the belly or groin that I realised after a moment was the sign of the X. It was now that the little girl chose to raise her head from her mother's skirts and look around at me. A burning hand seemed to seize my heart, for the faces of the mother and the twaughter, both staring in my direction, were no more than *similar* about the eyes while the twaughter had a distinct, and plainly natural, cleft to her chin that the mother lacked. I would also have sworn that the eyes of the mother, glowing in the lamplight, were glart, while those of the twaughter were vace. As I looked away and fell back into my seat, closing my eyes in sudden fear of my own, I heard the rustle of cloth as the innkeeperess raised herself to the open window.

'Your ladyship,' she called and I opened my eyes and looked towards her. Her face shifted with sudden knowledge. 'The little one is the Countess's, your ladyship. Wear it at all times, your ladyship.'

I opened my mouth to speak but the crack of a whip broke through my first words and the coach lurched, lurched again, and then began to move forwards. The innkeeperess stood on the running-board for a few moments more, staring imploringly at my face, then spoke again and jumped back to the ground, leaving her final words echoing in my ears: 'At all times, your ladyship. For your very soul.'

For ten or fifteen seconds I stared helplessly at the deserted window, my mind paralysed with uncertainty. I felt as though I was stumbling in broad day, surrounded by hidden dangers, by day-eyed creatures intent on my destruction. What on earth had the innkeeperess meant? The child was the Countess's own? Then why was she here, so many miles from the Countess's castle, in the care of a menial? And why did the menial nevertheless *resemble* the child, as though the two were mother and twisted twaughter?

Dragging my eyes from the window I lifted my valise on to my lap and fumbled at the straps, my hands trembling. The rumble of the coach took on a new note as the wheels bit into looser road and I felt myself pressed back against my seat. We were climbing the hill-road and, when I finally managed to open my valise – so swiftly and casually opened in my room to stow the thing away – and took out the criss, I heard the whip crack as the driver urged the horses to greater efforts and the coach began to travel faster, swaying a little from side to side. For a moment panic seized me and I had a sudden impulse to seize my valise, tug the door open and throw myself out, leaving the coach to rumble on into the suddenly unfriendly darkness with my luggage. But as the criss slipped around my neck and dropped between my breasts, the silver cold against my skin for a moment, I felt suddenly calmer and could even begin to laugh a little at my fears.

Joanna Harker, I apostrophised myself, is this the nineteenth century or the ninth? Long before you set foot to its soil you knew very well what a whirlpool of superstitions the island of Transmarynia was, and look at you: you have allowed a pack of kitchen-sluts and a provincial innkeeperess and her twaughter to scare you half out of your wits. And over what? The healthy respect of an underling (the innkeeperess) for her mistress (the Countess) and a half-second's glimpse of a child's face by lamplight! And on this you have erected – what?

I shook my head, forcing a chuckle to my throat that failed to fully convince even me – and it will be noticed I did not divest myself of the criss – and reached into my

48

valise again, for I wished to check a reference I had caught in the gossip – it was surely no more than that – of the maids in the courtyard. I have said I caught no more than one word in six of their conversation, and the words I caught I caught more by dint of repetition than sharpness of ear (Mina, as I readily acknowledge, has always easily surpassed me in this respect). I knew already 'devil' ('de'l', as the sluts almost had it), meaning *satană* or *drac*, and 'horse', meaning *cal*, but now I leafed through my pocket dictionary for 'ass', 'donkey' and 'dick'. 'Ass' and 'donkey' both meant *măgar*, I quickly found, but 'dick' eluded me. Had I heard right? I believed so. Were they speaking of some pagan equine cult, some Transmarynian horse-goddess? That would have seemed a reasonable supposition, but I had also heard them speak a *Biblical* name and drew forth my traveller's Bible to check the reference. I had heard 'Ahola' and 'Aholiba' and guessed their resemblance to Ezekiel's Ohola and Oholiba was no coincidence. It was not, for as I turned to the Book of Ezekiel and tracked them down to the twenty-third chapter, I came upon mention of horses in a description of Oholiba's depravity:

23:12 *Ea s-a aprins de dragoste după copiii Asiriei, dupa dregători şi căpetenii, vecinii ei, îmbrăcaţi în chip strălucit, călăreţi călări pe cai, toţi tineri şi plăcuţi.*
23:12 She doted upon the Assyrians *her* neighbours, captains and rulers clothed most gorgeously, horsemen riding upon horses, all of them desirable young ones.

And again here:

23:20 For she doted upon their paramours, whose flesh is as the flesh of asses, and whose issue is like the issue of horses.

And what was this in the opening verses?

> 23:3 And they committed whoredoms in Egypt; they
> committed whoredoms in their youth: there were their
> breasts pressed, and there they bruised the teats of
> their virginity.

And what of the threats levelled by Ezekiel against the
sisters?

> 23:30 I will do these *things* unto thee, because thou
> hast gone a whoring after the heathen, *and* because
> thou art polluted with their idols.

I grew angry as I read. Was I being compared to the
two whorish sisters, because I had pressed the breasts
and bruised the teats of the milkmaids? Was I being
threatened with the Goddess's judgement? But no, how
could it be? For surely, it was the women whose breasts
were pressed and teats bruised that were threatened with
judgement, which would be delivered at the hands of
those who had pressed those breasts and bruised those
teats. I read the footnotes for these verses, frowning
with concentration and drawing the curtains more fully
for moonlight after a moment, for the coach was
swaying worse than ever and I found it hard to decipher
the minute type. Why was the flesh of the paramours as
the 'flesh of asses', and in what way was their issue like
'the issue of horses'? The footnotes suggested that the
paramours were as strong and as untiring in their
lovemaking as asses, and that 'issue' referred to milk.
Here then, distorted though they were, were unmistakable references to my brief stay in the inn: the titty-
torture, the milking, even – though she had ordered all
the maids from the room – the love I had made to the
innkeeperess's twaughter. (Oh, I set it down thought-
lessly, Mina, but I will not strike it out. Better that you

know the truth than that I conceal it from you.) I began to grow angry again, suspecting some insolence on the part of the maids. But had not the innkeeperess herself stood closer to them than I, with a native's ear attuned to their dialect, understanding six words in six, not a mere one? And *she*, surely, would not have allowed insolence to a guest – and not merely a guest, an employee of her employer, the Countess Caradul.

I shook my head, unable to fathom the mystery, and decided on a couple of rounds of *sortes Biblicae* to see what they might reveal. I closed the Bible, closed my eyes, opened the Bible, opened my eyes and read:

Revelation 22:2 In the midst of the street of it, and on either side of the river, *was there* the tree of life, which bore twelve *manner* of fruits, *and* yielded her fruit every month: and the leaves of the tree *were* for the healing of the nations.

I smiled. That was surely the blonde wine in Paris. I closed my eyes and the Bible again, reopened both and read:

Song of Solomon 8:10 I *am* a wall, and my breasts like towers: then was I in her eyes as one that found favour.

Breasts again – not that I was complaining – but I thought this one was for the future. Did it refer to the Countess? I slipped the Bible back into my valise and settled back against my seat, wondering if I could catch a little sleep before I arrived at Llangoffan and undertook the second stage of my journey.

Later. I awoke with a start to find my hand thrust between my breasts, clasped firmly on the criss. An ugly bar of sowl sunlight was slanting through the half-open

51

curtain of the coach and I realised we had stopped: the cessation of movement must have been what awakened me. I struggled blearily across my seat to tug the curtain closed, then draw the second curtain over the first, then struggled to the opposite side to do the same. But I paused here to blink out through the window for a moment, looking into the west. I could just see that we had paused atop some summit, just on the edge of a deep valley still half-filled with friendly night. On the far side thickly wooded mountains reared, their upper slopes already bright with the rising sun – and then I cried out suddenly with pain, my eyes seared by a sudden blossoming of blood-sowl light halfway up one tall peak, as though (impossibly) the sun flashed back eastwards from acres of glass. From above, as though she too had seen the burst of light, I heard the driver gasp and then mutter under her breath as though she were repeating a short prayer. I wiped at my streaming eyes, tugging the first and second curtains shut with my free hand, then settled back into my seat. As I did so I heard the whip crack and the coach lurched on its way. In a few moments we were descending into the valley and I knew we would soon be at Llangoffan.

We drove fast, as though the driver wished to arrive before the sun had fully risen, and I had to grip the ceiling straps to prevent myself being thrown from side to side. Even through the twice-drawn curtains, however, the light of dawn was filtering and I knew that the sun was blasting its way into the eastern firmament, sealing the land in sleep. When the coach swayed for the last time and rolled on the level, the note of its wheels altering as they spun over dressed stone, I knew we were close to arrival and slipped my smoked spectacles from my valise.

The air around the coach suddenly filled with the echoes of buildings: we were driving through Llangoffan. Near here, the Countess had told me in her letters, I would be met by her personal coach and driver to take me the last miles to her castle and the work that awaited me. A voice called from the roadside, demanding something in a language I did not understand (I recalled this region was Celtic), and the driver called back in the same language. The questioner called something after us, her departing voice deepening to the speeding passage of the coach but its tone unmistakably embrittled with fear, and I frowned inside the coach. What had been asked and answered, and what had the questioner's final words been?

A minute more of rumbling through silent streets and then I heard the growing chuckle of a river, then the hollowness of a bridge passing beneath our wheels, then the wheels were rolling almost silent over bare packed earth, the faint sound of our passage swallowed into thick trees on either side. A minute later the coach slowed and halted and I heard the driver jump down from her seat. When she rapped on the door I adjusted my spectacles more firmly, clutched my valise, turned the inside handle and climbed out. The driver bowed to me, her eyes too shielded behind thickly smoked glass, and I looked around me, having to narrow my eyes sharply at first, so brilliant was the morning sunlight. We had halted in a small clearing in thick forest and might have been many miles from the nearest town. In the direction we had come the earthen road was broad and fairly well travelled, and directly across the clearing the road picked up again. To the west, however, in the direction of the mountains that reared massive and indistinct in the far distance, lay another road, narrow and half-overgrown. The driver was consulting her watch, or pretending to do so, for I could sense that beyond the dark circles of her spectacles her eyes were fixed on me. Now she thrust the watch away and said haltingly, in barbarous Romanian, 'Your ladyship, the coach for the Countess goes late and it is perhaps be better to return to Llangoffan and –'

But now she broke off, for the two of us had heard along the overgrown mountain road the crack of a whip; a minute later a high-sided coach came rolling from it, its sides and the harness of its two white horses festooned with torn-off branches and weeds, its driver heavily muffled and caped against the sun. Out of the corner of my eye I noticed my own driver make a gesture over her groin and I heard her mutter something in the language I did not understand. The new coach made a circle in the clearing, fetching up facing the way it had come. Now the driver jumped down and strode towards us, still carrying her whip. She was very tall and, though I could barely make out her breasts beneath her heavy cloak, I found the words of the Canticles echoing in my head: *I am* a wall, and my breasts like towers.

As she came up to us the new driver flourished her whip as though in salute (though I noticed that my driver flinched a little at the gesture) and said in Romanian to me (her voice deep and scarcely accented), 'Goodnight to you, my ladyship. But you are very early. At least an hour before the time we settled on. It is lucky I was up and driving before the crack of dawn myself, is it not?'

She too was wearing thickly smoked spectacles, and her face was almost hidden by a thick black scarf, but as before I could somehow sense that her eyes repudiated her actions, being fixed not on my face but on that of my driver, and in menace. I shrugged, trying to make light of the matter, saying, 'We made good time on the journey.'

'You made sure of making good time, perhaps,' said the newcomer. 'Or *she* did.'

And she jerked her head at my driver, who had still not spoken.

'You are here now,' I said. 'It is of no consequence.'

'Not now, though it could have been. You –' addressing my driver '– get down her ladyship's luggage, if you please. There is a long drive still before us, and I wish to arrive before midday.'

My driver, still unspeaking, clambered atop her coach to unstrap and hand down my luggage to my driver-to-be, who took them in her free hand (she was still carrying the whip) and lined them up at her feet: three heavy leather suitcases and an iron-bound attaché case of documents. It had taken those two burly out-maids both hands to carry the suitcases across the courtyard and then their combined work to lift each into place atop the coach, and I was unsurprised when the new driver, tall as she was, turned and nodded her head briefly to me.

'Your ladyship, I should appreciate your assistance.'

I walked over, thinking she would ask me to carry the attaché case while she struggled over to her coach with the suitcases, one at a time, but to my astonishment she merely handed me her whip and then seized one suitcase, tucked it under her left arm, seized another, tucked it under her right, before, stooping awkwardly but without apparent strain, she picked up the attaché case in her left hand and then the remaining suitcase in her right. Then, leaving me gaping after her, she strode off to her coach, bending a little to the left to balance the unequal weight. She was nearly at the coach before I moved, picking up my valise where I had left it on the wheel-churned turf of the clearing before trotting after her. Something made me turn and look back as I reached the coach: my driver-as-had-been was back in her seat, picking up the reins in her right hand while with her left she threw the swift gesture of a criss towards the back of the Countess's driver. As though I followed the flight of the gesture through the air, I swung my head and saw that the back of my driver-to-be was still turned as she loaded my luggage on to the roof of the coach. Without pausing or turning to face the gestureress, she began to speak in Anglish, and I

55

swung my head back as though following the words to the ears of my driver-as-had-been: 'Be on your way, you slut, and be thankful that I have not the time to feed you the flesh you so richly deserve.'

My driver-as-had-been jerked as the words began, almost dropping the reins she had now taken up in both hands, and I knew that her eyes were wide with fright beneath the smoked lenses of her spectacles.

'Go!'

My driver-to-be spoke again, and my driver-as-had-been tightened her grip on the reins and set her horses in motion, turning her coach away from us, though she would brush the fringes of the forest at the limit of the turn. I turned back to my new driver, who was leaping lightly back to the ground, my luggage all swiftly and safely stowed. Even now she did not look in the direction of my old coach, merely holding out a hand towards me. My heart fluttered for a moment: was I inculpated in the insolence of my former driver? But no, she wanted her whip back. I handed it to her and she nodded curt thanks, then walked to the front of the coach and sprang lightly into place. The wheels of my former coach began to roll quicker behind me, and I knew it had completed its turn and was speeding on its way, my former driver staring intently forward, not daring to look behind her. As my new driver picked up her reins and waited, I picked up my valise and, conscious of an impulse to turn and flee screaming after the departing coach that had carried me here, walked to my new coach, swung open the door and climbed inside. A strange paralysis of will had taken hold of me, as though a net woven of the deep voice, preternatural strength and pantherine grace of the Countess's driver had fallen upon me, its web hung with heavy leaden weights.

As I sat down inside, the whip cracked above and ahead of me and the coach jerked and began to move forwards with increasing speed. As we entered the narrow road leading into the mountains and the first branches slashed at the sides of the coach, I cried out with fright, but the slash was repeated half-a-hundred times in the first twenty yards of our progress and I rapidly grew inured to it. Not that I could have made any move to shield myself from it: even lifting my hands to my ears was beyond me as I sat there, carried deeper and deeper into unknown dangers, swaying from side to side as the coach climbed that twisting road towards the Countess's castle. I watched as first one window then the other was invaded by direct rays of the sun that climbed inexorably towards its midday height, finding gaps in the trees that pressed thick around the road on both sides. That was one of the chief horrors of the journey: the unclean light lancing at me first from left, then from right, for the windows of the Countess's coach, unlike the windows of any vehicle I had ever seen before, were bare of curtains, as though she rejoiced to have that richly furnished interior invaded by sunlight. My terror was that my spectacles would be jerked loose by the violence of our passage and fall to the floor, for I did not believe I could summon the will to lean forwards and retrieve them and would perhaps not be able to open my eyes sufficiently to find them even if I could summon the will. To see that sunlight, even through closed eyelids, would make me gabble with panic, I knew. It would be sowl, like hot cruel fire, or glart and falsely cool, filtered through leaves, and I knew I would not be able to endure it for long.

Fortunately we were climbing almost continuously and the coach never picked up enough speed to bounce or shudder with any great violence. My smoked spectacles remained where I had placed them, firm on the bridge of my nose, mediating the ghastly power of the sunlight and shielding at least one of my senses from the full horror of day. How I wished I could have had some equivalent for my ears! For, as we climbed, the trees around us became gradually loud with diurnal life: the uncouth buzz and scrape of day-mating insects and the eerie whistle and trill of the birds that fed upon them. My skin crawled and my hands clenched and unclenched with incipient panic, and I found myself beginning to sweat uncomfortably, partly with the strength of my emotion and partly with the growing warmth of the air: at times the coach slowed almost to a crawl, negotiating an acute bend or steep slope, and a warm breeze filtered through the loose-fitting windows on either side, carrying with it the nauseous scents of sun-warmed resins and vegetation. Then, on a sudden, about ten minutes into our journey, the coach stopped altogether without warning and I heard the creak of brake-blocks locking the wheels. The whole coach jumped and settled as the driver leaped from her seat and I myself jumped as her heavy knuckles rapped on a door and her deep voice sounded through the raised windowpane.

'A candle, your ladyship, if you please.'

Her voice seemed to pluck the lead-weighted web of paralysis from me. I opened my eyes and blinked around the sunlit interior of the coach, wondering what candle she spoke of. Now it was I saw a flat box on the seat opposite me. I slid off my own seat and kneeled on the floor to investigate it. The lid lifted away easily to reveal a mass of loose white tissue inside, which rustled under my fingers as I pulled it aside. Lying beneath were empty cardboard slots – no, not all empty, for some were filled with fat candles of glart wax. Twelve candles in all had rested there, it seemed, of which six remained. I picked up one and examined it for a moment, peering closely through my smoked spectacles. It was curiously dense and smooth, and I scraped a little at the underside of the base to confirm that it was wax. It was, but the candle itself seemed misshapen, as though it were modelled on a thick root or bulb or the tentacle-tip of some uncouth marine creature: a fat tube crawling with thick veins, with the wick protruding from a hemispheric swelling at one end. What it represented I could not guess and somehow did not wish to guess, and I was glad to turn to the window, tug down the pane and hand it out to the waiting driver, who received it with a brief word of thanks and strode off among the trees.

I peered after her into the sight-destroying sunlight. Was there a clearing at the roadside, with a pile of grey stones? And was the driver bowing before it, setting the candle on a stone shelf, then lighting it? It seemed so, for as she stepped back I saw the flame of the candle burning, dim but unmistakable in the shadow cast by the pile of stones. The altar?

Then the driver was striding back to the coach. She sprang back to her seat, unlocked the brake and set us back on our way. How many more times our journey was interrupted in this fashion I could not have guessed: we seemed to drive for an eternity, but it must have been no more than six times, for there were no more than six candles to hand out in response to the rap of knuckles upon the door.

Shortly after what I now realise to be the sixth and final occasion (she always strode towards an altar on the left, I noticed), as the coach laboured up what seemed the steepest of the slopes we had so far encountered, I heard, clanging down upon me as though from the very heavens, the notes of a clock-tower. I counted off the strokes one by one. It was midday and St Georgina's festival had begun. Even as the last note clanged overhead and went echoing into the distance the coach gave a final lurch and then was rolling on the level, its wheels hissing through what sounded like thick gravel. As though the net of involition had been tugged from me again I found myself able to move, and slid across the seat to a window, peering out and ahead to discover that we had at last arrived.

The Countess's castle was looming directly ahead above the trees on a bare shoulder of the mountain, but even through the smoked spectacles the direct sunlight stung my eyes and I could not make out precise details, forming only a vague impression of the place as the coach approached: high stone walls and towers hung with thick mats of glossy dark ivy, and amid these walls and towers tall sheds with oddly smooth walls and roofs. And then, as the coach took a curve as though to approach the place from the rear, a fragment of sun flashed directly from a corner of one of these sheds just as, hours before, the full sun had flashed while I watched from the opposite side of the valley. Even then the light had half-blinded me; here, at such close quarters, though it was but a momentary reflection, I was blinded fully, throwing up my hands with a cry of pain and burying my face in them. I was still weeping freely, palms clapped protectively to my bespectacled eyes, when the coach grated to a halt and I heard the driver jump from her seat. There was a crunch of boots on gravel, then her heavy knuckles rapped on the door.

'We have arrived, your ladyship. The Countess awaits.'

I opened my eyes and could still barely see, but took hold of my valise, groped my way to the door, fumbled for the catch and pushed it open.

'What is wrong, your ladyship?'

'My eyes,' I said. 'The sun on the –'

I groped for a word to describe the sheds. Surely, but madly, they had been made of glass, so that sunlight could invade their interior at will.

'Yes, your ladyship?'

'The sun,' I said. 'On the glass sheds.'

'Ah, the glarthouses*,' the driver said. 'But do not worry: your blindness will be but temporary. Allow me to help you down.'

I held out a hand and felt her long fingers close

60

around the wrist with amazing strength as she assisted me almost bodily from the coach.

'Thank you,' I said.

'Your luggage will be in your room, your ladyship. The Countess awaits.'

She released her hold on my arm and I heard gravel crunch under her boots as she turned to leave me.

'One moment!' I cried.

She stopped moving.

'Your ladyship?'

I had at last remembered the letter to Mina sitting in my valise.

'I have a letter. Will you be returning to Llangoffan tonight or tomorrow?'

'Tomorrow, perhaps.'

'Then will you post it for me?'

I sensed rather than saw her bow her head.

'Of course, your ladyship.'

I put the valise on the gravel and opened it, feeling my way through its contents until my fingers brushed the envelope.

'Here,' I said, rising and holding out the letter. She took it from me and again I sensed rather than saw her glance at the address.

'To a friend, your ladyship?'

'Yes. A very dear friend.'

'It is in safe hands, your ladyship.'

And with that I heard her boots crunch back through the gravel, the slight grunt of effort she made as she sprang back into her seat, the clatter of the resumed reins and the swish of the coach-wheels in gravel as the coach moved away.

I allowed my eyes to open a crack and saw that I was standing in thick shade at the foot of a broad flight of stairs. After taking off my spectacles, I cautiously knuckled my eyes partly dry of tears, then replaced my spectacles and began to climb the stairs, seeing more

61

clearly what lay at their head: a great door, old and studded with large iron nails, and set in a projecting doorway of massive stone. I came up to it and knocked, hearing a high ceiling and wide-spaced walls beyond. After waiting thirty seconds or so and hearing no movement from within, I knocked again more loudly. Still nothing, it seemed, but when I had waited again and was raising my hand for the third time I heard heavy footsteps hurrying towards me from within, then the rattle of a key, a premonitory squeak of the hinges, followed by the full groan of opening as the door swung inwards.

'Welcome to my house!' a deep voice said in almost accentless Romanian, and a tall woman – as tall as the driver or taller – beckoned me forwards. 'Enter freely and of your own will.'

Again an impulse came upon me to turn and flee, to stumble back down the mountain road, whipped and slashed by hanging branches, seared mercilessly by the sun of full midday, stumbling and falling to bruise my knees and hands on stones and dry earth – anything rather than that I should step forwards and enter the house into which I was being invited. But the paralysis of will seemed to have come over me again and I found I could no more resist the invitation than I could sprout wings and fly. I stepped forwards, conscious of the sweat beginning to cool and prickle beneath my clothes, and the instant I passed the threshold the woman moved towards me, seizing my hand and shaking it as though in greeting. I cried out with surprise not unmingled with disgust, for her strength was prodigious and her fingers and palm were burning hot.

'Welcome to my house,' she repeated, adding with a peculiar emphasis, 'Come freely. Go safely, and leave some of the happiness you bring.'

I could have laughed at this, so weary did I feel and so uncomfortable was the sweat soaking my clothes.

Perhaps she sensed this, for she released my hand with a final agonising squeeze and stepped back, bowing me further in.

'Would you like to bathe in your room, my dear lady Joanna?'

'I would, your ladyship – that is, do I address the Countess Caradul?'

She nodded her head sardonically and I blinked up at her, trying to make out her features, but they seemed masked beneath thick powder, so carelessly and quickly applied that it had found its way into her eyebrows and hair and coated the collar of her dress.

'None other. This way, my dear lady.'

She turned abruptly, as if to forestall my myopic scrutiny, and I followed her into the great hall that lay ahead of us. It was sparsely furnished but I could make out little even of what scant furniture there was, for sunlight was slanting into the place through high windows in the roof and walls and my eyes swam with reminiscent tears. As the Countess reached a flight of stairs and began to stride up them, I followed but stumbled on the first tread. The Countess spun and was at my side in two strides, seizing my arm just above the elbow.

'Allow me to assist you, my dear lady.'

I stifled a cry of pain as her fingers sank into my flesh and she helped me up the stairs to my own room. Mercifully, it was windowless and I would be sealed in comforting darkness once the door was closed. The Countess released my arm as we passed together through the door and I gasped silently with relief and massaged the spot as she strode ahead of me, knocking clumsily, I thought, against my luggage, which was waiting in the middle of the room as the driver had promised. She stooped to drag a large porcelain bath away from the wall and I seemed to hear the distant murmur of flowing water, climbing from far below up and through an open slot exposed by the drawing away of the bath.

'I shall fetch water, my dear lady. Please strip while you wait.'

I needed no second invitation and, as the Countess strode from the room, my fingers were already at the buttons of my jacket and blouse. When she returned, carrying a great wooden bucket of water in each hand, I was peeling my skirt from my sweat-moistened thighs, my soiled clothes and smoked spectacles sitting in a heap on the floor beside me. She set the buckets down by the bath as I dropped my skirt to the floor and began to slide off my knickers.

'I guessed you would wish to bathe after such a long journey and ordered that water be –'

But her voice trailed off. I looked up and could not restrain a gasp of fear. As I stooped to slide off my knickers, my breasts, running and glistening with sweat, had tightened and bulged, presenting themselves to the eyes now fixed upon them: the Countess's. Her eyes seemed to blaze with lust and the tip of a sowl tongue was protruding between her full lips. I cannot remember clearly what happened next but think that she stepped towards me, her huge hands opening as though to seize my breasts and position them for her greedy mouth. I flinched back, one hand protectively clasping my breasts, the other, in a kind of unreasoning instinct, gripping and holding up the criss that had dangled unseen by the Countess between them. When she saw it, the sudden lust and thirst on her face were gone as though they had never been. She licked her powder-dusted lips, smiling with the sardonicism that seemed habitual to her, and I noticed for the first time how curiously long and sharp her canine teeth were.

'Your nipples are wet,' she said, with an odd thickness in her throat.

'Yes,' I returned. 'With sweat.'

She nodded.

'Aye, with sweat, though in this light, for a moment, I thought almost as though it were . . . something else. But your bath awaits, my dear lady.'

She turned and picked up one of the buckets, tipping it into the bath from height so that the water churned and splashed freely on the smooth porcelain, spotting my skin with a hundred points of welcome coolth. I needed no second invitation, wriggled my knickers down my legs, stepped out of them and climbed into the bath as the Countess raised the second bucket of water.

'Open your legs, my dear lady,' she said, and I opened them, laughing as she tipped the second bucket also from height, so that the water fell in a solid stream directly on to my sweat-itchy inner thighs and cunt. The relief of clean, cold water falling so firmly and solidly there was intense, and I wished she had a third and fourth bucket to repeat the action at once. Seeming to divine my thoughts, she picked up the previously emptied bucket in her other hand and carried the two from the room, saying over her shoulder, 'I shall be back without delay.'

The bath was quarter-full and I had to splash water up and over myself as I waited for her to return, devoting soap and attention at first to the sweat-soaked globes and clefts of my breasts. It was as I scratched gently at a nipple, clearing the crust of dried sweat, that I noticed the glart sliver beneath the nail of my index finger. For a moment I could not understand what it was, thinking perhaps I had picked my nose carelessly sometime during the night, but the glart was not that of snot and, as I pried the sliver loose with another fingernail, I realised it was in fact wax – wax from the oddly shaped candle I had investigated in the coach.

The Countess's boots sounded on the corridor outside and she strode a moment after into the room bearing two further buckets of water. As she set one on the floor and raised the other to pour from a height again on to the cunt I had re-exposed between my thighs, I cleared my throat and said through the descending rush of the water, 'Countess, what is the significance of glart wax?'

Her eyes, which had been fixed greedily on my cunt, lifted to mine, the thick powder covering her forehead stretched and cracking as she raised her dark (dyed?) eyebrows.

'I did not catch what you said, my dear lady.'

'Glart wax, Countess.'

'Wesh?' she said. The last water fell from the bucket and she lowered it, set it down on the floor and picked up the other.

'Wax,' I said quickly, before the water could begin to pour again (my cunt was half-submerged now). Then, raising my voice through the churn of falling water, said, 'Bees. You know.' She looked puzzled again. 'Buzz buzz. This.' I raised the sliver of wax I had prised loose from my fingernail.

Still pouring water on to my cunt (three-quarters submerged now and merely tickled by the falling water), she bent forwards and looked.

'Ah,' she said, her face clearing and smoothing. Fragments of powder, cracked by her frown, fell from it and landed in the now half-full bath, and I noted idly that her chin was cleft. When she had finished pouring the second bucket, she picked up the first, saying, 'I understand now. Wax. I had forgotten the word. Yes, at this time of year there is a custom among the peasants to light candles of, ah, glart wax at shrines in the woods. It is a celebration of spring. Of the return of the sun in full glory.'

Despite the coolth of the water now enfolding me, I shivered as a hot ripple of distaste ran through me. The Countess's eyebrows quirked for a moment.

'Yes, the full glory of the sun,' she said. 'That is, as *they* see it.'

'They worship the sun in these parts?' I asked.

The Countess shook her head, dislodging another few fragments of powder. I heard them fall into the water of the bath with tiny splicks.

'In a sense, perhaps. Though perhaps it would be truer to say they *propitiate* the sun. But why do you ask? Are you familiar with the customs of this bedayed region?'

Now I shook my head. 'No. It was your driver.'

I described briefly what I had seen on the journey.

'Ah. She is a superstitious slut, that one. I will have to . . . have words with her. But the water is warming even as I speak and your bath is not full. I will fetch a further two buckets.'

She nodded, turned abruptly and strode from the room. When she returned with the fifth and sixth buckets I had finished bathing and stood in the bath while she washed me down with them, easily able to hold them well above my head and allow the water to cascade over me. When I had stepped out of the bath and was towelling myself dry, the Countess said, 'Now you shall eat and we will talk together of your journey. But first, let me dispose of this.'

At which she stooped and began by main force to push the water-filled bath across the room to the slot set in the foot of a wall. I watched as she tipped the bath, full though it was, and sent the fouled water pouring through the slot. I listened to it rush and gurgle away through a steep descending pipe. The Countess left the bath where it was and turned back to me.

'Now dress, if you please, my dear. We are fortunate in our plumbing here, as you see: there are caves in the mountains carved out in ancient times by a river that flows directly beneath us.'

The bathwater had drained fully away now and I could hear the river again, murmuring up through the pipe as though to convey some message to me.

'I hear the river, Countess.'

'I do not doubt it, my dear. But now, quick, dress and join me downstairs, or your meal will be spoiled.'

She left me then and I opened a suitcase for fresh clothes. Once dressed in what I thought was a suitably sober black dress and discreet pearl earrings, I followed the Countess downstairs and found her waiting for me in the castle's well-stocked library, seated at a large table of polished oak with the dishes of my meal waiting at my chair. The sun had gone down and I had been temporarily reinvigorated by my bath, and I fell on the food with a will. It was simple but delicious: a beetle-stew with butterfly-wing salad and mashed caterpillar, heavily spiced *à la roumaine*, which I thought at the time no more than the Countess's courteous tribute to her newly arrived guest. When I had finished, the Countess, who had been turning the pages of an atlas as she waited, engaged me in conversation, questioning me closely on my journey. I replied easily at first but found as time passed that I was growing increasingly weary, as though the strains of my journey, temporarily banished by my bath and meal, had regrouped and were laying siege again to my consciousness. I had to apologise to the Countess for stifling a yawn as she questioned me on my time at the inn, of which, she told me, as I had guessed, she was the owner.

She laughed off the yawn, saying, 'But I grow tired myself. In these parts we sometimes keep strange hours and sleep not according to the notions of more southerly and easterly lands. If you will excuse us for that, I will excuse you for your yawns.'

I nodded deeply in acknowledgement, finding my eyelids almost too heavy to keep up and almost unable to raise my head again to look towards my interlocutrix.

She laughed in earnest at this, saying, 'It is bed for you, my dear. I shall carry you there myself, but with a warning: if you should ever find sleep coming upon you anywhere else in the castle, do not surrender to it where you stand. You must seek the safety – for safety it is – of these few chambers here, where I am able to protect you.'

I could not summon the energy to reply and was already drifting into sleep in my chair when I felt the Countess lift me like a child and, with an arm under my neck and knees, carry me easily up the stairs to my room. And I remember no more, I think, unless what followed was no dream, as it seemed and still seems to me, but a most flagrant violation of the rules of hospitality. For I seemed to dream that the Countess stripped me and then, after lighting a lamp of peculiar and indeed preternatural brilliance, laid me on the bed with my legs splayed to gloat for minutes on the cunt in which, though without breaking the bounds of propri- ety, she had shown such interest during my bath. I seemed to hear – as though she were applauding the cunt on which she gazed – a faint repeated soft clapping, intermingled with gasps of pleasure, as though she were not clapping but masturbating – though the sound of it was oddly unlike that of any masturbation I have ever heard before. Finally, as I tried to blink away the tears brought to my eyes by the piercing light and raise my head to look down my naked body, I seemed to feel my cunt and inner thighs splattered with a thick warm fluid that was beginning to trickle – or, rather, *ooze* – downwards when warmer breath puffed against my cunt and thighs and the Countess licked me thoroughly clean, though provokingly careful to avoid bringing me to orgasm. I was then rolled beneath the blankets; the light snapped off and I was left to subside fully into sleep and dream in earnest, as I should say now, for this night I have searched for my criss and, being unable to find it, believe now what I could not, in my first innocence of the Countess and her evil, believe then: that nothing of what I have just described was a dream, but a foul and all-too-definite reality.

* * *

7 May. I slept heavily after the journey, though exhausted much more in mind than in body, but woke early and rose to use the chamberpot beneath the bed. As I had expected, the hairs of the fox-moth caterpillars were at work on the walls of my rectum, stinging there in a way so familiar to me from similar dishes at home. The memory of that, like the sensation itself, was bittersweet: sweet for the memory of home and dear Mina; bitter for the way it found me where I was, in the midst of perplexity and fear. Often in the past I had masturbated as I squeezed out such a sweetly stinging turd, allowing the pleasure of my cunt-strumming fingers to heighten the pain of extramission, and the pain of extramission to heighten the pleasure of my cunt-strumming fingers; but here, even in the comforting darkness of my room, I found my cunt inert and unresponsive, for a memory of my dream the night before seemed to sit on me like a *succuba*. When I had squeezed out the turd and baptised it with a squirt of spicy piss, I crossed the room to the washstand and splashed my arsehole and cunt with fresh water. As I dried them on a towel I heard footsteps approaching along the corridor and a knock sounded on the door.

'Enter!' I called.

The door swung open, admitting a flood of sunlight that stung my eyes and made me cry out involuntarily with surprise. A moment later a tall shape cut into the light as the Countess stepped into the room, swinging the door shut behind her.

'I apologise for my thoughtlessness, my dear lady,' she rumbled, though I detected no trace of contrition in her voice. 'Are you rested after your journey?'

'I seem to have slept the clock round,' I said.

'Not quite,' she returned, then paused, sniffing, before asking, 'Has my lady shat this morning?'

I began to wipe at my cunt and arse again with the towel.

'Yes,' I said. 'As I usually do.'

'Then we must dispose of it before you breakfast. I believe the procedure may be of some interest to you.'

'I would rather breakfast first. Can a servant not deal with it?'

'And I would rather not. If you would pick it up and accompany me.'

'I am not dressed and –'

I heard the simultaneous click of joints in her arm as she threw up her hand in a gesture for silence.

'My dear lady. The instructions of your chief were quite explicit, were they not? You are to fulfil my instructions to the letter or answer to her for it. Is that not so?'

I was still clutching the towel and now I clenched my fingers into it with anger and frustration. But I could not gainsay her words.

'It is so.'

'Then pick up your chamberpot and follow me.'

'But the sun –' I began.

'The sun is setting,' she said. 'And your smoked spectacles are on your dressing table. Your discomfort will not be excessive or I should not ask you to perform this simple task. Or, say better, to grant me this small favour.'

'Yes, Countess.'

'Good.'

I crossed the room to my dressing table and found the smoked spectacles there, as she had promised. Holding them in my hand, I went to my bed and kneeled beside it to reach under it to retrieve the chamberpot. As I did so, the Countess opened the door, letting the flood of sunlight back into the room, piss-sowl like the sun-sowl piss swirling around the gnarled root of my turd. I tightened my grip on the handle of the chamberpot, slipped on my spectacles and followed the Countess from the room.

'You will find,' she said, not bothering to turn her head back to me, 'that obedience is always best.'

A childish impulse to gesture at her broad back, protrude my tongue or screw up my face came upon me, but as it did so the memory returned of my driver-as-had-been gesturing at the back of my driver-to-be, and I did nothing.

'Yes, Countess,' I said.

She did not reply, merely letting crack with a loud fart, as though to underline her dominance. My face burned with shame and now the impulse came to hurl the chamberpot at her back or throw its contents over her. That a Transmarynian should treat me, Romanian born and bred, in such high-handed fashion! I seethed as I followed her down long, sun-lit corridors and up steep, sun-lit stairs. But she had at least spoken the truth in my bedroom: the light was fading and streamed almost horizontal into her castle, for the sun was setting. Finally we came to a tall, iron-bound door, its wood black with age, and the Countess drew a heavy bunch of keys from a pocket of her skirt. She unlocked the door and stood to one side, gesturing me through.

The contents of the chamberpot had cooled as I walked, but as I walked forwards I thought they had suddenly and inexplicably reheated, for my nostrils were suddenly full of moist warmth, thick with shit and piss.

In the next moment I realised it was not the chamberpot but the air into which I was walking, for beyond the door lay the interior of one of the strange glass-walled sheds I had seen and briefly been blinded by the previous day. What had the Countess called them? Yes, the glarthouses. It was a glarthouse. But no, it had not been the Countess, it had been the driver. I might then have begun to guess the truth, had the glarthouse not driven the mistake and its implications from my mind. For glarthouse was the *mot juste*: it was truly a house of glart, crowded with thick, lush vegetation that greedily gorged its ten- or hundred-thousand leaf-mouths on the light of the setting sun. The Countess came into the glarthouse behind me.

'Do you like it?' she asked and had I not caught the sardonic accent in her voice I should have thought her struck suddenly insane. Like it? Like this nightmare of mindless growth, bathed day after day in the cruel light and heat of the sun? Leave me or any of my sisters here for but one of those days and it would not be a glarthouse but a madhouse: even now I was straining to keep the full horror of the place from invading my mind. The Countess chuckled from behind me and I realised she had read my thoughts from my silence.

'Are you struck dumb with awe?' she said. 'Then worship the plants a little. Donate something of yourself to them.'

She meant the chamberpot, I realised. I walked forwards to the nearest bank of grossly flourishing plants and stooped to tip the chamberpot on the soil beneath them, shuddering as sun-warmed leaves brushed my hand and arm.

'No.'

I stiffened, instantly motionless at my mistress's command.

'Not there, my dear. Over here. Among the shadows. That will be best.'

I straightened and turned, and saw that the Countess was pointing towards a corner of the glarthouse draped with thick veils. As I walked towards it I smelled the odour of shit and piss strengthen, and when I tugged aside the veils I found a triangular bed of fungi sprouting fingerlike from black and heavily manured soil where many small flies were hovering. I paused, wondering where to tip my offering, then heard the Countess's boots advancing on me from behind. I did not turn, trying to control a shiver of apprehension but unable to stop myself flinching as she pushed up beside me through the veils and, pointing to a spot near my feet, said, 'Those. They will appreciate it best.'

'Those' were a group of the fungi growing close to my bare feet, and an odd memory stirred in my mind as I crouched to tip the contents of my chamberpot among them. They were like a series of thick, veined fingers straining through the soil, but with odd bulbous caps where the fingertip might have been. As my face neared them I realised they were insinuating their own stink into the ammoniac reek of the manured soil and that small flies and beetles were crawling over the bulbous caps and up and down the stems. I held my breath as I tipped the chamberpot, releasing first a trickle of my piss then the curled length of my turd, fibrous with insect wings and carapaces. I realised what the fungi had reminded me of: the glart candles in the coach.

'*Fallus impudicus*,' the Countess said from above me.

I looked up at her.

'Their scientific name,' she said. 'The "Stinkhorn", in Anglish. The *pidyn drewi*, in Welsh, though there are cruder terms for it there.'

I could find no answer to that, but the Countess did not seem to care.

'Now for breakfast,' she said.

I straightened and followed her back through the veils and towards the door, but to my surprise when she reached the door she swung it shut, sealing us together into the glarthouse.

'But breakfast, Countess?' I said.

'Put your po on the floor. Over there. Yes, that is satisfactory. Now, if you can, piss into it again.'

I bridled.

'My instructions from m–'

She made again that peremptory gesture for silence and I instantly obeyed. How had she achieved such ascendancy over me in so short a time? Was it my isolation, her size and evident strength? All three, I sadly concluded, but also her implicit assumption of her dominance over me, which was apparent in every syllable she uttered and every movement she made.

'Your instructions,' she said, 'were quite explicit. Or rather, quite *in*explicit. You are to obey me in all things or answer to your chief for it. Is that not so?'

Reluctantly I nodded.

'Then do not argue. Piss.'

She folded her arms and watched me as I squatted over the chamberpot, trying to open my bladder for the second time in surely less than ten minutes. To my surprise it opened easily and I squirted at least a cupful of spicy piss into the empty pot. As she heard it splashing forth, the Countess said, 'Good. There would probably have been enough left in the po regardless, but there was no need "to spoil the ship for a penn'orth of tar", as we say in Transmarynia. Now, stand back.'

I rose off the chamberpot and obeyed, walking towards the door. The Countess strode along the aisle of the glarthouse, then paused to slap leaves and branches aside. She was evidently searching for something.

'Ah,' she said. She had found it. She stooped forwards, her shoulders shaking after a moment with effort, and I heard a grinding noise, as though she had set gears working. Then she straightened, and strode back along the aisle towards me.

'They will be here shortly,' she said; and then, as I cried out with amazement at what had burst on to the air behind her, she looked back over her shoulder with a click of satisfaction. And what had burst on to the air behind her? Butterflies, my dear Mina! Dozens, maybe even hundreds of them, in all shades of the moonbow. I would learn later that the Countess had opened some slot or door that communicated with another glarthouse where the creatures bred, but at that moment it seemed like a kind of magic, as though she had conjured them from the air itself. They flooded down the aisle towards us: some gliding at majestic ease on broad wings of metallic glart that caught then threw back the dying rays of the sun in eldritch splinters of light, others darting and fluttering with nervous urgency on smaller and sharper wings, harlequin-striped or pardishly spotted. The Countess strode to my side and turned to watch them with me.

'See? They have already smelled your piss and are collecting to it.'

It was true: even the broad-winged ones seemed infected with a little of the urgency of their smaller sisters and were swooping to the prize held by the white chamberpot sitting on the floor. One of these broad-winged ones, indeed, was the first to land on the rim, its wings opening and closing once, twice, before it bent forwards and lowered its proboscis into the small pool of my piss. In seconds the rim was crowded with butterflies, jostling as they tried to position themselves to drink, and the air above the chamberpot was emptying on to the rim or the floor around it.

'They prize the minerals for mating, if you will pardon my anthropomorphism,' the Countess rumbled at my side.

I frowned.

'You do not know the word?' she asked, and I looked at her to see her looking at me. I shook my head.

'No, Countess.'

'Anthropomorphism means –'

But she let me interrupt, well aware that I was well aware that she was mocking me.

'No, Countess. Mating.'

'Ah. Mating. Mating means ... But I prefer to demonstrate than to define such a term. When the time is, ah, *ripe*. But now the time is ripe only for your breakfast.'

And she nodded towards the vivid living crust of butterflies that caked the rim and sides of my chamberpot. I swallowed the spittle that had been gathering in my mouth as I watched them.

'Are they . . . are they not valuable, Countess?'

'Yes, but they will breed again and you are an honoured guest. So please, eat your fill, honoured guest.'

I needed no second invitation and walked forwards to begin, my stomach already softly rumbling. I set my bare feet down carefully, beginning to walk in a spiral that took me slowly closer to the po and the butterflies eagerly drinking at its rim. Finally, I was crouched at arm's length, my heart pattering in my breast as I scanned the jostling line of butterflies for my first prey. It was almost as though I had been thrown back centuries into savagery, hunting naked at dusk for insects in some Goddess-forsaken wilderness. I shot out a hand and plucked one of the broad-wings from the row, pinching its wings shut as they kissed for a moment and jerking it off its feet, leaving its companions undisturbed. As I nipped its head off with my teeth, my nose was tickled with the creamy scent of its wing-dust and I had to restrain a sneeze. Once it was dead I plucked its wings off and slipped the body into my mouth, chewing, savouring its flavour. It was good: spicy and dry, like butterflies I had tasted in southern Italy. I swallowed and pushed the wings one by one into my mouth, licking at them, holding my breath as their dust momentarily clouded the air in front of my face. They crunched like stiff paper in my mouth as I reached out for a second butterfly, forgetting in my concentration that the Countess stood and watched me. I finished a dozen or more and then, wiping at my dust-covered lips and chin, rose and turned back to her. The sun was almost set and the glarthouse was full of shadows.

'Shall I take the po?' I asked her.

'No. Leave it where it is. You have eaten your fill of them; let them drink their fill of you. I will have it returned to your room.'

77

I followed her from the glarthouse, waiting while she locked the door again when we were on the other side. Somehow the action of locking the door made my heart sink, and I noted the weight and number of the keys she drew and returned to her pocket as I had not noted them before.

'Now,' she said, turning from the door, 'you shall dress and converse with me. I have much to ask of Romania before I undertake my journey.'

Later. When I had dressed, I searched for my criss, meaning to wear it permanently thenceforth, but I could not find it. Nor could I, when I conversed with the Countess in the library, bring myself to raise the matter, though from the way her eye rested occasionally on me I believe she knew well what was troubling me. We talked for perhaps an hour and then, despite the freshness of the night, the Countess seemed to grow weary, stifling a yawn as she found some pretext to bring our conversation to an end. She left me with instructions to draw up a timetable of her journey from the railway guides I would find in the library, together with food for my midnight and morning meals. I bowed in apparent acquiescence, secretly vowing to complete the task as speedily as possible, retrieve my diary and write up the events of the past few days, and then set out on an exploration of the castle.

Once the timetable was drawn up I set out on my exploration, apprehensive that I would disturb servants and be reported to the Countess for prying. In the event no such thing occurred. I saw no one and heard nothing, but discovered that the bunch of keys was not carried by the Countess for show. Doors, doors, doors everywhere, and all locked and bolted. In no place, save from the windows in the castle walls, is there an available exit. The castle is a veritable prison, and I am a prisoner!

3

Joanna Harker's Journal
Continued

12 May. When I awoke on this day my first thought –
as, to my shame, it had not been on the previous nights
of my stay – rather say, my *imprisonment* – was of Mina,
as though in my extremity my soul clung to what was
best loved and best familiar, as a sailor will cling to a
spar of her smashed ship in the midst of a howling
sea-storm. If it had been sent as I requested – though I
knew it had not – the letter would have been four or five
nights in her hands by now and tonight she would have
been preparing for our simultaneous masturbation.

I lay still for a moment, trying to review my memories
of the Parisian waitress's bared buttocks, the tremors of
apprehension that had shuddered juicily through them
as condign punishment first threatened, then descended
with thundercracks upon their marmoreal purity. But
the images of those white curved buttocks and their
cruel violation, though laid so recently to the pages of
my memory-book, were faded and desiccated and even
the thundercracks of punishment, ringing from that
rubbery youthful buttock-flesh, were weak and distant
in my ears. I had suffered and experienced too much in
the few nights of my stay – my *imprisonment* – in the
Countess's castle and it is as though I view the previous
years of my life from the far bank of a wide river
flowing under brightest sunshine.

No, I can push the memories of the last few nights away from my mind no longer: they come crowding in, forcing themselves upon me, filling my eyes and ears and nostrils so that I seem to find myself back among the scenes of horror that lie beneath this cursed place, where the Countess keeps and drains her wretched slaves, or once again on the roof, where the Bitch-Mistress herself lies like a bloated leech in that obscene glass coffin of hers, befouling the pure light of the moon and stars. Vomit rises to my throat even as I set the words down, but somehow the horror of the memories is lessened by the act of writing and I can find the will to force myself to proceed. If words here and there are illegible, dear Mina, you will forgive me for it, for my hand trembles as though with ague. I promise to pause and breathe myself back to semi-calm when it gets especially bad.

So, to proceed: on the night on which I discovered that I was a prisoner rather than an *employée* I found myself again growing sleepy very early, shortly after I had eaten my midnight meal from the tray left for me in the library. I sought my bed and awoke while the sun was still high in the sky, as I somehow sensed even in the sealed and comforting darkness of my room. It was confirmed when, as before, I had used my chamberpot and the Countess's footsteps sounded along the corridor outside. She rapped on the door, I called 'Enter', and she entered, admitting, as before, a flood of sunlight. This time I had my smoked spectacles already in place and could quickly obey when she ordered me to bring my chamberpot, as before, to the sunbathed glarthouse, where, as before, I manured the fungi, remoistened the po with piss and breakfasted on the butterflies the Countess released to drink of what I had provided. Then, as before, we returned to the living quarters to talk, on this occasion for nearly two hours before the Countess, as before, grew tired and found some pretext to retire, leaving me as before with some trivial but time-consuming task and some cold food for my midnight and morning meals. This time, however, I paid close attention as she departed, listening to discover in which direction she walked, for I wished to undertake a more thorough exploration of the castle and had no desire to stumble across her sleeping-quarters. Frowning in concentration at the library table, I heard her feet ascend a long stair, then the creak and closing of a heavy door, then another, fainter ascent of a long stair, another, fainter creak and closing of a heavy door, a third, faintest ascent of a long stair, a third, faintest creak and closing of a heavy door, then finally silence. The direction in which I would explore was now fixed: not up, but down.

First, I completed the task the Countess had set me: making translations into Romanian of selected entries from an Anglish encyclopaedia. If I had known what awaited me later in the night, I feel sure my pen should have fallen from my nerveless fingers as I translated the entry on '*Milk, production of*', but at the time my mouth merely watered and my stomach began a faint but strengthening grumble that carried me, when I had completed the translation, to the waiting tray of food. As I drew away the cover, however, a thought struck me: why had I felt sleepy on not only the first night but the previous night too so soon after finishing what I had intended as merely my midnight meal, not my final meal of the night? Was the Countess drugging my food in an attempt to adapt me to what I had already deduced were her wholly unnatural patterns of sleep and waking? I sniffed carefully at the food – beetles in maggot sauce – but it was, as usual, heavily seasoned *à la roumaine* (ground wasp-sting and spider-fang) and I could not be sure that I detected any unusual odour. But I asked myself: was this spicing a hostess's consideration for an honoured guest or the seizing of an opportunity to disguise some soporific drug? To pose the question in such terms was to answer it: was I an honoured guest, when not four hours before I had been crouched pissing in the glarthouse as she watched? Was I an honoured guest, when she had cunnilingued me (as I now believed) less than three hours into our direct acquaintance, without so much as a by-your-leave? No, the food was almost certainly drugged and, though I would, in the end, have no choice but to eat it, I could delay until I had completed my planned exploration of such lower levels of the castle as were accessible to me.

I almost wish now I had eaten the food before setting out, so that my exploration had been cut short by sleep well before I made the discovery that awaited me. But it was not to be and, leaving the food untouched behind me, I slipped from the library, the box of matches for its lamps snug in one of my pockets, and cast about in the corridors outside for a descending stair. After finding and being frustrated by three locked doors, I found what I sought: a stair descending for what, from my preliminary whistle, was many feet. I positively smiled as I set foot to it and began to climb down, moving further and further from the Countess sleeping far above, and even dared hope that I should find some means of escape below: an unlocked door or a tool with which I might lever one of the doors at higher level. Goddess forgive me for my presumption! I be–

I have just sat back for a minute to recover my calm and hope I shall be able to continue. Yes, I believe so.

To resume then: I began to descend the stair I had discovered, pausing frequently at first to whistle out the way below me, but growing in confidence as nothing untoward reached my ears. All I could hear, faint but strengthening, was the sound of the subterranean river described to me by the Countess. The thought of escape occurred to me again and I wondered if I would find some passage that led to the river and whether it would have banks that I could follow downstream until it debouched into the valley. I had studied maps of Transmarynia in the Countess's library and believed it was none other than the river Llangoffan, which was shown springing from the mountain at almost the very point one would have expected if it flowed roughly eastwards beneath the castle. All thought of this was, however, driven from my mind when I heard, cutting through the growing clamour of the river, a distant but perfectly distinct moan: the very first evidence I had had that the castle was inhabited by any but the Countess and myself (I had already decided that the Countess and the driver of the coach were *una et ibidem*, and I had mentally consigned Mina's letter to oblivion). I descended faster, my ears pricked for the sound again, and the echoes of my hastening feet were sufficient to tell me that I neared the foot of the stair where awaited what seemed to be two passages sloping yet deeper into the mountainside.

When I reached the foot of the stair I found I had heard true: two passages sloped downwards ahead of me, veeing apart like the middle and index fingers of a benedicting goddess or the splayed thighs of a lustful giantess. I took the passage to the left, and soon the echoes of my feet against the smooth stone slope of its floor, mingling with the murmur of the river still far beneath me, told me that another pair of passages lay ahead, veeing apart in the same way. Were there two such passages at the end of the passage to the left? And did each of these new passages divide in the same way? I took the one to the left and discovered that it at least did divide in that fashion: after I had walked perhaps half as far as before I found two more passages at its far end.

From the way the length of the passages was shortening I deduced this could not go on for ever, and I was proved right when I took the right of the two new passages that confronted me. As I paced along it, it was

83

my skin and nose that brought me evidence of other inhabitants of the castle: the air was growing faintly warmer around me and I could detect a waft of sour sweat and, faint but distinct, fresh *milk*. The smell had strengthened almost to a cloud when, at the end of the passage, I reached a half-closed door. Why it was not locked I did not pause to wonder, for the moan I had heard already was repeated from the chamber beyond, and I slipped through (not caring to tug the door wider and risk a creak) and discovered what had awaited me since I first conceived the idea of exploring the castle while the Countess slept: the Countess's chained and cruelly exploited herd o–

I was forced to break off again just now, and have brought myself back to some semblance of calm with deep and regular breaths.

To resume: I slipped through the half-open door, the smell of sweat and milk intensifying sharply in my nostrils, and discovered myself in a long, low-ceilinged chamber at right angles to the door, which was about halfway down its length. I sensed immediately that the room was occupied and whistled, hearing softer shapes directly ahead and to left and right. However, there was a smell of oil and fire in the place too and I knew a lamp was nearby that had been alight and glowing within the twenfer*. I sniffed more carefully, slowly swinging my head, and discovered the lamp was to the right. As I turned to find it, the moan sounded again from behind me, much louder between the walls of the chamber, and showing me softer shapes along the walls of the chamber ahead of me as its echoes bounced into silence. It was the moan of a young woman in troubled sleep, I thought as I walked carefully down the chamber, finding the stones below my feet oddly warm, as though low fires were burning beneath me. When the reek of oil rose to a pitch in my nostrils I reached out and was soon lifting up the lamp, which had rested on a shelf at the

84

far end of the chamber. It was the work of a moment to light it from the box of matches I had brought with me from the library, and as the flame strengthened from a glow to a glare I turned and cast its light down that long chamber to see whether the softer shapes against the walls were, as I thought, the bodies of sleeping women.

I wonder even now that the lamp did not slip from my fingers and smash upon the floor, for the horror of that first sight of the Countess's herd – there is no other word for it – will live with me for ever. Seventeen sleeping women – eight down one wall, eight down the other, with one on the end wall opposite to that where I stood – met my horrified gaze, chained naked on what seemed like low stone thrones. Their breasts were large and obviously swollen with milk and two open pipes ran down the chamber left and right at breast-height (there were levers by each throne, I discovered, to jack each prisoner up or down as required), extending wings of themselves under each set of breasts – save for the breasts of her on the end wall, which seemed to feed neither pipe, though they were largest of all. It seemed as though the women would be milked by hand into the pipe-wings lying under their breasts, whence the milk would flow into the pipe and be carried down the chamber to where it disappeared on an unknown journey through an opening in the end wall where I stood. When I had got over my first horror, I noticed that the light of the lamp had disturbed the women: heads rolled and eyelids fluttered, and some mumbled and muttered in their sleep, while the largest-breasted of them all, the woman chained on the end-wall, emitted another of her moans.

I realised they were all drugged and sleeping as I should have been, had I eaten the food in the library far above. After setting the lamp on the shelf (I first retrimmed it so its light was not excessively bright), I tried to wake one of them, then, when I had failed with her, tried another and another. But they would not respond to my whispers, my rattling of the chains that bound them hand and foot or my gentle nose- and ear-tweaking, but merely mumbled or muttered more loudly in what I realised was Welsh: these were peasant-girls, kidnapped by the Countess and chained here to be milked for her profit beneath her castle. But just then, as I straightened from an unsuccessful attempt to waken a fourth girl, the girl on the end wall moaned loudly again and woke up, as I discovered when she spoke. Her first words were in Welsh but, as I turned in surprise and looked towards her and she saw my features, she substituted Romanian.

'Who are you?'

For a moment I could not penetrate the thickness of her accent, but then, with a hurried 'A friend, I hope!', I flew down the chamber to her. She blinked at me blearily and I almost sobbed to see the suspicion born of suffering on her sweet young face. She licked her cracked lips and said, 'A friend? No friends of ours come down here. None come at all but that arch-fiend and her twaughters.'

She looked upwards at the ceiling with mingled fear and defiance, as though her gaze could pierce the many feet of rock that lay between us and the sleeping chatelaine of the castle. The movement made her splendid tits, full and fertile as twin moons, jiggle lusciously and I had to swallow away a sudden constriction in my throat before I was able to ask huskily: 'The Countess?'

'Aye. Though better call her a Duchess of Hell.'

Despite the thickness of her accent, she spoke good and grammatical Romanian, and I realised that she was a woman of some education. Though I was bursting to question her about the Countess's twaughters, of whose existence I had so far received not the slightest intimation, I decided to discover first who she was and why she was here. I questioned her and quickly learned that

86

she was the twaughter of a local schoolmistress and forced to repay a debt owed to the Countess by her mother.

'When she has drunk her fill of me, I can go home.'

'Drunk?' I said. 'And what of the others?'

'I have the biggest breasts,' she told me, 'and am therefore *honoured* –' she spoke bitterly and laughed without mirth when the word left her lips '– with her ladyship's special attentions. When I came poor Blodwyn there was in my place.' She nodded forward and I followed the gesture to see a girl with what seemed the second-largest pair of breasts in the chamber. 'But the *Countess* –' again a mirthless laugh '– was pleased to tell me that I had usurped her with ease.'

'And when was this?' I asked.

'Three weeks on the morrow of tomorrow. I have seen girls come and go in that time, for she ensures a steady supply of *debtors* –' again the laugh, which was worrying me now, for it spoke of incipient hysteria '– to supply her business. I must remain till she tires of me, and that night may be long in coming.'

At this she began to weep, and I sought for a way of distracting her.

'Her business?' I said gently.

She sniffed and continued, 'Aye, her business. The bitch supplies half Europe with her cheeses and yoghurts, growing rich off our young breasts and milk.'

'Of this I knew something already,' I said, and quickly told her of my purpose in the castle – that I was a lawyer come to arrange the Countess's passage to Bucharest, where she planned to set up an academy for underprivileged young women of the lower classes.

The Big-Breasted One (I had still not learned her name) laughed bitterly again.

'That will be merely a cloak for some far brighter purpose, I promise you. The bitch's cruelty and ambition know no bounds, as I can testify. Doubtless she means to set up another milking-station in your capital, and add fresh cheeses and yoghurts to her range.'

I shook my head.

'No, that will not be possible. In my country women lactate only after giving birth and can spare only a little milk from nourishment of their twaughters. That is why cheese and yoghurt were such luxuries and so prohibitively expensive, before the Countess began to export from Transmarynia.'

But now she shook her head.

'No, that will not impede her. It is not natural for the women of Transmarynia to lactate as I do either, but the Countess has means of imposing it. None of us here were lactating before we were imprisoned, least of all I, but look at us now.'

Sensing that I was on the brink of uncovering a great secret, I asked how the Countess brought about lactation out of season, but the Big-Titted One shook her head.

'I do not know, but some here suggest there is a poison in the bites she regularly delivers to our breasts.'

I was horrified.

'The bites?'

For answer she merely nodded downwards at her own ample globes, and I stooped to examine them. Tenderly though I lifted and parted them, she shivered and whimpered with pain, and I realised they were even fuller of milk than they appeared. I paused, feeling an excited pulse starting in my throat as I looked up from my examination and said, 'You are very swollen. Would you care for me to draw a little off and relieve the congestion?'

She paused, then shook her head.

'I – I dare not. She is punishing me by leaving me unmilked for two nights. If she finds less milk than she expects when she drinks from my breasts again, I fear what she will do.'

'Very well,' I said, resuming my search for the bites of which she had spoken. In a moment more I had discovered them: a pair of sowl-rimmed holes on the inner underside of her left breast.

'Here?' I asked, pointing.

She nodded.

'Yes. Each of us endures it every few nights, though I believe, even if it had nothing to do with our lactation, she would still indulge herself in it, as cruelty for cruelty's sake.'

I bent forwards and kissed the bites gently, pressing my lips first over one, then the other.

'Thank you,' she whispered, 'you are very kind.'

I looked up to see tears streaming down her face and gathering on her chin to drip to her breasts. She twisted her head to one side, as though she feared to let the tears fall there, saying, 'Please – wipe them clean.'

'Your breasts?' I said, puzzled.

'Yes. She hates to find tear-salt on them when she licks them before milk-drinking, or pretends to do so, as an excuse for punishing me.'

I began carefully to wipe her breasts dry of tears with alternate hands, licking my fingers clean as I lifted a hand away, but realised after a moment that traces might be left no matter how carefully I wiped. I looked at her.

'I shall have to lick them clean,' I told her, adding, for this was no servant-slut, 'With your permission?'

She nodded and I put my face forwards and began, working my tongue at first up and down the tit-cleft, confirming my fears that hand-wiping would not have been enough, for I could distinctly taste tears as I licked. Then I roamed the globe of her left breast with my tongue, spiralling slowly up to the summit, before licking the large nipple with the tip of my tongue, but careful not to provoke milk from it. Then I roamed the right globe, licking away the salt of her tears, slowly

89

spiralling to the summit, but leaving the nipple unmilked as before. She sighed with relief as I finished and I looked up to see her smiling brokenly at me, her face glistening with drying tears.

'Careful!' I said. A tear-drop was gathering on the point of her chin. She swung her head to one side and it dripped harmlessly on to her flank.

'Does she not object to tears on your face?' I asked.

She shook her head.

'No. Only on my breasts. Sometimes she twists my nipples before she drinks from them, to make me weep. Then she will lick my face, to cleanse her palate for the sweetness of my milk, she says. Oh, she is cruel! Cruel!'

Big-Tits (as I was now, to my shame, mentally apostrophising her) began to weep again, holding her head to one side as before, so that her tears dripped clear of her breasts.

'Hush,' I said. 'I am your friend, I will help you – all of you.'

She sniffed, shaking her head helplessly.

'A friend perhaps, but what help can you offer us?'

'I can help you to escape.'

'You have a key for our chains? A crow to prise them loose?'

'No, but surely –'

'Look at them,' she said.

I examined her chains in earnest for the first time. She was fastened by her ankles and wrists to the low stone throne I had already noted and whose seat was moulded, I now saw, to the shape of her thighs and buttocks. I lifted the chains fastening her, rattling at them, tugging them. They were rusted but sound and each link was twice as thick as my thumb.

'Are they all like this?' I asked, looking back at the other girls, who seemed to have grown accustomed to the lamplight and were sleeping quietly again.

'Yes,' she said.

'But does she never release you?'

'She releases our right or left hands every twenfer, that we might eat and –' the bitterness was back in her voice '– that we might be milked.'

'I do not understand.'

'Look at them,' she said. 'Do you not see how each girl is within easy reach of one of her companions?'

I nodded.

'Every twenfer she releases their right or left hands, so that each girl can be milked by the girl to her left or right.'

I swallowed, suddenly and cruelly longing to be there to see such a milking, then frowned as a thought occurred to me.

'But the girl on the end of the row?'

'She is milked when the others all are done, by the girl whom she has just milked herself.'

'But she never grants you full release, for exercise or to meet the calls of nature?'

'For exercise we are released every two twenfers, but in the interim we stay chained, for we meet the calls of nature where we sit: there is a hole beneath our buttocks. Some say she allows our piss and dung to fall directly into the river, but I do not believe she would allow it to go to waste like that.'

'I think you are right,' I said, remembering the ritual chamberpot-emptying she had forced me through for the past three days.

'Rhiannon there –' she thrust out her chin in the direction of one of the other girls '– she thinks the bitch heats these lower levels with our waste, allowing it to ferment somewhere and generate gas. I believe it may be so. It would suit her cruel sensibilities to heat our backsides using the product of our backsides.'

I nodded slowly.

'It's possible,' I said. 'Seventeen girls could perhaps shit enough to heat seventeen girls.'

'Then could a hundred-and-thirty-six shit enough to heat a hundred-and-thirty-six?'

'I do not understand.'

'How did you get here? Once you reached the foot of the stair, I mean.'

I started to describe the branching passages.

'Yes, yes. They branch. And how many branches did you pass, to reach here?'

I thought back.

'Three, I think. Yes, three.'

'There is a chamber such as this at the end of every final branch. Which makes how many chambers in all?'

I thought.

'It is . . . two times two times two. Eight.'

'So eight chambers, with seventeen girls in each. Eight along each wall to supply her cheesery, and one, her with the biggest tits, on the end wall to quench the Countess's personal thirst. Seventeen times eight. A hundred-and-thirty-six.'

I was staggered.

'You have seen them?'

'Every two twenfers we see each other, when she exercises us by marching us to a new chamber. On the second twenfer we walk as far as the first node; on the fourth as far as the second; on the eighth as high as the third. We pass each other in the passages, and sometimes are able to exchange words, though she punishes us severely if she catches us.'

'And she does all this alone?'

'The exchanges of chamber are staggered, so that only two chambers' worth of girls are involved each night and she or her twaughters can well manage that number.'

'Against thirty-four of you?'

'Our feet and hands are shackled and she carries a cruel whip that she uses on the slightest provocation, or on none at all, if the whim strikes her. It is often a relief to be chained to our thrones again, so that our poor abused arses are dangling over nothingness. And look at us. We are kept permanently drugged and in no fit state for rebellion. Why else do you think they sleep so soundly?'

'You woke,' I said.

'The girls she drinks from are drugged but lightly. She says a stronger dose would taint our milk.'

'And does it not taint their milk?'

'Their milk is for cheese and yoghurt, and the drug is destroyed during fermentation. She is too cunning to damage her profits unnecessarily.'

I was silent for a moment, thinking over what she had said, then asked, 'Then there is no way I can help you?'

'None, unless you can find her keys, and there is small chance of that. No, you will have all your work cut out to help yourself. Do you think she means to let you leave this place, now you know even a few of her secrets? You will be kept safe here until she is well established in Bucharest and has bribed her way to the same immunity from your accusations as she enjoys here in Transmarynia.'

She had spoken the plain truth and I was silent for a few moments more.

'Nevertheless, I shall try,' I said. 'For your sake as much as for mine.'

'I thank you for it,' she said, 'but now you had better go. If she finds the oil in our lamp markedly diminished she will grow suspicious and will take it out on our bodies as well as yours.'

I nodded and kissed her.

'Then till we meet again in a happier place and time, farewell.'

'Farewell, mistress. You have a good heart and I pray it will avail you something against that she-fiend.'

A tear came to my eye at the nobility of this poor creature, so cruelly abused and exploited, yet preserving

93

within her remarkable breast an indomitable spirit that all the Countess's cruelty could not crush. I slipped back down the chamber and extinguished the lamp, hearing the murmur of the other girls, disturbed in their sleep by the sudden disappearance of light as they had been a few minutes before by its sudden appearance. Then, pausing only to kiss Big-Tits farewell a final time (I held and joggled her breasts comfortingly in my hands), I slipped from the chamber and began to retrace my footsteps through the passages. For a moment I pondered whether to explore the second branch of this lowest level, and see whether, in the second chamber, I would find the Countess's personal milkmaid awake and ready to talk, but it seemed unavailing: she could surely only repeat what the first had told me and I doubted that her breasts would match, let alone surpass, those I had already licked and fondled. It was then I realised I had neglected to ask the milkmaid her name, but somehow it seemed better so: she was like the personification of a milk-goddess or of Mother Mary, her spurting nipple buried in the mouth of Baby Jesa. And perhaps she was called Mary in any case, or whatever the Welsh equivalent was.

4

Joanna Harker's Journal
Continued

After my conversation with the big-breasted milk-slave – with Mary – I left the other subterranean passages unexplored, retraced my footsteps to the stair, and climbed back to the ground floor of the castle, sick at heart and gut with the new knowledge I carried. I was longing now for the oblivion of sleep and when I reached the top of the stair I ran for the library and the drugged food I knew was still waiting for me there on a tray. As I spooned it greedily down (for I combined true hunger with my hunger for sleep), I reflected that *she* (the Countess) did not mean me for a personal milk-maid yet, if she was drugging me so heavily: any milk my breasts secreted would be tainted and suitable only for cheese or yoghurt. Soon, more apparent now that I anticipated its coming, I felt sleep overcoming me in a slow tide, but a spark of paradoxical rebellion seemed to light as it rose and to flare brightly beneath the waves. I would not sleep here, where the Countess had commanded I sleep, but would instead seek out some distant spot. Perhaps – yes, the door of the glarthouse. Perhaps it too, like the door of the milking-chamber far below, would have been left neglectfully open and I could sleep amid the plants, blessed by the light of the moon and stars.

Accordingly I rose from my seat and walked to the glarthouse, already beginning to stagger a little. My hopes were unfounded and the door was securely locked, but I curled up nevertheless on the floor and surrendered myself to sleep. So it was that, by my own wilful defiance, I exposed myself to the second of that twenfer's twin horrors, either of which I sincerely believe might have threatened the reason of a woman much less troubled than I had already been.

The hardness and sun-warmth of the stone floor proved no match for the strength of the soporific drug with which my food had been laced, and I fell asleep quickly, waking I know not how long later to hear a key rattling in the lock of the glarthouse door – from the other side, that is to say, from *within* the glarthouse itself. I opened my eyes and saw sunlight spilling beneath the door: it was dawn and the glarthouse was filling with light. Who then could be within it? The Countess herself would approach from this side and was perhaps even now knocking on the door of my room to collect me and my chamberpot. The key seemed to rattle interminably, as though wielded by a clumsy or un-skilful hand, and my heart, already beating apace, seemed to leap into my throat as I heard a stranger's voice sound in slurred Anglish: 'Let me try, you fool.'

I tried to push myself up from the floor and stand but, whether my food had been drugged especially heavily or my limbs were cramped from contact with the bare stone of the floor, my body refused to obey me. Another voice slurred in reply, too thick with tiredness or emotion for me to distinguish the words, but seeming to challenge the verdict of the first voice. Then there was a yelp and the key fell silent in the lock for a moment before resuming its attempt on the lock with new confidence. The hand now guiding it was unsteady, but steadier nevertheless than the hand it had replaced, and after a moment I heard the lock surrender and the door creak open, releasing a flood of light over me in which I screwed my eyes tight, consigning my body and even perhaps my soul to the Goddess's care.

Heavy feet tramped forwards, loud even through the surge of blood in my ears, and I thought for a moment they would pass me by. A cry of surprised discovery disabused me of this notion, however, and then hot hands were laid on me, dragging me upright and propping me against the wall. I could barely understand the Anglish they were speaking: as I have already noted, it was peculiarly thickened and slurred, as though they were continually on the brink of rising from or sinking into profound sleep, and was heavy with the accent of the region, but I transcribe a brief passage with annotations, to give a flavour of it.

'Paul! [*which I understood to mean 'Paula'*] It's one of Pa's floosees [*or floozees?*]. From the milking-sheds. [*That at least was plain enough.*]'

'Nah. [*No*] It's that lawyer-bint [*?*]. From Rom'nee.'

'What's she doing here, like?'

'Like enough waiting for you, Jo. [*A contraction of Josephine or my own name, unpleasantly enough.*] She'll'a [*she will have*] heard all about you and your pocket-monster [*?*].'

'His [*?*] trouser-snake [*??*], more like. Eh, darling?'

My eyes had grown slightly better adapted to the light and I was peering out at them between quarter-opened eyelids. Three flushed and sweating faces met my gaze, leering at me from a few inches away and wafting over me a reeking halitus, as of some strong chemical of the foundry or tannery. I sneezed and spluttered with disgust. (I abandon my annotation from now on, and leave my future readers, if any, to make sense of their words as best she may.)

'Nah, she don't like your boozy breath, Jo. Look at her.'

'Give her a mouthful then, like. That'll cheer her up.'

One of the three raised a bottle (I now noticed that all three clutched one in their right hands) and unsteadily offered the neck to my lips. I turned my head aside, sneezing and spluttering again, for the chemical reek rising from it was worse even than – and without doubt responsible for – their foully tainted breath.

'She don't want that neither, Jo.'

'She do, she jus' don't realise it yet. Here, hold her nose shut and I'll tip a splash down her throat.'

Hot hands fumbled at my face and sudden rage rose to overthrow my fear and disgust. I struggled to free myself from their clutching hands, saying aloud in my best Anglish: 'Unhand me! Unhand me at once! Your mother shall know of this and I promise you merciless retribution!'

For I had guessed, you see, and guessed half-correctly, as it turned out, that these three were the Countess's twaughters. But they did not seem inclined to pay much regard to my words.

'Here,' said the one I had decided was called Jo, 'she's a Rom'nee. I'd recognise that accent anywhere.'

'Me too,' said Paul. 'One of the most potent dick-stiffeners known to man.'

'And when,' chimed in the third, whose name I did not learn, 'did your dick ever stiffen in the presence of a Rom'nee?'

'Last year. Remember, when Pa sent us down Margate way to sort out that pilfering in the cheese warehouse?'

Jo shook her head.

'I don't remember that.'

'You didn't come. You were in disgrace. But I don't remember there was a Rom'nee down there.'

'There was, I tell you. She had an accent just like this one and the proof is right here: look.'

I heard a strange buzzing sound.

'See? Why's my dick gone that stiff that quick just

98

through hearing a Rom'nee accent if I hadn't already been sucked off by a Rom'nee?'

The other two were silent for a moment, as though pondering the evidence presented to them. I struggled to focus my eyes through the flood of sunlight and see it for myself. Paula seemed to be clutching a thick grey club between her legs but, before I could lean forwards a little and make it out properly, I had to blink away tears and close my eyes again. Had she opened her skirt? Was 'dick' a slang term for 'cunt' and 'stiffen' a local metaphor for 'become aroused'? Was she – my stomach lurched at the thought – pleasuring herself with a (forgive me, Mina) d*ld* in preparation for an assault on me?

'And was she any good?' resumed the one called Jo, grudgingly.

'She had a suck on her like the tide at Clanecly. The spring tide, mind you.'

I sensed that their eyes were fixed suddenly on me.

'And do you reckon she'll be any good too?'

I could not understand them fully but knew well enough by now what they were planning: to force me to cunnilingue them. I opened my mouth and screamed on my highest note, knowing it would easily reach the Countess's ears, wherever she was in the castle, but to my surprise they took no notice at all.

'Let's suck it and see.'

'No, let *her* suck it and see.'

'Get that mouthful down her throat first. Warm her up, like.'

Strong, burning hands seized my head and the neck of the bottle was forced between my lips. I struggled hard, but my cries of protest were stilled as a fiery, reeking liquid was tipped into my mouth. It burned like acid wherever it touched and the stink of it scorched the back of my throat and seared through my sinuses, making warm tears positively squirt from my eyes.

'No, stop her! She's trying to spit it out!'

I was indeed, but the bottle was plucked from my mouth and one of the hot clutching hands clamped under my chin, forcing it shut while stern fingers, searing with an unnatural heat, pinched my nostrils shut. My whole head was on fire now, my mouth a scalding pouch of agony, and I was convinced that if I swallowed I would scar my throat and stomach for what little remained of my life, for this was surely a deadly and fast-acting poison. But I had no other choice: it was swallow or asphyxiate. In fact, it was swallow *and* asphyxiate, for the stuff stopped me breathing freely for at least a minute after it had scorched its way down my throat. As I choked and spluttered I dimly heard that strange buzzing sound again, this time twice, and through the fantastic jewels of my pain-and-sunlight-spawned tears I could see that the three women were pressing close to me, clutching in their right hands thick grey clubs that seemed to sprout from their groins. The poison they had forced down my throat was searing in my stomach now, eating (as I imagined) like acid at the lining, but the warmth was growing somehow not so unpleasant. If I *were* poisoned it was almost pleasurable to be so.

'Who's first, then?' asked the one called Jo.

'Me,' said the one called Paula (or rather say, Paul'). I heard Jo shake her head.

'You've already had a Rom'nee, you said. It's our turn.'

'Fuck off. I suggested it first.'

The third broke in.

'Lads, lads! Let's not argue over her. She's young and wet-gobbed. There are blow-jobs for us all.'

By now, so swiftly had the liquid forced down my throat been working on my unaccustomed tissues, I had decided that being poisoned *was* a pleasure: the warmth in my stomach had communicated itself to my breast

100

and loins and seemed to be riding to all parts of my body on the suddenly quickened tide of my blood. My lips and fingertips tingled and bells and whistles sounded in my ears, and I no longer feared what they proposed to do with me: I longed for it. I longed to suck them, to uphold the honour of 'Rom'nee' womanhood, to efface the memory of that tidal cunnilinctrix in Margate with the memory of myself. Perhaps I murmured lustfully as those three she-fiends leaned towards me, convincing them that their potion had had its desired effect, or perhaps they read its workings in my face and drooling lips. In either case, the first attempt on my virtue was made.

'Here, darling,' the unnamed one said to me, leaning her face well forwards to breathe her now sweet halitus into my face, 'get your hand around this and get sucking.'

And my right hand was tugged open and forced around what seemed to my befuddled senses like a fleshy member. But it was like no member I had ever handled before in my life: a hot hand-thick tube perhaps seven or eight inches long. It had a bone-stiff core on which rode soft skin, crawling with thick veins that ticked to the beat of her heart. At the upper end (she gripped my hand by the wrist and slid my fingers up, allowing me to explore this wonder) I found the skin was fastened in a loose curtain that slid open as I tugged at it, exposing a glowing bulb or cap of spongy flesh that throbbed beneath my clutching hand. I peered too, trying to match what I felt to what I saw, and could almost convince myself that this tube was sprouting between the woman's thighs. The horror of the next instant will live with me for ever, for my hand –

As before I was forced to break off and breathe myself back to a semblance of calm.

To resume: my hand fell back down the thing and brushed what was unmistakably cloth: the slit in her

101

skirt through which the thing was jutting. And then, as poisonous knowledge burned through the befuddlement they had forced on me, I began to gather breath to shriek in unendurable horror, for my hand had dipped between the unfastened slit of her skirt and was delving within. There was a bush of hair there, clustering around the upper slopes of the base of the fleshy tube. Below there hung a large and leathery bag containing what seemed like a pair of stones that evaded my fingers as I grasped at them. But my fingers, probe as they might, could detect no trace of a cunt: the fleshy tube was rooted firmly between her thighs as though it had always stood there and always would. My scream was still shrilling down the corridor (though again they ignored it completely) when I heard the heavy racing footsteps of the Countess, and my hand was suddenly and mercifully released. Now I could pluck it from between those thighs and the horror that couched there. I could barely see and could not have raised myself to watch even if I had been able, but my ears were sufficient witness of the storm of wrath that was breaking over my three would-be violatrices. A minute or two into it, my face pressed to the cool stone floor as phrases of white-hot fury still beat like foundry hammers above me, I was quietly and comprehensively sick and lapsed finally and mercifully into unconsciousness.

I awoke in my bed to hear, as on previous mornings, the Countess's knuckles rapping on the door. Memory of what I had experienced – rather, *endured* – during the previous twenfer instantly filled my head, but they were accompanied by a misty sense of unreality that might almost have convinced me I had dreamed. But at the first move I made to struggle up in bed and answer the knock, my mouth, throat and sinuses provided unmistakable evidence of the liquid I had been forced to swallow. They were exceedingly sore, in short, and my brain throbbed; my eyesockets ached and my stomach rolled. The Countess's knuckles were peremptory now and I thought that in another moment she would call out.

'Please enter, mistress!' I called, and the act of submission was somehow – and, to my spirit, sickeningly – enough to soothe my bodily pains. The door swung open, admitting a flood of sunlight in which, as the Countess stepped carefully aside from it, I was held secure as I slid naked from the bed, suppressing a groan, and kneeled to draw my chamberpot from beneath the bed and use it. She seemed to time her first words to the moment my anus opened to emit a turd.

'I warned you.'

'Yes, mistress.'

I knew instantly of what she spoke: my choosing to sleep away from the part of the castle she had told me was safe. I baptised the turd with piss, then rose to wipe and wash myself.

'Later,' she said. 'You have slept long tonight and I have already knocked twice on your door. Come with me now to nourish the falluses and break your own fast.'

I nodded silently and picked up the chamberpot to follow her to the glarthouse. When we reached the corridor leading to the door I looked for the patch of vomit I knew I must have left there, but the floor was clean and unmarked, unless one patch, near where I might have expected the vomit to have lain, were a fraction cleaner, as though recently scrubbed. Then I raised my eyes to the door, feeling my heart beginning to thud in my breast, for I seemed to hear the key rattle again in the lock on the far side and the voices of the three young women, thickened and slurred with the poisonous liquid I now realised they had all been drinking from those bottles. What had the liquid been? Why could anyone wish to torture their body with it? But my stomach, even as it fluttered with fading nausea,

103

seemed to supply an answer: the warmth, it said; and I remembered the glow that had begun to occupy my body once I had swallowed.

The Countess's broad back almost hid the door from me as she took out her bunch of keys and rattled at the lock herself, and my heart skipped as I remembered the promise I had made to Big-Tits – to Mary – in the milking-chamber far beneath our feet. The Countess's keys: how could I take them from her? She pushed the door open and I followed her in to perform the ritual of manuring we had established. This done, I set the emptied chamberpot on the glarthouse floor, crouched over it, squinting in the bright sunlight that filled the glarthouse, and readied myself to trickle fresh piss into it. Barely had I crouched, however, when the Countess spoke.

'No! Not today. Put the chamberpot against the wall. We will see whether you can take its place.'

I did not understand and the Countess growled – the *mot juste* – with impatience.

'Against the wall. Put the chamberpot there, then return and lie on your back. Lift your legs up and over your head till your toes are resting on the floor. Then open your thighs and pull your buttocks apart. Your cunt and arsehole are unwashed. Let us see whether they can attract butterflies in their own right.'

I understood now and took the chamberpot to the nearest wall, leaving it there before I returned to follow her instructions: lying on the floor, with my legs lifted up and over my head, my thighs open and my buttocks levered apart. The floor shook beneath me as the Countess strode down the glarthouse to operate the machinery that released the butterflies from some ad-joining glarthouse or chamber. I waited, straining my ears to catch the first faint whisper of wings, but it was a shadow that told me the butterflies were loose in the glarthouse: it fell on my face as one passed between me

104

and the declining sun. Another shadow fell on my face, then another and another, and I squinted upwards to see the air full of the butterflies, dancing in the air above me. I held my breath, wondering whether I was a suitable substitute for the chamberpot: would my moistened cunt and unwiped arsehole attract them? Then I sighed with relief as I felt the feather-brush of disturbed air on my raised buttocks and the sudden tickle of delicate feet: a butterfly had landed on me. It strode forwards confidently for the exposed disc of my arsehole and I felt the thread of its tongue probing at my buttock cleft and the still moist smear of unwiped turd.

Another followed it, then, in a sudden rush, two and three and four more, till I had lost count and butterflies were crowding to the unwashed tissues of my arsehole and cunt, jostling on my thighs and buttocks and on the backs of my hands, sending puffs of disturbed air tickling across my skin as in ones or twos they were forced briefly back into the air by the overcrowding. My fingers were beginning to ache from the strain of holding my buttocks apart and I heard the Countess's next order with relief: 'Now you may breakfast on them.'

Very slowly and carefully I let go of my buttocks, allowing the gluteal hemispheres to slide slowly together, re-forming the buttock-cleft and resealing my anus between it. The butterflies feeding from my anus crowded more closely to it as it slipped from them, jostling each other more severely than ever, and when it was finally inaccessible again to all but a few they were positively fighting for it. My hands were finally free, but still half-gloved with butterflies, and I had to shake them gently free before, peering up and between my splayed thighs, I could begin to pick butterflies off my cunt and lower them to my waiting mouth. As I did so, I heard a sound immediately familiar but not, for a moment, identifiable. Then I remembered: it was the faint repeated soft clapping of my first twenfer in the castle, when the Countess had carried me to bed and violated all canons of hospitality by laying me naked and drowsing on my bed, with splayed thighs over which she had gloated before splattering me with some fluid and cunnilinguing me. Here I was again, of course, with splayed thighs and cunt on open display, or at least as open as the butterflies clustering to it allowed. I could not look towards the Countess, and doubt that I could have made out much in the sunlight anyway, but whatever it was she was up to seemed, as before, to be pleasurable: she was gasping faintly as the sound continued.

I plucked and ate butterflies, and was on my seventh or eighth when her gasps turned into a low groan; the soft clapping stopped and I heard a splatter of some thick fluid being thrown to the glarthouse floor. What on earth was she doing? Or rather, for silence now reigned, what on earth had she done? I plucked and ate a ninth butterfly, nipping off its head with my teeth and severing its wings with practised ease, even in my inverted posture, then said to the Countess, 'I am full now, mistress.'

'Then rise,' she said. I wafted my hands at the cunt-clustering butterflies, trying to shoo them from me, but they remained stubbornly in place until I swung my legs back from over my head, whereupon most took to the wing. I rolled on one side as I straightened my legs, not wishing to press my buttocks to the floor and crush the butterflies still feeding there, then got back to my feet, my body veiled for a moment by fluttering wings, though a few stubbornest butterflies were still clinging to me, probing at the mineral richness of my cunt and anus. The others were already fluttering to the traces of piss in my chamberpot where it was pushed to the wall.

'Come,' said the Countess.

I followed her, trotting a little to catch up, and wailed with surprise as my bare feet flew suddenly apart and I thudded on my back and buttocks, crushing a final clinging butterfly in my fall. I had stepped unaware into the patch of thick fluid I had heard being spilled there moments before. I could feel the patch beneath my legs and buttocks as I lay groaning: moist and sticky but oddly *warm*, even against the sun-warmed stone of the glarthouse floor. The Countess strode back to me, looming above me in the dying sunlight.

'On your feet, you careless slut.'

I was dazed and shook my head to try and clear it, but the Countess misinterpreted the movement.

'You dare disobey? On your feet at once.'

And her demonic hand seized me by the wrist and heaved, lifting my upper body clear of the floor. The pain as her burning fingers bit into my flesh cleared my head in an instant and I struggled to my feet, feeling the fluid smeared and sticky on my back and buttocks. The Countess released my wrist and strode off again with another peremptory 'Come!', and I trotted after her, peering at the floor for further patches of the fluid and wiping at my soiled back and buttocks. I had time for a fleeting sniff at the stuff as I passed through the glarthouse door and the Countess paused to lock it, then for another as she strode past me and I trotted in her wake. It had an odd, almost herbal smell, but with a briny undertone. For a moment I was tempted to lick my fingers, then remembering my experience of the previous twenfer decided not. Later I would discover that the stuff had dried on my skin, peeling away in flakes and shreds, but a minute after we left the glarthouse all thought of it had been driven from my head, for the Countess was leading me not to the library and our usual conversation but down the corridors to the regions of the castle I had explored illicitly the previous night. My heart began to beat faster. Was

~~Big Tit's~~ Mary's warning that the Countess could not let me free for months to come about to materialise? Was the evil bitch leading me to imprisonment among the milk-slaves? I feared it was so when, having led me to the very stair I had descended less than a twenfer before, she turned to address me.

'It was intended that you returned to Romania soon, was it not?'

I nodded, saying, 'If the Countess had no further need of my services. And dare I hope she has not?'

Cracks appeared in the thick white powder on her face as she smiled sardonically for a moment. Then the cracks disappeared as her face relaxed, and she nodded.

'Yes, you dare. My use for you is almost at an end, you will be glad to hear. But I do not wish you to return to your home and your loved ones carrying certain – how shall I say? – *misapprehensions* about your hostess. I believe there has come to your ears during your stay certain unsavoury – how shall I say? – *rumours* of what lies beneath my castle. I need not say that they are wholly baseless, as you shall now see with your own eyes. Follow me.'

And producing then lighting a small lamp, she began to descend the long stair that led, as I had already seen with my own eyes, to the foul scene of her fouler profiteering from the unnaturally lactating breasts of a hundred-and-thirty-six unjustly imprisoned young women. I followed her, trembling with apprehension, for I feared that this was all a monstrous jest on her part and that she was leading me underground not to dash the 'rumours', as she put it, but to confirm them on my very own person: *viz.*, by forcing me to milk-slavery myself. When we reached the foot of the stair and the twin passages, we turned, as I had done, down the left; then down the left again; then down the right, and were confronted by the same door I had slipped through to find the chamber beyond crowded with chained and drugged young women. But now the door was locked and the Countess was fumbling in a pocket of her dress for her massive bunch of keys. To my surprise she did not use them herself, but held them out to me.

'It is key 37,' she told me.

I took them from her, my heart thumping again in my chest, and searched for key 37. The keys were of all shapes and sizes, and even degrees of antiquity, some tarnished with age, but all were stamped with an identifying number. I found 37 and stepped forward to use it on the door, drawing breath carefully into my nostrils. I could smell the sweat of the previous night leaking around the door but it was cold and the scent of fresh milk that had so strongly accompanied it was faded almost to nothing. The lock turned with a groan, surrendering to the key, and I pushed the door open.

'Enter,' the Countess said from behind me, and I obeyed, stepping into the darkness of the chamber beyond, shivering with apprehension as air much colder than the previous night's folded around me, and I wondered why I could hear the river much more clearly now. The Countess followed, lifting the lamp high as she came, and I did not need to look at her face to know that her mask of powder was again cracked with that sardonic smile of hers.

'As you see,' she told me, 'see with your very own eyes, the rumours are baseless.'

The milking-chamber was bare and unoccupied, and only the stone thrones remained: the chains, with the young women they had fastened, were quite gone.

'These,' continued the Countess, nodding downwards at a row of thrones and the gaping hole in the seat of each, 'are for the disposal of rubbish. Pray see for yourself. With your very own eyes.'

She was lifting the seat of one of the thrones and inviting me forwards. My throat tightening with horror, I moved to the throne and looked down the mouth of the huge pipe she had revealed to me. What was she telling me? That my disobedience had resulted in the sacrifice of her milk-slaves? That she had flung them to their deaths down their own lavatories?

'Can you hear it?' she asked.

I nodded as I looked down the pipe. The river was sounding up from below it very clearly, as though it lay but a few tens of feet distant. But had Mary not told me that the piss and dung of the milk-slaves were preserved for fermentation, to heat the milking-chambers?

'As you see,' said the Countess, 'anything dropped in meets the river in a few seconds. But that is enough: you have seen all you need to see and I notice that you are shivering. Let us return above, where you may dress and join me again for the conversation I have come to value so much. It will be one of our last sessions, now that my use for you is coming to an end and you will soon leave the castle.'

The threat, it seemed to me, was unmistakable. That twenfer or the next I would follow the milk-slaves down one of the lavatories. The river would bear all evidence of her crime away while she travelled at her leisure to Romania and brought to hellish fruition the vast scheme of wickedness she nursed even now in her cruel and calculating bosom. I could see only one shadow of hope in a sun-blasted desert: that when the bitch found her pretext to break off our coming conversation and retire to her unnatural nocturnal slumber, I might penetrate her lair and steal her keys. These secured, I could open any door in the castle and doubted not that within minutes I should be fleeing back down the mountain. Even daylight would not stop me, I vowed, though the words rang hollow in my mind as the Countess led me back up the passages to the stair. She was so tall, so strong, and the only advantage I held over her, I had come to believe from my observations of her, was that her hearing and night-sight were much less acute than

110

my own. Could I find some way to turn this to my advantage?

I mused on the matter as I accompanied her back to the middle level of the castle, where she allowed me to bathe and dress, and I was distracted, despite my best efforts, during the conversation we held in the library. She noted my wandering thoughts, the bitch, and asked me with that characteristic risory *craquelure* in her mask of powder, whether my attention played on my coming departure from the castle. I had to dissemble my consternation at the question, and thought I had carried it off well enough. Some time later, as she grew obviously weary, she found a pretext to break off our conversation and left me with some especially trivial task of research and transcription to perform on the library table. I did not make even a pretence of beginning it, for in the coming twenfer I should either have fled or been flung from the castle's precincts. Instead I listened with especial care as she left the library and made, as I thought, for her sleeping-quarters. But no! To my surprise, and then growing dismay, she did not take the usual turning and instead I heard her walk back the way she and I had already travelled: to the stair and the branching passages of the milking-chambers. I lost her footsteps as they descended the stair and sat shivering with misery at the library table. Was she going below to prepare my sacrifice to the river? Would the drugged meal I next ate – already waiting on its tray – be the last of my life?

It seemed an age before the faint sound of her reascending footsteps reached my ears. I listened as they came back along the corridors to reach and ascend the stair I had thought she was first making for, the first of the three that led, I believed, to her sleeping-chamber. I listened with growing hope as she ascended the stair, then smiled as I heard the creak and closing of that first heavy door. Twice more I heard a similar ascent, a similar creak and closing, then all was silence. I would wait now till I was sure she was well asleep, then set off in pursuit of her. I was gnawed by one remaining fear: that she should have locked or bolted each – or any – of the doors as she passed through. No such sound had reached my straining ears, it is true, but perhaps that meant the mechanism of either lock or bolt were well oiled.

While I have been waiting I have completed this diary entry and now prepare to seek out the Countess's sleeping-quarters. Later, if I am able, I will continue and record my success or failure.

Later. Imagine my suspense when I at last set out to find her sleeping-quarters: creeping down the corridors to the first stair, climbing it with murine stealth, reaching that first door and pausing with hammering heart to feel for the handle. Ah, the Goddess was with me! It was not locked and the handle turned smoothly and silently under my hand. Then came the next stair and the next door, and again the Goddess was with me. These two successes merely heightened my apprehensions, however, for it fitted well with what I knew of the Countess's character that, divining I had by now determined on a burglary of her sleeping-quarters, she should raise my hopes for a comprehensive dashing, and leave the first two doors unlocked but not the third. I climbed the third stair and stood, heart knocking against my ribs with sufficient violence, it seemed, to be audible for yards, before that third door, on which all my hopes now rested. With a silent prayer I groped for the handle and turned. My knees melted and I nearly fell as it turned as smoothly and silently as the two before and I slipped through that final door.

For final door it was: on the other side lay the Countess's sleeping-quarters: a flat roof of the castle, bare beneath the moon and turning stars. The moon, at her fullest, was bathing the roof in brilliant light and my dark-adjusted eyes were blinded for a moment. Then, as the moon slid behind a veil of clouds, I saw the Countess's bed in the middle of the roof, raised to the open heavens on a framework of iron. 'Bed', I say, though it was no bed in truth, as I soon discovered. How could one expect a beast of such a nature as she to lie in a bed? And 'she', I say, though in truth 'she' was no she. Like the momentarily hidden moon, my cup of horror was its fullest and I was about to drain it to the dregs.

I crept out on to the roof, approaching the platform and the foul burden it carried: the Countess's coffin of clear glass, in which even now she was stretched and sleeping. My eyes were adjusting to the moonlight filtering through the veil of clouds, and I could see as I approached that she was lying naked there – her clothes hung from hooks on the framework. The moon licked through a rent in the veil of cloud and for a moment I could see the Countess's sleeping face with an awful clarity. My gorge rose with horror as I saw the fresh milk oozing from her lips: she had evidently descended to the milking-chambers to feed from milk-slaves she had not yet sacrificed to the river. It seemed as if the whole awful creature were simply gorged with milk. She lay like a filthy leech, exhausted with her repletion.

But now the veil of cloud was passing from the moon and her light was licking across the roof like a great silver tongue. As the tongue licked across the platform my heart, which in the next instant would be twisted with horror and disgust, sang with delight in my breast: the keys were glittering inside the coffin at the Countess's hip and if I could lift the coffin-lid without waking her they would soon be mine. But the moon-tongue was licking over the whole coffin and the sleeping foulness it enclosed, and detail upon detail of the Countess's body was laid bare in merciless detail before my astonished and horrified eyes. Even now to recall them brings a deadly sickness to my throat: the *glartness* of her skin, which she had concealed from me with that thick facial powder; the *hair* that sprouted on every limb and on her *flat* chest, with its stunted and dwarf-nippled breasts. But worst of all was to come: for my eyes had fastened on the centre of her body and the extravagant bush of dark and curling hair at her groin. What was that beneath the bush, hanging between her grotesquely muscular and hirsute thighs? *Dear Goddess: what was that beneath it, beginning to stand upright as though the flood of unimprisoned moonlight had called it to full and foulest life?*

I turned and fled from that accursed rooftop, seized by overwhelming panic, racked by horror, my mind permanently blasted, it seemed, by what I had seen – the unspeakable member the Countess wore in lieu of a cunt between her hairy thighs. Down, down, I fled, down those three stairs, flinging back the doors with reckless violence, down and ever down, and when I reached the middle level I raced for a fourth stair: the one that would lead me to the milking-chambers, to the milking-chamber the Countess had shown me that day, where I had determined to unburden myself of my horror in the quickest and cleanest way I knew: by throwing myself down one of those lavatory holes into the subterranean river.

I raced down the branching passages, taking left, left again, then right, and then threw myself sobbing against a locked door. It was now I discovered that the shocks to which my overburdened frame had already been subjected were not complete, for as I beat with my fists in an access of despair upon what separated me from the oblivion I sought, I heard a voice suddenly upraised within: *the voice of big-titted Mary*, whom I had believed sacrificed with the other milk-slaves that very twenfer by the Countess. Superstitious dread seized me and I could barely croak in reply to ask through the door whether I were addressed by mortal woman or ghost. When the voice replied affirming the former, I nearly fainted with relief, and it was some time before I could compose myself to answer the questions she, evidently as surprised as I, was pouring at me.

Slowly, by question and counter-question, we pieced together the two halves of our story and laid bare the Countess's plot: all occupants of the milking-chamber had, Mary told me, been moved by the Countess's twaughters earlier in the twenfer without explanation, and had lain chained on the floor of the neighbouring milking-chamber for some hours before being moved back again. In that time, plainly, I had been shown the empty chamber and believed the Countess as monstrous in deed as she was in soul and body. I remarked exactly this to Mary, telling her of what I had just seen far above on the castle roof: the glass coffin; the Countess sleeping naked within it; and the teratoid horrors revealed to me by the moon. When I completed my nefandous narrative with a description of the more than obscene member I had seen rising between her hairy thighs, reply came there none for some moments, and I believed Mary had fainted clean away inside the chamber for excess of horror. Perhaps she had, for when she spoke again her voice was trembling and low, though this was due in part to what she now had to tell me: that what I had seen confirmed an age-old Transmarynian legend concerning a race of women cursed in the very depths of antiquity for some monstrous crime that cried to the very face of Heaven for vengeance. They had been punished by being half-stripped of their humanity, retaining the mind of a human being but not her true and wholesome corporeality, that they might know and eternally bewail their transgression. Thus the bestial hair I had seen on the Countess's limbs and chest, her lack of full breasts and the obscene tentacle between her thighs. She was no true woman but a creature of a different order for which a name no longer existed. My gorge rose as I listened, for I realised that the Countess's three twaughters were of the same kind, so that the Countess was not, as one might have hoped, a solitary survival of a race – or, rather, *breed* – of creature doomed, on her passing, to utter and final extinction.

Then, as Mary continued, it was my turn to grow faint with horror and clutch at the wall for support. There was only one course now open to us: that I should return to the roof and burgle the Countess's coffin, returning with the keys to release Mary and her milk-slave sisters, whom the two of us could then lead in rebellion against the Countess and her monstrous brood. My heart turned to water in my breast at the thought of it (it turns to water still), and it took all Mary's eloquence, and then the briny barbs of her tears, clearly audible from within, to send me back up the stair to complete the task.

The night is passing quickly, but I have paused to add this final entry to my diary before I again ascend the three stairs to the roof, the glass coffin and the milk-gorged monster that lies within it. Perhaps she – or, rather, *it* – lies awake, waiting for me; perhaps she – *it* – still sleeps. I will soon know, but I will hide my diary on a high row of the library before I go in the hope that, should I fail, it might one night expose the horror I have uncovered in this cursed place.

5

Letter from Miss Mina Harker to Miss Caliginia Vestenra

9 May.

My dearest Caliginia,

Forgive my long delay in writing, but I have been simply overwhelmed with work. The life of a legal assistant in a successful firm is never a restful one, but the preparations for the Countess's arrival have made all previous storms seem like the merest summer breezes. Last month we were reviewing applicants for teaching posts at the academy she means to set up; this month, while continuing apace with that task, we have been drawing up and publicising the terms of the scholarships she is offering for the poor and under-privileged of all Europe. One term at least seems most curious, and I mean to raise it with Joanna when I have her direction in Transmarynia, that she might question the Countess more closely about it. I speak of the medical inspection each girl is to undergo before she sits and passes the entrance examination: the Countess's instructions stipulate that the doctor is to pay close and careful attention to the breasts, ensuring that they are above a certain ratio to the girl's height and/or weight, and that the left should deviate in size and sphericality from the right (or vice versa) by no more than 5 per cent! Of course, we have all heard of eccentric millionairesses from America, but do you ever hear of anything half so eccentric as this in a millionairess from *anywhere* in the world, let alone such an out-of-the-way place as Transmarynia?

Ah, I promised not to brood on it, but I have written the fatal word twice now and my thoughts have flown, willy-nilly, across the miles of plain, forest and ocean to Joanna's side. I do hope she is taking care of herself and eating well, and that Transmarynia is as civilised these nights as she assured me it was before her departure. I should not have wished her to go, but it was such good business for the firm and Joanna had not the heart to refuse her dear old mistress Haukina, after all she has done for the two of us. Nor indeed had Joanna the inclination: if the Countess establishes herself in Bucharest, there will be work for many years to come, and if Joanna's diligence and efficiency impress her in exotic Transmarynia – as surely they must! – what could incline her to change lawyers in mundane Romania? Nothing, so far as I can see.

But I must not babble of my own hopes and fears, especially when I am bursting with curiosity to hear more of your own adventures, if all that I hear of you and a certain tall and curly-headed young woman is true. Write and tell me all, omitting nothing that might bring a spark to my eye and a tingle – and trickle! – to the pussy you know and love so well. Joanna has promised me at least one thorough pussy-tingler from Transmarynia, and I long to hear of her encounters with one or two of the snow- or fire-capped maids for which that island is famed. Ah, the ten o'clock bell is ringing and I must take Haukina her morning coffee. Write soon, omitting nothing!
Your loving
Mina.

Letter from Caliginia Vestenra to Mina Harker

17, Craiova Street
Wednesnight.
My dearest Mina,

Oh, you sly bitch! I thought I had concealed my liaison successfully from all prying eyes, but your espionage corps has been too efficient for me. Yes, it is true: a 'certain tall and curly-headed young woman' and I have been making the mattresses of my mother's house groan with sincere complaint a month come Monnight. Or twenty-past two in the morning, Monnight, to be precise: you can tell it is serious if I have been counting the minutes, can you not? Oh, Mina, I am so happy: she and I have been destined together from the first starlight that shone at the Goddess's command on the fair face of Earth. You know – who could know better? – how I love to be dominated, nay enslaved, in the act of passion, and she, my dearest and most dolorating Domina, matches my love of submission with her own love of command. I am all over bruises, and bless every one!

But you ask for details and I shall supply some. I take, as merely the most recent pearl on the shining necklace of our nights, the Tuesnight just passed. She had been out and returned with a package for me whose contents she teasingly refused to reveal until she and I were safely in our pre-nuptial chamber. When we were there, she ordered me to strip and advance on all fours to the bed, where she sat waiting for me, still fully dressed, and with the package, still securely wrapped, resting on her knees. As I came up to her, she presented it to my face, ordering me to sniff out the contents like 'The true little bitch you are, snuffling in the gutter for your pleasure'. I tried to obey, but whatever lay within had been drenched with aniseed before wrapping, and all I could detect was the merest momentary suspicion of leather. I confessed my failure and she ordered me flat to the floor while she stood atop my bare buttocks in her boots. I obeyed and she mounted me, bouncing so that my pussy, already inflamed by the orders she had issued, was pressed hard to the carpet, though without sufficient friction to give me any true satisfaction. How I longed to lower my hand and wank, but I knew that our game must go on a little longer. With a final bounce, she jumped free and sat on the bed once more, ordering me up to sniff again at the parcel. I obeyed, but as before I confessed my failure, and as she harangued my ineffectuality and ignorance I felt a trickle of pussy-juice starting to creep down my inner thigh.

She then ordered me to open the package – but with my teeth. As I have said, it was securely fastened, looped with tape and tied with string. The paper was tough and fibrous, and tasted most unpleasant as I began to lick and suck at it, having to moisten it with my spittle before my weak teeth could make any impression on it. And all the while I struggled she, of course, was abusing me for my dilatoriness and ineffectuality. I longed to answer that my *dilat*oriness was entirely her responsibility, but it was not the moment to interrupt the game with insolence or innuendo, and I licked and sucked on, slowly gnawing a first opening to the package. Here she stopped me and ordered me to sniff again. I did so and this time, amid the reek of aniseed, I could detect a definite leathery tang: the package contained some item of fresh new leather. I told her so and she nodded, a cruel smile beginning to spread with almost solar menace across her handsome face. My pussy tingled more than ever, and I knew revelation was at hand. It came swiftly when she ordered me away from the bed to crouch on all fours on the floor with my eyes closed. I obeyed and heard her walk up behind me, then straddle me as her strong hands tore the package fully open. String and tape landed softly on the floor beside me, followed by fragments of the discarded wrapping. Whatever had been in the package was now loose and in her hands. I kept my eyes tight shut, shivering with anticipation, and almost cried out for joy as I felt something loop into place around my neck and slowly tighten.

'You may touch it,' she told me, 'but keep your eyes closed.'

I reached up and explored it with my fingers. Cool brass studs met them as they slid around it, then an iron clip for the thin, strong lead that dangled upwards into her strong fingers. It was a bitch-collar, and the proud humiliation of wearing it made my pussy squirm with delight, almost spurting juice, so that my inner thighs grew slicker and slimier still. She tightened it a further notch, so that I found it almost difficult to breathe, and asked me, 'What is it?'

'A collar, mistress,' I strained out.

'No! It is more than a collar. Name it in full.'

'It is a bitch-collar, mistress.'

'Good girl. Very good girl. And who is the bitch?'

'It is I, mistress.'

'And are you a disobedient bitch?'

I tried to nod as I replied, but she had dragged back on the lead and I could not move my head.

'Yes, mistress,' I managed to say.

'You are right. That is what you are. That is why you wear a bitch-collar and lead. But those are not all that are required for the training and punishment of a disobedient bitch, are they?'

'No, mistress.'

'Then what else is required?'

Even had I not been wearing the collar, I should have croaked when I answered, such was the lust that tightened my throat, churned in my belly and sent rippling fingers through the gushing walls and lips of my overexcited pussy.

'A – a whip, mistress.'

'Yes.'

And I jerked with surprised delight as I heard her slash a whip down beside my cheek, which was kissed with disturbed air.

'So now, disobedient bitch,' she breathed, leaning forward to put her lips close behind my head, 'are you ready to be punished?'

She had given me a little slack on the lead and I could nod this time.

'Yes, mistress.'

'Yes, *please*, mistress.'

I swallowed with difficulty, finding it hard to fit a bolus of pleasure-fear down my collar-constricted throat. My ears were buzzing with a mixture of asphyxiation, excitement and apprehension.

'Yes, please, mistress,' I said, and then shrieked aloud as the whip descended full on my buttocks, leaped aloft and descended again, slashing at them in a frenzy of strokes of which my poor buttock-cheeks, already bruised and tender, reported every nuance. She had tugged back on the lead, pulling my head up so that I stared at the ceiling, somehow noting through my pain a constellation of piss-splatters from a game we had played in the chamber the night before. And then, as my buttocks seemed about to burst into flame from the violence to which she had subjected them, and as my pussy seethed with pain-joy and pleasure-grief, she ceased to whip me and was kind in the afterseethe of her cruelty. She flicked the full length of the whip up between my legs, pressing its dangling length hard to my oozing pussy. Then she ordered me to close my thighs tight on it. I did so and slowly she began to drag it free, drawing its hard

122

leather up over my pussy-lips and pussyhorn. She paused as halfway through I began to shudder and gasp with impending orgasm, then resumed more slowly, timing the sliding-free of the whip to my final and cataclysmic release. It came as the very tip of the whip was tickling its way up my pussy, and I collapsed full length on the floor, pounding my hips at the carpet and rasping my inflamed nipples left and right against the carpet as what seemed like an ocean of pussy-juice dripped and oozed between my shuddering thighs.

There! Has that brought a spark to your eye and a tingle or, better still, a trickle to your pussy? If so, you know my tongue would be at her service were I there in your company, as it was at the service of the pussy of my love when she stripped too and we continued the game we had begun. Of which more later, I promise. She is away on business tonight and I must find my own pleasure with my fingers for the nonce. I am about to do so again, and will leave a token of it with my signature. Sniff the spot please if you pleasure yourself over this letter, and kiss it in remembrance of me as you come, my darling.
Caliginia.

Letter from Caliginia Vestenra to Mina Harker

24 May
My dearest Mina,
   Have we set a new fashion? If so, well, you know me, I must always be *à la mode* and with this letter I shall enclose something that will, I am sure, recall some at least of the many happy hours of pleasure we have spent together. If you like you can pass it on to dear Joanna when you write to her – and do not worry yourself, I beg you, if she delays in writing.

That Countess of hers (and yours!) sounds somehow a *stern* taskmaster (just writing her name makes me shiver with foreboding – and moisten just a little, I confess) and I am sure she is keeping poor Joanna so busy she has not been able to snatch a moment to herself, save perhaps to write the diary she promised to keep for your instruction, and delectation. I long to read it too and to hear of Joanna's conquests among the fair maids of Transmarynia. Rest assured, however, that her heart remains with you, wherever her fingers, tongue and pussy stray.

But to business: I shall continue the description of the game my love and I played when she gifted me the bitch-collar and whip. You will recall how she fitted the former to me and plied my greedy backside with the latter before employing it to bring me to orgasm. Thereupon she, till then fully clothed, stripped herself as bare as I had been from the beginning, and we played a little more. I was sopping wet from the whipping and the orgasm she had induced, and oozed still more as she scolded me for it, telling me that my thighs and belly were quite coated with my foul and fishy exudate, which was stinking worse with every passing moment. She ordered me on to my back, legs wide apart, and I shivered with joy, for I thought she meant to tongue me clean. Well, she did, but not in the way I had imagined: she laid her hand flat to my pussy and rubbed at it hard, then presented her dripping palm and fingers to me to lick clean. Then she coated the back of her hand with my juice, and presented that to my tongue. I was shivering again, for I sensed some hidden purpose in the ceremony, but had to wait out two more pussy-cleanings, when she scraped at my pussy-lips and inner thighs with her fingers, soaking them thoroughly before raising them to my mouth. Her complaints were redoubling, for of course the sensation of her hand on my pussy and the taste of my pussy on her hand were arousing me more and more. Now she began to muse aloud, and again I shivered with joy at her words.

'It is no use: the stuff oozes out faster than I can sponge it away . . . I must . . . yes, I must find a way of cutting the time of travel from hand-soaking to licking . . . Or perhaps – could it be possible? – Perhaps find some way of *eliminating* hand-soaking altogether . . . Some way of introducing mouth directly to pussy . . .'

I thought, of course, that she meant by this introducing her own mouth to my pussy: but not a bit of it! Her next words hollowed my stomach with trepidation.

'Perhaps . . . But is the bitch flexible enough? I doubt it. If only there were two of her, one to lick the cunt of the other – or, rather, one to lick the cunt of the other as her own cunt is licked. But wait a moment –'

And now I knew for certain that my love's eloquence had worked its way with my dear mother, and that we should all three celebrate the coming nuptials of two of us. My mother, as you know, is of scrupulous correctness and (to my mind, though if a whisper of it came to her ears I know I should die of chagrin!) a certain *provinciality* of morals, and in her night and district it was little known for twaughters to couch with mothers. But times change, and some whisper that the finest pleasures are between two women of the same blood but twenty-three years' difference in age, for the elder knows how she herself was, and the younger learns how she herself will be. Be that as it may, I know my second orgasm of the night, provided for me for the first time by my mother, was finer almost than the orgasm provided for me earlier by my lover.

Oh, forgive me, Mina, for I have wandered a little from the point: the musing of my lover (I will not yet

125

reveal her name, for I plan to bring you together very soon and wish you to hear it from her own lips) on the possibilities of mutual cunnilinctus between me and a hypothetical twin. But downstairs, dozing over her embroidery, was my actual twin, persuaded to the deed earlier in the twenfer by my lover's eloquence. Thus it was that she (my lover) stamped barefooted on the floor in a certain rhythm, and then arranged me on the floor with my legs wide-parted, so that the first sight my mother had, having climbed the stairs and knocked and been told to enter, was of my pussy, oozing with fresh juice. Her eyes widened at the sight and a sparkle of pleasure lit her dull eyes – for you know that recently she has not been in the best of health. Indeed, my lover later confessed that this was one of the cards she played in persuading my mother to the mutual cunnilinctus: the fresh juice of the twaughter's quim was, she told her, regarded as a sovereign remedy for all manner of ills among the mothers of – where else?! – northern Transmarynia.

Thus it was she too had soon stripped, peeling her clothes from her smooth limbs then dropping to the floor with almost youthful carelessness before she came to me. When she reached me she reversed herself and crawled atop me to present her face to my pussy and her pussy to my face. I peered up at it, recognising my own there in the pout and fleshiness of the lips, though hers were fleshier than mine. Then my lover gave the order and her face was lowered to my pussy, and her pussy to my face, in the same movement. Her tongue was deliciously warm and soft, lapping gently at my juicy pussy-lips and thigh-hollows, and for a few moments we synchronised our tongues, licking and lapping in close harmony. But the difficulty of maintaining the synchrony soon persuaded us to abandon it, and I gladly sent my tongue roaming over the loosening folds of her pussy

126

at my own pleasure – and hers too, I hope! Nay, I know, for she began to juice and leak with reassuring celerity, and the sound of the soft lapping of her tongue on my pussy was joined by the sound of the soft lapping of mine on hers. Another order from the Comptroller of Cunts who was peering between our thighs, and we began to work on each other's pussyhorn, sucking and nibbling each other towards orgasm. I had to move my head downwards to obey the order and my forehead was soon running with pussy-juice, making me wonder if mother-juice were as good for twaughters as, in Transmarynian lore, twaughter-juice was for mothers. I certainly suspect pussy-juice of any kind is good for one's skin, for – as who knows better than you, dear Mina? – my face is always glowing after I have performed a lengthy cunnilinctus on a gushing pussy!

I thought of this as I licked my mother, and began to supplement tongue-work with pushes and prods of my nose and chin, with feline cheek-slidings and purrings. Evidently the variety of pussy-pleasuring I was now offering pleased her, for she began to ooze more freely than ever (my eyebrows and widow's peak was positively stiff with dried pussy-juice later) and to pay me back in my own coin, so that my purrings began to stutter with moans of oncoming orgasm. My lover, whose attention had never wandered from the two pussies whose simultaneous pleasuring she was supervising, ordered us into the final straight and we discarded all refinements and supplementary pussy-pleasuring for a straightforward tongue-gallop at our stiff and aching pussyhorns. Soft and warm as my mother's tongue was, it was almost painful to be pleasured so directly, to have unrefined sensation poured so fierce-floodingly into the nerves of my pussyhorn, almost as though I was drinking molten silver from the cunt-chalice of Luna herself, in the tale of Mariah and the Moon-Chariot. (Do you remember how we used to giggle over our book in Mistress Cecilia's lessons, because of the drawings someone in an upper form had left in the margins of the text?) Perhaps my mother felt the same, or perhaps growing years had brought a new resilience to the pussyhorn I now bore proudly between my thighs, crowning the sacred portal of my pussy-lips. Certainly she did not relent a fraction of her tongue-galloping at my pussyhorn, whose sensitivity she must have known for herself at my age, and I took this to be a sign that I should endure and suffer her to gallop as long as she pleased.

I was right to read her intentions so for, even as the pain of direct pussyhorn-pummelling, clitoris-cudgelling, nymph – oh, foo, I cannot think of an alliterative verb to accompany that – for, even as I say, the pain of direct pussyhorn-pummelling (etc) grew, the pleasure began to outgrow it, like a naked young woman fleeing up a long stair of melting wax. She reaches the top while five or six treads are still solid, and throws herself headlong into what awaits her: a room full of swansdown where pleasure-maids lie waiting with expert tongues and fingers for the simultaneous servicing of every inch of her body. But I do not believe I could have come harder in such a setting than I did to my mother's ministrations. My thighs arched up involuntarily, tightening on her head and ears, and when I began to come my pelvis pounded up at her quite independently of me. She tells me that she was almost frightened by the violence of my orgasm, and would have been so, had she not known – and who better than her? – of my capacity for powerful and prolonged pussy-bliss. Her own p.b., felt with streaming moisture on my face, was nigh on as powerful and prolonged, and I tickled it out seconds longer with a tongue just barely flickering at her pussyhorn.

128

And then, as we lay gasping on the floor, she atop me and I beneath her, my lover offered us a token of the pleasure she had received in merely watching. Perhaps you will not believe this – it is only Caliginia and her imagination, you will say (or at least you will say till you meet my love and see the strength of her arms and chest) – but this is what she did. She kneeled close to the two of us, sliding her arms and forearms under my neck and thighs, and then, with barely a murmur of effort, barely a pause, lifted the two of us clean off the floor and carried us to the bed! She told me later that watching us tongue each other to orgasm had filled her with such *joie de vivre* that she felt as though she could lift Bucharest and fling it clean into the Black Sea. What she did next, having deposited her gasping, post-orgasmic parcel of mother and twaughter in the scented depths of the bed, you will learn, my dearest Mina, in the next instalment from your ever-licking, ever-leaking, ever-loving,

Caliginia.

PS I am reopening the letter to enclose the new token that, in my excitement of reminiscence, I forgot I had promised you. Do you not see how it glows with health? I should be *most* pleased to hear that you have returned it, after a fashion, whence it came, and tickled yourself a little diversion in the midst of your work and your anxieties about dear, distant, but (I am perfectly sure) hale and hearty, Joanna. My licking, leaking and loving again and always. C.

Cîmpulung & Twaughters, Building Merchants, Bucharest
24 May

Dear Madam,
We are in receipt of your instructions and will construct the subterranean cells according to your specifications.
We are, dear Madam,
Yours respectfully,
Pro Cîmpulung & Twaughters.

6

Mina Harker's Journal

24 July. Constanţa.

Lucy met me at the station, looking sweeter and lovelier than ever, and we drove up to the house at the Crescent in which she and her mother have rooms. The troilism C has so vividly and movingly – in two senses! – described in her letters certainly seems to have agreed with her mother, for she glows nearly as much as C, and seeing the two side by side one might almost mistake them for twinsters*, not mother and twaughter separated by a tweth*. A few moments into the drive, however, I caught C looking at me with that secret smile she always wears when she is up to mischief, and I knew some surprise was waiting for me in the house. C refused to reveal what it was, despite repeated questions, and I asked her mother permission to spank her as she (her mother) sat opposite us and watched. Smiling, the dear middle-aged lady granted her permission, and from the way C wriggled into a corner of the carriage I knew she had plotted this and allowed me to catch that smile on her face. Still, one does not look a 'gift horse in the mouth', as the Transmarynians say, and I dragged her squeaking and protesting (and giggling too, despite her best efforts to seem outraged) from her corner, planted her firmly over my knees, and began to haul up her skirt. The flounces of her petticoats fanned the air and I smelled, as I expected, the spice of her pussy as her naked thighs and bottom were exposed. Her mother watched, eyes shining with amusement, as I held C's petticoats and skirt clear with one hand and prepared to administer the first spank with the other.

But the first stage of this preparation was, of course, to reacquaint myself with C's beautiful bottom – with her glorious gluteus – her phenomenal fesses – her nuzzlesome nates (she is sitting beside me in her bedroom giggling, for I read aloud the words as I pen them, and she is censuring me for satirising her prose-style). Accordingly I sent my hand roving and rummaging over the curves and crevices of her bottom, testing the ripeness of the fading bruises that patterned its silken surface. She wriggled, squeaking that my hand was disgustingly hot, though her voice was muffled, for I had thrust her face into the seat (telling her to keep the strictest silence). I paused in my manual exploration of that silken bumscape, its slopes and bays and soft central cleft, and sniffed disdainfully.

'Then the remedy,' I told her, 'is at hand.'

And without warning, taking great care not to allow the movement to be apparent in my body, I raised my hand and brought it down with a thunderclap on her bum. She cried out into the carriage-seat, and told me later that the blow made tears squirt from her eyes almost as though a wave of compression had shot through her dainty frame, forcing her lachrymal glands to discharge. Now I paused again, staring down at the hand-shaped mark glowing sowl against the bruised silk field of her right buttock. I mused on it, beginning to trace its outlines with a fingernail, stroking gently at it and the skin that surrounded it, trying to read the increasing heat as blood rushed to the place. Then, raising my hand with the same care as before, I said, 'Well, my disobedient darling, did that h–' and splin-

tered my own words with the thunderous descent of my
hand, aimed this time at the left buttock. Then, into the
echoes of that, and of her yelp of pain, I breathed the
word I had auto-interrupted, 'Hurt?'

She began to speak but I silenced her with a sharp
'Shush. I will see for myself. Lubrication speaks louder
than words.'

And I inserted my spanking hand slowly between her
thighs, slipping it millimetre by millimetre to that
reliable indicatrix of arousal: her silk-locked, satin-
lipped pussy.

'Ah!' I said. My fingertips reported moisture. She was
oozing with pleasure, excited by the spanking as quickly
as I myself had been. I pushed my fingers deeper,
brushing the swelling fringes of her pussy-lips, sliding
each fingertip in turn up and down them, from pollex to
minimus, and then held the hand up for her mother's
inspection, turning it left and right so that my moistened
fingertips caught the lamplight within the carriage and
shone.

'Do you see, Mrs Vestenra? Do you see what a slut
your twaughter is?'

Silently, with a glance of amusement at her oblivious
offspring, Mrs Vestenra leaned forwards from her seat,
eyebrows lifting and mouth opening. I read her intent at
once and held my glistening fingertips forwards to her.
She closed her mouth on them one by one, beginning at
my thumb, licking first clockwise then counterclockwise,
inserting the tip of her tongue carefully beneath my
fingernail to remove the very last trace. I felt her
twaughter wriggle impatiently on my lap as her mother
silently licked and sucked the pussy-juice from my
fingertips, and told her, 'Sit still, slut.'

Her mother completed the fingertip of my ringfinger
and moved her mouth off and down to the fingertip of
my little finger. C wriggled again.

'Sit still, slut. I am preparing myself. Mentally.'

Her mother finished the fingertip of my little finger, then, after planting a departing kisslet on the nail, leaned back silently to her seat with a wink. (I shall leave a space clear here for C to record her own thoughts on this betrayal, when she reads the diary: *I knew all the time, Mother dearest: a slut twaughter is a slut's twaughter*). I blew Mrs Vestenra a silent kiss and lowered my cleaned hand to C's buttocks, to outline and stroke the hand-marks, measuring the heat again. My fingertips, cooled by her mother's spittle, were highly sensitive now and reported the increased heat perfectly: her buttocks were glowing fiercely and she could not complain that my hand was hot *now*.

C wriggled again under my attentions, pressing her mouth harder into the carriage seat and mumbling something I could not catch (she tells me now that it was 'Go on: spank me!'). I rubbed the knuckles of my index and forefingers on her buttocks, riding its smooth and snowy curves for a moment or two, then drew a slow breath, raised the hand, and began to spank her again, firing the blows at her from low-down at first, with a loose wrist, but gradually raising the height and increasing the speed and strength, so that the carriage was filled with a fusillade of crisp ringing, like the hooves of a horse galloping madly on firm frosty earth. Starting to pant with the effort, I looked up and caught her mother's glowing eyes, and saw that she had inserted a hand up her own dress and was rocking to and fro in her seat, evidently wanking like a woman possessed. My own pussy, bubbling with juice between my Caliginia-burdened thighs, longed for similar attention, but I knew C would see to that on her arrival and continued, starting to sweat now a little as my spanks grew higher and heavier and harder yet, my wrist locked firmly as I hammered the milky mounds of her buttocks to a deep and glowing vace.

How long I would have kept up the spanking I do not know: the excitement of meeting C again; the knowledge

134

that C's own mother was watching me administer the punishment to her twaughter; my guess at what awaited me in their house and desire to prepare C properly for it – all this seemed to turn my muscles to untiring steel. But the journey, unlike my potential spanking, had a limit set on it from the start, and somehow my ears, feasting though they were on the blows, reported that the carriage was slowing, as though to stop.

Still keeping my hand busy on C's bum, I looked up at C's mother again and, though her face was twisted with the final seconds of wanking before orgasm exploded in her firmly fingered loins, she read the meaning of the look and nodded. We were nearly there. I stopped spanking abruptly, inserted my hand brusquely and brutally between C's thighs, and began to rub her to orgasm with my blistering fingertips, racing to bring her off simultaneously with her mother, whose mouth had come open with a gathering groan as her skirt positively bounced and billowed on her lap, so vigorously was her hand working at her pussy beneath it. My fingers almost slid off C's pussy as they touched it, she had leaked so freely. Would I be able to time her orgasm to that of her mother, which was seconds away, at most? I need not have worried: C's pussy was a pile of gunpowder awaiting the smallest spark. Verily I believe that my fingertips, superheated with the spanking I had administered with that hand, could have ignited true gunpowder if they had been pushed into it. Certainly C's pussy-powder, packed densely into the neat sex-triangle of her pelvis, took fire with the first touch and blew her into ecstatic oblivion with the second, so that mother and twaughter groaned out their orgasms over the same moments.

Then we were arrived, and I tugged down C's petticoats and skirt, swung her upright on my lap and pushed her to her feet. She tottered for a moment, the muscles of her thighs and knees still plainly spasmic with orgasm, then stooped to push open the door and climb out. I rose to my feet, offering my sticky hand to her mother, who accepted it with a smile and allowed me to pull her to her own slightly tottering feet. I assisted her from the carriage and we stood in the street while the cabbie wrestled my luggage down from the rack and staggered up the path behind the three of us as we strolled to the front door. I wondered for a moment whether to double the cabbie's tip and invite her in for what I had guessed awaited me, but there is, I have learned as I have grown older (I read that aloud, but C has not said a word in praise of my youth, for which silence she shall suffer, I promise – and I did not read *that* aloud, so it will come as a cruel and complete surprise), a law of diminishing returns at work in spintries: one cunt and pair of tits added to two cunts and pairs of tits increase possibilities markedly; one cunt and pair added to three less so; and one cunt and pair of tits added to four less so still.

So I paid the cabbie off once she had carried my luggage inside and then listened without regret as she slammed the door on her way out, her cheerful whistle fading as she strode back down the street to her waiting cab. C, who had guessed what had been in my mind (I hired cabbies by the hour and even night when we two were lovers in Bucharest, though that had been one cunt and pair of tits added to two), quirked her eyebrows at me, but I shrugged and followed her through to the sitting-room, where her mother had preceded us.

I heard a tinkle of tea-things as I entered the room, and the murmur of her mother's voice, to which – from a tall chair whose back was to me as I entered – the deeper voice of a younger woman replied. From the way C coloured and quivered, and positively rushed forwards around the chair to throw herself on to the lap of its occupant, I knew my conjectures had been correct: C's secret smile had foretokened my first meeting with her mysterious lover. I came around the chair myself, and C's smile met me again, pleased and proud as she sat firm on the knees of a handsome young woman in military uniform. C turned her head to address this worthy, whose eyebrows were lifting in enquiry.

'Can you feel it, Artemisia?' she asked. 'My bottom is positively on fire from what Mina has just been handing out to me in the carriage.'

I smiled, holding out my hand.

'I am very pleased to meet you, mistress. Caliginia has written a great deal of you, but did not tell you, I see, that I should be arriving tonight.'

A strong dry hand took and clasped my own and, as the dark eyebrows lifted again at the feel of C's pussy-juice on my fingers, I confess that my own knees weakened a fraction, little though I am given to submission myself. This was a dominatrix of dominatrices, I could see, and I blessed the happy chance that had brought her into C's orbit, for C is, of course, a dominanda of dominandas. With a final squeeze, the stranger released my hand.

'Yes, she told me nothing,' she said in her deep voice, speaking with military crispness and precision. 'And I shall punish her for it with great severity.'

C bounced happily on those strong knees, beaming up at me.

'Did I not tell you, Mina? What a great bully she is, and how cruelly she treats me?'

'You did at that,' I said.

A rustle of cloth and squeak of shoe on the carpet from behind me made me turn, and there was C's mother holding out a cup of tea with a smile. I took it and sat down in a chair facing Artemisia and C, taking a sip and watching with a smile of my own as C whispered in Artemisia's ear. When she took her mouth away Artemisia was chewing her lip as though reaching a decision. She looked at me, and my stomach rolled a

137

little at the clear light of her dark eyes. I became suddenly more aware of the trickling pussy between my thighs. Now a smile quirked Artemisia's lips.

'Caliginia tells me you are in need of servicing, and asks my permission for her to extend it to you with her tongue.'

I raised my cup to my lips and took a sip before lowering it and nodding slowly, not wishing to seem uncouthly eager. I nodded, saying, 'Yes, I have leaked considerably. Spanking her, as you may know yourself, is a highly arousing business. Mrs Vestenra herself will testify that merely watching and wanking has rewards beyond the bliss afforded by the beaten bottoms of lesser girls.'

Mrs Vestenra smiled too, holding up her wanking hand, which was still stained with pussy-juice.

'And here is the unwashed proof,' she said in her clear, sweet voice, a tone lower than C's.

Artemisia – I feel I need to know her a night or two longer before I can sincerely call her Art – laughed and said, 'Unwashed proof indeed. But my little slut will attend to your hand, Mrs Vestenra, when she has finished between the thighs of her dear old friend here.'

My spanking hand, still soiled with C's pussy-juice, shook fractionally as I lifted my cup and sipped again. C slipped eagerly off A's lap, lowered her knees to the carpet and knee-walked across to me. She pouted up at me, putting her hands to either side of her firm breasts and pressing them together before joggling them up and down.

'Pussy-purification, mistress? I'm very cheap, but very good.'

I took another sip of tea, determined not to let the minx see how eager I was to be serviced.

'Then if you are very good, why are you so ch–?'

But I spluttered on the word, for C was performing that trick of licking her own nostrils, her tongue-tip

138

sliding first up one, then the other. She lowered her tongue and then, as though I had completed the question, said quietly, 'Why am I so cheap, mistress? Because I love my work.'

It was too much for me. I needed – nay, craved – her tongue on my pussy, which had woken and begun to throb between my thighs, glowing with lust like the midsummer moon. I put my cup of tea down on the table at my side and hoisted my skirt and petticoats up, sliding forwards on my seat so that I could open my legs to the fullest. C watched with narrowed eyes.

'Does madame want the quick service?' I shook my head. 'The long service?' I shook my head again. 'Or the extra-long service?'

For the third time I shook my head. C lifted her eyebrows.

'Then madame must be jesting with this humble little whore, for those are the only services she offers.'

I leaned forwards, took her by the shoulders and tugged her down and on to my waiting pussy, not even presenting my soiled hand to her first. I glanced up at A, who was watching closely but calmly enough, and she nodded when she saw I was signalling with my eyebrows for further permission. Having received it, I said slowly to C, 'What I want, you gorgeous slut, is all three services at once. Quick, long. In that order. Very well?'

C's voice sounded from between my thighs, muffled and hollow. 'Very well.'

'Then supply them.'

And she put her face forwards and down the final inches and began. The first few strokes of her tongue were enough to remind me of what I had been missing since she and I stopped sleeping together regularly. C once told me that she lived for and through cunt-licking, and though since then her horizons – partly at my instruction I am pleased to say (she has just laughingly denied this, and added more weight to the punishment that hangs above her unsuspecting head – or, rather, above her unsuspecting bottom) – but, though her horizons, as I say, have expanded since then, the active aspects of her love-making will always be dominated by her expertise on a pussy, which she can play, I truly believe, like a harp, ringing a whole symphony's worth of sensation out of it, playing chords or arpeggios upon the pussy-lips with her tongue, nibbling at and around the pussyhorn with her teeth, and able to provoke orgasm in the most unresponsive pussy merely with her lips.

On me she played all the variations of her repertoire: the kisses, the licks, the nibbles, the tongue-trembling, the pouts, the sucks, the puffs, the hums and lip-buzzes, the spittling, the nose-insertion and snorts, the pussy-hair tweaking and plucking and teasing, the expected and the surprising, the gentle and the cruel, the worshipping and the insolent: in short, all. My pussy-juice had not had time to crust or cake, and her tongue lapped it away easily, only to find that more was leaking forth from the secret cells of my pussy. She slobbered greedily, satirically, and strove womanfully to master the new flow.

One sign of a truly expert cunnilinctrix is that she is able not only to pleasure but also to amuse: I have laughed quite as often as I have come, with C's lips and tongue upon my cunt, and did so again now, as she pretended to choke on my pussy-flow, snorting it into her nostrils and blowing bubbles with it, which I could feel burst minutely against my thighs. Then she played another of her tricks: using my pussy as a telegraph, flickering her tongue against the lips in the dots (flicks of her tongue) and dashes (licks of her tongue) of Morse. A bittersweet rush of nostalgia filled my breast, tightening around my heart for a moment before breaking with a shiver that ran through my whole body.

She and I had learned Morse together by practising on each other's pussies, using our tongues or tweaking at our pussy-hair, and had been able, at the height of our expertise, to carry out long conversations in this fashion: once, when J and C had important news for me, C refused to impart it until she had cunnilingued me for two minutes – at the end of which, to J's astonishment, I was in full possession of all that they had to impart.

I was not at the height of my expertise in Morse now, and had to concentrate closely to decipher the Morse C was transmitting through my pussy-lips. She, as though realising I would be rusty, warmed up first with a simple SOS SOS SOS, then began to tell me that she was drowning in my pussy-juice. I laughed aloud and A – who had apparently not yet been initiated into this aspect of C's cunnilingual technique – looked at me in puzzlement. Then C's tongue, dotting and dashing (flicking and licking) against my pussy, suggested a trick to play on A and I assented by tightening my thighs for a moment. After clearing my throat (though my voice remained tremulous with the pleasure of C's pussy-licking), I told A I would demonstrate my powers of telepathy. She was to ask me questions that she knew I could have had no means of learning before my arrival, and I would search her mind for the answers. Still looking puzzled, she shrugged her own assent and asked how often she and C had made love in the previous twenfer, and how often C had achieved orgasm on the *second* occasion. There had been no time for C to inform me of these facts by letter, and she presumed I had not been told in the carriage (of which C's mother nodded confirmation). Even before she had finished speaking, however, C's tongue was transmitting the answers to my pussy, and I bowed my head a little and pretended to frown with concentration.

'You have made love . . .' I said, 'five times . . . or five-and-a-half, counting the snatched . . . fuck . . . I'm sorry, snatched *fumble* ... strolling on the promenade before lu– yes, before lunch. On the second occasion you were ... aiming to beat a record ... and Caliginia came –'

I paused, frowning harder (though C's tongue had already told me the number), and then looked up triumphantly.

'Thirteen times. Which is –' C's tongue was busy again '– once more than your pr– your previous record.'

A's eyebrows rose with surprise.

'I am right?' I said, gasping a little as C set to work again with a new message. A nodded.

'And,' I asked her, 'would you now like to hear details of the moles and birthmarks on your body? And other distinguishing characteristics?'

She nodded again, saying, 'I know Caliginia has not informed you of those facts, for I have seen all her letters to you before she sent them. Unless she concealed one from me.'

At this C, still with her head buried between my thighs, wriggled her bottom and forced out a disdainful fartlet in A's direction. A shiver of vicarious fear was added for a moment to the shivers of pleasure filling my body, for A's eyes had settled on the insolent rump with a flash of menace, before raising again to mine.

'No, I will accept that she has not revealed them to you. So proceed.'

I had already been given details by C's busily Morsing tongue, but as before bowed my head a little and pretended to frown with concentration.

'On the upper right slope of your left breast ... a black mole. And the nipple of that breast is larger and slightly ... darker in colour. Caliginia has often commented on it, despite punishments. Your right breast ... is perfect. Or at least, perfect by comparison with the rest of your body –'

A snorted, realising then (she told me later) that somehow I was receiving the information from insolent C.

142

'For it is not ... absolutely symmetrical. On your pussy, the left *labium majus* ... is fleshier than the right ... and tends to droop sadly in detumescence. You have a small sowl birthmark on your left inner thigh also – it is shaped like a ... like a piss-pot.'

At this, A's face brightened with anger for a moment, then she broke into hearty laughter as she slapped one heavy hand on her knee.

'I have it!' she cried. And on the arm of her chair she began to rap out a message in Morse with her fingers. I listened, frowning with genuine concentration now, for she was transmitting fast, then nodded. C told me later that she did not catch the first message A tapped out, nor the whole of the second, so that it was a complete surprise to her when A sprung up in her chair and pounced forwards on her, lifting her petticoats and skirt to expose her arse, which still glowed with heat from the spanking in the carriage.

'Now, my dear,' A said. 'You shall tell me why you concealed this facility in Morse from your military lover, and threw away so many weeks in which we could have practised it together. You shall transmit your answer, *en claire*, through your old friend Madam Mina, or I will demonstrate that her hand in the carriage was as light as a falling feather or snowflake compared to mine.'

I was starting to gasp with the onset of my first orgasm, which C was skilfully inciting even as she transmitted a further message.

'Is she transmitting?' A asked.

I nodded, feeling the muscles of my thighs beginning to tremble and tighten.

'And what is she saying?'

I swallowed, trying to hold down the tremors in my voice as I said, 'She is saying she had no idea ... that someone as co– as bovine as you could have learned something so ... complicated.'

A snarled with gratified anger and set to work spanking C's bare bottom. Her blows shuddered through C's body, making her mouth jerk against my pussy, and the sensation of this, plus the sound of A's meaty blows meeting C's firm buttock-flesh, was sufficient to tip me groaning into orgasm. In the afterseethe, however, as C opened her thighs wide to be fingered to orgasm herself by A's strong fingers, the curve of her beaten bottom glowing vace even from my angle, I found myself a little maudlin, thinking of J far away and the last orgasm we two had shared. When C, easily excitable as always, had shuddered out her orgasm and (despite owing me the long and extra-long pussy-lickings) been carried back by A to the chair for bottom-kissing (C was stretched on A's knees, bare bottom raised), I found myself growing more maudlin still. To be in the presence of lovers when one is oneself loverless always twists the strings of one's heart, even when one of the lovers is as dear to me as C. But C is right: I shall have had a letter from J within a week, at most, for she would not let another week pass without writing to me, I am sure. In the meantime, I must lick up the honey that is offered to me, for A, C and C's mother are happy for me to join their circle, and to substitute for C's mother when she feels her age and wants merely to watch and wank a little, with an occasional word of advice.

30 July. Tonight is the sixth twenfer of the week C spoke of, within which, she assured me, I should hear from J. But I have heard nothing, and believe that I shall hear nothing tomorrow. Has her letter been lost *en route*? But surely even Transmarynia is not so uncivilised that letters go astray there with any frequency. Certainly the Countess's correspondence, which was copious in the early nights, arrived without interruptions or losses, so far as we could tell. My heart sinks more the more I

think – *brood*, C would say, ~~but her lover is safe with her, or no more than a few streets away~~ – on the matter, and a sense of foreboding comes upon me. J is in some great peril, or has been so, and the outcome is unclear. No, I will strike through what I wrote of C. It is unworthy: for all her scatterbrain she recognises that anxiety without the possibility of action is worse than useless, and I am sure she would say the same were J in the house with us now and A far away on some military errand in Transmarynia, or Siberia, or wheresoever. But C is calling for me to come and join a new game. I must conceal my woe and savour the fruits of the moment. You will understand, my love, when you read this, I am sure.

Later. After the game to which C had invited me (and from which my pussy is still oozing, even now) we took a stroll on the seafront in the pearly light of pre-dawn, yawning a little, and before turning for home paid a few *bani** to look through one of the public telescopes bolted to the railings there. There was mist on the water and nothing seemed visible at first, till C, her eye fixed to the telescope, cried out that she could see a ship. I exchanged a glance with A, as C's old lover and new, both of us smiling at her girlish excitement, but her next words made us reconsider: the ship, she said, was being crewed by *naked* women. A's thick eyebrows quirked and she asked C whether she was joking. C shook her head, her eye still fixed to the telescope, and her own mouth quirked in almost identical fashion, as though in telepathic sympathy.

'The poor things,' she said. 'They must be getting very damp in that mist.'

I caught the accent of authentic pity in her voice and realised that she spoke the truth about what she saw, or at least about what she thought she saw. I asked for my turn at the telescope and C reluctantly surrendered the

145

device to me. I stooped to it and peered, seeing nothing for a moment, then realising that the long, low, vague smeared outline in the field was the ship of which C had spoken. But I could see no detail until I realised that perhaps C's eye had focused fractionally closer or further than my own. I touched the focusing screw and gasped at what I saw. A puffed her lips out behind me, evidently convinced by my reaction as she had not been by C's. The ship *was* crewed by naked women: I could see them stumbling to and fro on the deck like dolls of white porcelain, animated by some sorceress's spell, though the illusion of porcelain solidity was disturbed by the way in which their breasts and buttocks, made tiny with distance, bounced and joggled. They were evidently struggling to trim the sails, though why they should be so anxious in such a calm sea with the air so still I could not understand.

A's boot scraped on the pavement behind me, and I took the hint and relinquished the telescope to her. The sowl rim of the sun, rising in the east, was staining the water as though with blood as A stooped to the telescope and stared at the drama taking place far out over the water. Again there came over me that sense of foreboding I had already felt for J.

'The wind is picking up,' A announced, straightening from the telescope, 'and I do not think they will have the sails set in time. They may be driven ashore.'

She paused, looking up and down the promenade, lips pursed, her mind obviously racing as she considered what to do. Then she looked at me and my stomach somersaulted happily with the authority that had begun to glow in her eyes.

'Madam Mina, you must run along to the coast-guard's hut that way –' she jerked her strong chin '– while Caliginia and I will run for the hut this way. There is something very wrong here and I fear a tragedy may be in the making.'

I nodded, and turned to obey without a second thought, glancing out to sea as I did so. The mist was being whipped away in streamers by a wind that was picking up with preternatural speed, and the ship, the dark outline of its deck and spars dotted with the white hurrying dots of the naked women, was already creaming through the water, set on a course that would dash it against the shore somewhere very close at hand. I looked away from the sea as C's and A's feet began to pound the promenade behind me, put my head down and ran.

Cutting from *The Bucharest Daily*, 8 August
(Pasted In Mina Harker's Journal)

From a correspondent.
Constanţa.

This bustling port, whose inhabitants have long prided themselves as much on their nautical common-sensicality as on their Black Sea cuisine, has been buzzing over past nights with all the frenetic excitement of an overturned hive. Rumour is easier to get at than solid fact, but when grasped, like the mist which figures at the very beginning of the tale, leaves the hand no heavier than when it began. The solid facts are these: that a Transmarynian-registered vessel, the *Demeter*, was driven ashore with extraordinary violence on Monnight morning, snapping its keel with the force of its impact and shedding two of its three masts; that the crew, a mixture of Transmarynians and Scandinavians, was not seriously injured but in some cases suffered severe bruises or strains; that the cargo, a collection of sixteen glass tanks for a private aquarium planned to open in the New Year in Bucharest, was, in paradoxical concomitance, entirely undamaged and has already gone on its way by rail. Beyond this there is only conjecture and rumour, centring principally on the *manner* of the vessel's grounding and the *condition* of the crew. Earliest reports spoke of a wind of preternatural power that seized the vessel as it drifted in an offshore mist, but this has now been discounted and it is rumoured that the ship came ashore *under its own power*, employing some revolutionary marine engine working a species of subaqueous 'propellor', as the new-fangled nautical jargon has it. This rumour has been by no means discouraged by the speedy arrival of government officials or by the tarpaulins that now shroud the vessel's stern and the sturdy police who patrol the shore, keeping all enquirers (including your own correspondent) at a discreet distance.

As for the condition of the crew, they are rumoured to have come ashore entirely naked, nor was a stitch of their clothing discovered on the vessel when it was searched by coastguards. All but one of the crew-women, like the town officials who first questioned them, have now gone into *purdah*, and the best efforts of your correspondent have proved unavailing to obtain an interview, even at second hand, with even a single one of them. But if further rumours are to be believed, they would be in no fit state to answer questions even in their mother tongues, for they were said to be in a state of near complete psychological collapse after some very great and harrowing ordeal endured during the voyage from the Transmarynian port of Llanelli. Certainly it is true that at least five members of the crew are presently held in a sealed ward in the Constanţa Royal Memorial Hospital, while more are said to have been taken up the coast to a private asylum for treatment. A search is presently being undertaken for a final (and fully clothed) crew-woman who is said to have been seen leaping from the prow of the vessel even as it crashed against the shore. She should be easy to find, for she is said to have been a giantess who would overtop head-and-shoulders ninety-nine out of a hundred of the town's inhabitants, at the very least. Because she has not yet come to light, fears are being expressed that she is lying injured and undiscovered somewhere, perhaps having fled from the scene of the wreck in a state of understandable panic. Those metropolitan sophisticates who are inclined to treat these rumours of giant fugitives and revolutionary engines as symptoms of provincial hysteria are urged to reconsider, for metropolitan sophisticates of a very high order are undoubtedly numbered among the government officials rushed post-haste from the capital after first reports of the grounding were telegraphed there early on Monnight morning.

Log Of the *Demeter*, Llanelli To Constanţa (held in secret Romanian government archives).

Written 18 July, things so strange happening, that I shall keep accurate note henceforth till we land and briefly sketch the history that has led to this point. My misgivings began in Llanelli on 6 July, after we had finished loading the cargo of glass tanks (fifteen of them for an aquarium, so I was told, in Bucharest) and wood for some connected project. I had hoped to catch the tide and be at sea before dawn but our preparations were interrupted by the arrival of a further item of cargo: a sixteenth glass tank, which was, unlike the others, not of clear glass but translucent, and which was far heavier. The instructions I was given for the stowing of this tank were so curious that they would have made a strong impression on me had nothing further of note happened on the journey; looking back on them now, they seem the first intimation of the horror that awaited us.

I was told by the self-appointed supercargo who accompanied the new tank to ensure that the tank sat in a cleared space all of its own in the hold, so that it might be surrounded by, and regularly bathed in the light of, a series of electric lamps that were to be set up around it. This 'supercargo' (whose height and breadth of shoulder somehow set my nipples crawling) supervised the stowing and the setting up of the lamps, then conducted a test of the latter: they were powered by a kind of wheel-less bicycle on which, I was curtly informed, a crew-woman was to pedal every twenfer for at least fifteen minutes. I nodded, keeping my temper as best I could, and was about to order one of the cabin-girls atop the bicycle saddle when the 'supercargo' forestalled me, issuing an order herself to the cabin-girl I had already selected. Blushing, the girl (who is normally of a piquant insolence but seemed abashed in the presence of the 'supercargo') climbed atop the saddle and commenced to pedal. Normally the sight of her long legs working would have attracted all eyes (and, hearing of the electric lamps, which were the first some of them had seen, half the crew had gathered in the hold) but, as the mechanism warmed and the first flicker of light spilled from the lamps, all concupiscence was driven from our heads, so searing and brilliant was this aforementioned light, even at much less than half or even a third strength. I flung up a hand myself and I could hear the poor cabin-girl, who had been staring eagerly at the lamps in elaborate unconsciousness of the eyes that watched her pumping legs, almost fall off the saddle with the violence of the movement she made to shield her own eyes.

When I was able to lower my hand the 'supercargo', suppressing what I believed was a smile of sardonic amusement, began to apologise, adding (her hidden smile momentarily stronger) that she blamed herself (she said) for neglecting to mention that the light was so powerful (though I noted even through my tears of pain that she, alone of those who watched, seemed unaffected by it). She then produced a pair of dark goggles which she said were to be worn by the girl selected to power the lamps. And with that, and a final reminder that the tank was to be bathed in the lamplight at least fifteen minutes a twenfer, for preference at midnight, she left us, chucking the cabin-girl under the chin as she went with a murmur of sympathy. That the cabin-girl was weeping from inflamed eyes for at least an hour afterwards seems proof that the sympathy was as genuine as it was efficacious. Even then, moved by some instinct of coming danger, I should have dearly loved to dispatch the sixteenth box into the sea, but my loyalty to my employers held me back. Would that I had put into the opposite balance my loyalty to myself and my crew!

11 July. At midnight I ordered a cabin-girl below to operate the lamps, noticing her reluctance, for the victim of the lamp-testing had evidently been at work with her tales. I told her that she would earn an extra thruppence a week for her efforts, and the immediate smile on her face reassured me that she would work with a will. Later, however, when she had returned from the hold, I saw her on deck whispering to one of her fellows, evidently much downcast, but I could not find time to question her.

12 July. The cabin-girl was reluctant again to go below, though I reminded her of the extra thruppence.

15 July. The cabin-girl's reluctance tonight was such that I resolved to find time to question her, this twenfer or the next, on her experiences in the hold.

17 July. I questioned her and found that she complained of a strong dislike of the translucent tank, though she

151

had smelled, seen and heard nothing that could explain this. Had I not been present when the tank was brought aboard, I might have dismissed what she said; as it was, I ordered that she be accompanied by a companion when she next pedalled those eye-searing lamps into life. The ship's carpenter produced an additional pair of smoked goggles, which were rough and ready enough, but serviceable. We were to put into Gibraltar docks that night.

19 July. We will be in Gibraltar longer than I anticipated, for a telegram has been waiting at the shipping agent's the past week and was brought aboard by the agent herself. 'Repairs' are to be made to my ship and, though I could and can see no justification for them, what may I do but submit? Even in the midst of my anger and perplexity, however, I remembered the cursed tank and ordered the two girls below into the hold at the requisite hour. A fear shared might almost be a fear doubled from their reluctance to descend again. I ask myself whether I will have to send them down in threes next, and wonder whether we will reach Constanţa with the entire ship's crew below decks in goggles, watching a cabin-girl pedal for fifteen minutes around midnight.

Later. Would that I *had* sent them down in threes! At one bell the second mate remarked that she had not seen the girls since they went below and, though she joked that they would be sharing a hammock somewhere, tickling each other's pussies while their fellows toiled, I was immediately apprehensive and ordered a search. They were found in the hold a little distance from the translucent tank, lying unconscious on the deck, lips, chin and breasts wet and stinking with vomit, and have not recovered yet. I have ordered the ship's doctor to question them and report to me privately.

152

20 July. The doctor made her report this morning but left me little the wiser, for the girls are now suffering from a light fever and speak in a semi-delirium. They remember nothing of how they came to find themselves lying unconscious on the deck, or at least will say nothing of it, though the doctor noted that the lightest allusion to the tank plunged them into acute anxiety and fear. The cursed thing is occupying my thoughts almost to exclusion of the 'repairs', or 'refitting' as the agent, who is down here every twenfer, has begun to call them, seeing my scepticism written plain on my face. Tonight, Goddess willing, they will be complete and we can sail finally for Constanţa.

21 July. We are under way again and my heart is a little lighter. Both cabin-girls are on their feet and though I was resolved to order neither of them below again – the tank can stay sealed in clean darkness for the rest of the voyage, so far as I am concerned – to my astonishment they approached me at the usual hour and requested permission to leave the deck-scrubbing I had ordered them to, that they might go below and pedal! Perhaps we have left some evil influence beyond the straits, and have only clean sailing and a safe landfall before us.

Later. Again the second mate remarked on the belated-ness of the girls, though not quite half-an-hour had passed, but one of them almost immediately appeared on deck, licking her lips in a curious manner but otherwise apparently free of cares. When I asked her where her companion was, she told me she was still below, adding an extra ten-minutes' light to the tank. Perhaps my worry now will be to keep them away from the thing!

Later. My apprehensions are back redoubled, for the cabin-girl who stayed below has been discovered in

153

almost the same condition as before, lying on the deck of the hold, her face and clothing stained with vomit, but almost fully conscious this time. Her little companion, a blonde Swede like herself, was among the crowd that carried her up on deck, and I thought I heard them exchange a few low words. My Swedish is not what it was but I would swear that they were 'You drank too much' – from the girl who came up earlier – and 'Yes, but it was sweet' – from the girl who stayed below.

22 July. To my renewed astonishment, the girls were again more than willing to go below to bathe the tank in light, and to further astonishment they had persuaded a third to accompany them. My vision of the entire ship's crew below deck at midnight rises again before me. Is there some game they have invented, or have they discovered some means of broaching the tank and stealing its contents? Perhaps it contains some valuable foodstuff or drink? If so, I am responsible for any loss or damage. They are below now, and I have ordered the second mate to see what she can spy out from the door of the hold.

Later. The second mate has reported that she could see nothing but the flaring of the lamps, but she heard giggling and laughter and a deep voice that she swore belongs to none of the three girls. I have decided to have them all into my cabin for questioning this morning, after dawn if needs be.

23 July. I have questioned them and am almost convinced that their tale is true, particularly now that I have been given some kind of proof. They were ordered to my cabin after six bells, and I lined them up in front of my desk, letting them await my pleasure while I finished some pretextual marking-up of my charts. Then I lifted my head and fixed them sternly with my eye. Their lips quivered at first, and I knew they were finding it hard to suppress laughter, but I let the silence draw out, then slowly slid open a drawer of my desk and lifted out and on to the surface of my desk my trusty birch. This had the desired affect, for blood drained visibly from the face of one of them, and the other two went taut-lipped and blinked. They are a pretty trio, two blonde Swedes and a dark-haired Dutch girl, and I should prefer to see them smiling, but fear on a pretty face has its attractions too.

'Now, girls,' I said. 'There is a simple choice before you. A parting of the ways. One path leads downwards, into darkness and pleasure; the other upwards, into light and . . . pain.' I lifted the birch a little and let it fall to the surface of the desk as I said this. 'And it is for you to choose which path your tender feet tread. Your choice rests on your answer to a simple question: what are you doing below in the hold with that tank?'

Silence. I fixed my eyes on the girl who had paled, the Dutch girl, reckoning reasonably enough that she was the weakest vessel of the three. She moistened her lips, her eyes meeting mine for a moment, then dropping. I looked at the other two. Their eyes met mine longer, then dropped too. It was apparent they were not going to speak, and I felt my pussy stir and begin to moisten at the thought of the stern step I would now have to take. I raised my eyebrows.

'Well, girls?'

No reply.

'Very well, girls. Trousers and knickers down.'

They did not instantly move to obey and I picked up the birch and lashed it down on the surface of my desk, sending charts and instruments rolling or flying to left and right.

'Do you hear me? Trousers and knickers down.'

The girl who had paled now obeyed instantly, the other two following her as I rose to my feet, birch in hand, and strode out from behind my desk.

155

'Move back two paces,' I ordered, striding further, to stand behind them. One of them, her trousers already around her knees, stumbled as she obeyed, and I could see that all of them were now shaking with fear.

'When your knickers are down, bend forwards.'

Knickers slid down and they bent forwards, raising three pearly bottoms to my greedy gaze, each buttock as perfect as the full moon, or rather more perfect, for the moon is mottled and marked. Well, their buttocks would be more perfectly lunar shortly, if my final threat was unavailing. I deployed it now, swishing the birch slowly to and fro.

'The parting of the ways, girls,' I reminded them. 'It now lies directly before you. A path down to dark pleasure and a path up to bright pain. I shall now count ten. If I reach ten and have heard no word from you, I shall know which path you have chosen. One. Two. Three. Four. Five. Six. Seven. Eight. N–'

Something shone suddenly between the bare thighs of the girl who had paled, and I realised a moment before the splutter of piss falling around her feet that her bladder had loosed, constellating my carpet with shining droplets and filling my cabin with the spicy smell of piss. I reached out with the birch and gently flicked her bottom. She shivered at the contact.

'You, my dear,' I asked her. 'Are you ready to speak?'

She nodded, but it was not she who spoke, rather one of her companions, who twisted her head to look back at me, saying, 'Ve vill speak, captain.'

'Very well, speak,' I told this one, one of the Swedes, as I walked back to sit at my desk. As I went I caught another whisper between the Swede and her compatriot, the ones I had heard whispering on the 21st. I did not catch it, I thought. I sat back in my chair, putting my birch on my desk again in silent threat, letting them stand with their trousers and knickers still down (piss was still dripping from the Dutch girl's pussy), and nodded for them to begin. The nostrils of one of the Swedes, the girl who stayed longer in the hold on the 21st, flared for a moment, and then she said, 'Ve play a game in de hold, captain.'

'Hmmm?'

'It is a game of our homeland. A game of pussy-lices.'

That had been the whispered word, I now realised. *Löss* – Lice.†

'Yes?'

'Ve keep dem in boxes, captain. De lices, dat is, captain. To play de game, von drops de lices on to a pussy, den von must catch dem using only von's mout and teet. Also nose. It is most usual dat it be a race between two teams, each team being two girls, dat is, von girl whose pussy is liced and von girl who catches.'

I nodded slowly, saying, 'But with two teams that is four, in all. There are only three of you.'

'Yes, captain. But it is possible also to adapt de game, when de circumstances press. Ve have played it dus: a girl is liced, den anudder girl catches de lices, while de tird girl pedals. Vhen her feet have turned von hundred times, de score is taken of lices, den places are changed, and de game played again. It is most entertaining.'

I had been watching her closely, trying to determine whether she was telling the truth. Now I asked, 'And how does this explain why you were found those nights lying unconscious with vomit on your face? You, and then she?'

I nodded at the other Swede. The first Swede swallowed nervously and I thought suddenly that I had caught her out in a lie.†

'It explains in a vay, captain. You see . . . ve also have been drinking someting . . .'

Ah. I had guessed as much. But were they robbing the tank?

'What?' I asked.

She paused, then said it quietly: 'Beer.'

My lip curled with disgust. I had suspected once or twice before that the foul concoction had been smuggled aboard a ship of mine, or even 'brewed', as I believe the term is, after we were at sea, but this was the first time I had had true confirmation of it.

'Is there any on board now?'

She shook her head.

'No, captain. It has all gone overboard. Ve have learned our lesson, I assure you.'

'And the lice?'

'Yes. Ve have dem still, for ve mean to play de game still. But not,' she went on hastily, with a nervous glance at me, 'in de company's time.'†

'In the company's time will be acceptable,' I told her, 'if it keeps you working happily at the task of lighting the tank. But of course you can show me your lice?'

'At vonce, if you vish, captain.'

I relaxed, no longer vigilant for an accent or gesture of mendacity. She had now to produce them or be revealed as an almost certain liar; therefore she must be able to produce them.

'Yes,' I said. 'I wish. And you,' I added to the Dutch girl, 'can go and wash. Return when you have done so and mop my carpet. Now.'

The first Swede and the Dutch girl pulled up their knickers and trousers and scurried off, and I was left with the second Swede, who was still standing to attention on the other side of my desk with her trousers and knickers down. I looked at her, musing. Her eyes met mine, widening slightly.

'It is a pity, is it not?' I said to her.

She nodded, understanding me instantly.

'Yes, captain.'

'Three fine arses. One fine birch. And never the twain did meet.'

She swallowed, passing her tongue along her lips.

'Dere is –' she began, then had to pause to swallow

away the constriction in her throat. 'Dere is von arse still, captain.'

Her voice was husky with arousal. I was silent for a moment, as though considering her words, then nodded.

'You are right. Take off your shirt.'

I watched her hands tremble as they took hold of the hem of her shirt and peeled it upwards, revealing the bare skin of a smooth flat stomach, then the twin small mounds of her firm breasts, tipped with stiff sowl nipples that protruded at me like insolent little tongues. Her shirt came over her head and she dropped it to one side, standing before me now bare to the ankles. I allowed my eyes to roam the pale perfection of her body, noting its curves and planes, the firm breasts, the smooth flanks and thighs, the deep belly-button, and the wave of pale pussy-hair, almost indistinguishable from her skin, that slid downwards – pussywards – from her mound of Venus, to curl around the sowl lips of her pussy. I raised my eyes to her face.

'Now clasp your hands on the back of your head.'

She obeyed, and I watched her breasts tighten and lift, elevating her nipples a few further degrees, like miniature sextants fixing on crepuscular Venus. I reached out and picked up my birch, then pushed charts and instruments left and right, clearing a wide space down the centre of my desk.

'Now close your eyes.'

She obeyed, her smooth moist eyelids coming down over her glart eyes like curved marble screens, so finely sculpted that they were almost translucent.

'Now lean forwards over the desk.'

Eyes still closed, she obeyed, leaning forwards over the desk, crushing her breasts against it, beginning to rub her nipples against the smooth wood.

'Stop that,' I said.

She stopped and in the silence I could hear that her breath was coming faster, sliding in and out of her like a length of silk. I pushed my chair back slowly and with exaggerated care, wanting her to hear every creak and scrape, got to my feet and walked around the desk with the birch. I stood behind her, feasting my eyes on the bare buttocks that confronted me, sitting firm and rounded above the shadow-cleft between her thighs whence her pussy-lips peeked, pouting.

'We have time, I think, for only one swipe. Will it be enough?'

She had quivered as I began to speak, the outline of her buttocks blurring a little as the movement ran through them. Now her buttocks tightened as she replied.

'I vill try my best, captain.'

'As will I, my dear.'

I took a step to the left, turning so that my birching hand was on the other side of my body from her, ready to swing through the maximum arc, achieve maximum speed before it burst upon the flesh of her expectant bottom.

'Are you ready, my dear?'

She did not answer for a moment, and I knew she was swallowing away her pleasure-fright and her pain-greed. When she spoke, it was a whisper, but it seemed to twist a lock open in my own trousers, inside my own knickers, and my own pussy gushed juice.

'Yes.'

I drew in a deep breath, swung the birch back, loosening my opposite knee – the knee nearer her arse – so that it was ready to sink as I swung, allowing my whole weight to follow through; and then I swung. Swung with all the strength in me; swung with all the anger I had experienced at hearing they had smuggled beer on board; swung with all the delight of inflicting pain on a beautiful young girl who accepts it willingly – a beautiful young girl whose pussy is oozing for it; is aching for it; is asking for it. The helmswoman later told me that the crack of the birch against those firm

160

Swedish buttocks was faintly but clearly audible on deck, succeeded by a bark of agony that must have been clearly audible throughout the ship. I swung the birch free and gazed on my handiwork, panting and sweating as though I had been hauling an anchor in for a minute. That white arse was now streaked and slashed with sowl lines that were darkening towards vace even as I gazed, and her whole body was tense with the agony of the blow, but not just with the agony of the blow: with the anticipation of my next order.

'Begin,' I said, and she started to rub her nipples at the desktop, hands still clasped on the top of her head, bottom shrieking with pain above a pussy that begged for pleasure, but was able to receive it only at second hand, from those stiff nipples being rubbed at the desktop. Being ground at it. Her pussy-lips were clearly open now, and juice was beginning to trickle between them down the smooth plains of her thighs. I have bet before now on the progress of such juice: on whether a drop of it sliding down the left inner thigh will reach the knee before a drop sliding down the right inner thigh, while the poor cabin-girl lies ordered into absolute stillness, unable to ease the pain in her bottom with nipple- or clit-joy. With this one the flow was so copious that the bet would have been over in seconds, and would have been difficult to call. And she was already moaning in the last moments before orgasm, her buttocks tightening above the glistening shadow-cleft of her upper thighs. Now she was not rubbing her nipples against the desktop but pounding them against it, raising her upper body and letting it fall, absorbing the whole impact into her breasts, punishing them. Then she was coming, writhing on the desktop, the muscles of her buttocks and thighs spasming as an intense orgasm seized her. As she was panting out its afterseethe, my whole cabin filled with the musk of her sweat and pussy-juice.

There was a knock at the door.

'Enter,' I called.

The door swung open and the second Swede came back in, carrying two small tobacco boxes. The first Swede, sprawled across my desktop, thighs splayed, juice-drenched pussy on full gaping display, the inner planes of her legs glistening as far down as her calves, groaned and tried to push herself up.

'Stay still,' I said.

The second Swede's eyes were fixed on her compatriot's gaping pussy.

'Too moist?' I asked her.

She blinked and turned her glart eyes on mine, the pupils wide and black.

'Captain?'

'Too moist?' I repeated. 'For the lice?'

'Um, yes, captain. De pussy must be dry, or at least de hair must.'

'I do not think the hair is dry,' I said. 'So lick her clean, then dry her with your own hair. The hair on your head, that is.'

Another blink, and my pussy pulsed as her pupils widened even further.

'Yes, captain.'

She walked to my desk, putting the tobacco boxes one atop the other, then stepped back and kneeled behind her compatriot, put her face forwards and between the splayed thighs and began to lap at the pussy that awaited her there.

A shudder of surprise ran through the first Swede, then a moan of pleasure. After a few seconds she asked, 'Agneta?'

The sound of soft, careful lapping stopped and the second Swede pulled her face back for a moment.

'*Ja*,' she said, then put her face back between the thighs. The sound of soft, careful lapping began again.

Another knock sounded on the door behind her.

'Enter,' I called.

The door opened and I heard the Dutch girl come in, her feet pausing in surprise for a moment as she saw the cunnilinctus taking place before her, or perhaps as she saw the birch still hanging from my right hand, or perhaps both. I wondered for a moment whether to order her to join the two, the cunnilinctrix and cunnilingued, perhaps to kiss and lick the birched buttocks, but decided not. The pain still blazing there must have been a delicious contrast to the pleasure of the second Swede's tongue on the pussy directly below, and I did not want to soothe it while the pussy-licking lasted. Or indeed afterwards.

I turned my head reluctantly and looked at the Dutch girl. She was carrying a bucket and cloth for the piss-splattered carpet, as I had ordered. I nodded at her to begin her work, then turned back to watch the pussy-licking as she came forwards on her hands and knees to scrub the carpet.

By now my suspicions were almost gone, though I had not yet seen the contents of the tobacco boxes. Soon I had done so, and my suspicions were entirely gone. Now the second Swede withdrew, turned around and put her head in between her compatriot's thighs upside down, so that she could lick deeper, up over the whole of the pussy and the hair that capped it.

The Dutch girl and I watched (she snatching glances as she scrubbed), feeling our own pussies respond to the sight and sound of a slender and beautiful blonde servicing the oozing pussy of another slender and beautiful blonde. But when the first Swede had shuddered to the first of what might have been many orgasms, I ordered the pussy-licking to cease and the pussy to be dried. The second Swede withdrew her head, turned to face the first Swede's pussy again, then pushed her head between the fork of the splayed thighs and towelled at the first Swede's pussy vigorously with her head, drying it for the licing. This done, I ordered the first Swede up on my desk, legs splayed, pussy just overhanging the edge of the desk. She obeyed, stepping finally out of her knickers and trousers, slipped up on to the desk, swung herself around and opened her thighs wide to expose her pussy. It was gaping, oozing and the pussy-licking had plainly only made matters worse, but her hair was dry and would remain so now that her juice could not trickle into it. When she was positioned I ordered the tobacco boxes to be opened and saw that they were crawling with pussy-lice, having been replenished, so the two Swedes told me, from the brothels of Gibraltar.

'They are larger than I expected,' I said, looking down into one of the boxes as though it were an arena of tiny gladiatrices exercising in pale, jointed armour. The lice were clumsy on the smooth floor of the box, their crooked forelimbs dragging them jerkily forwards as they cast about for the hair and heat of a pussy.

'Yes, captain,' said the second Swede, her blonde hair rumpled and glistening with the pussy-drying. 'Dese are specially bred lices, from Sveden. Dere is a Svedish madam at Gibraltar and she keeps two or tree pussies of her girls alvays vell stocked vid de Svedish lices. Ve Svedish seagirls alvays visit her ven ve are in Gibraltar.'

'I see,' I said. 'But please, begin the game.'

She nodded.

'I eat von first, captain. Dis is – how do you say? – de tradition.'

She then plucked a hair from her compatriot's pussy, with an accompanying squeak, and dangled it into one of the boxes, nudging at the lice. A louse caught the hair almost immediately and clambered up it like a little gymnast. The Swede put her head back and lifted the hair, which was so pale and slender that the louse seemed to be floating in clear air, until it hung above her mouth. Then she lowered the hair and started to nibble

164

her way along it, driving the louse before her until, just before it reached her fingertips, she snapped her mouth forwards over it and I heard it pop between her pearly incisors.

'Vould you like von, captain?' she asked.

I nodded, and she dangled the hair in the box again.

'It is said, captain,' she went on, lifting a new louse free on the hair, 'dat de *connoiseuse* can tell merely by de flavour of de louse vot is de race of de girl's pussy on vhich it has been feeding.'

I put my head back, opening my mouth, and she lowered the hair for me. I did not nibble my way up the hair as she had done but popped the louse beneath my teeth almost at once, pressing my tongue forwards to catch the minute pop of its bursting, then working the empty skin loose from my teeth and swallowing it. It was faintly sweet but insubstantial, and I considered that one would have to eat dozens before one could say truly what crab-louse tasted of.

'Now ve play de game,' said the Swede. 'First, ve comb de pussy.'

She slipped one end of the plucked hair into her mouth, allowing it to dangle there from a corner of her lips so that both hands were free, then put the lids back on the tobacco boxes, drew a fine-tooth comb out of a trouser-pocket and set to work on her compatriot's pussy, combing the silken blonde hair in two curls on left and right. She tilted her head to one side, then the other, checking the symmetry of the pussy-combing, then dabbed at the pussy-hair with the comb here and there, put her head one side then t'other again, and nodded with satisfaction.

'Now,' she said, mumbling a little because of the hair still in her mouth, 've introduce de lices.'

She opened one of the boxes, plucked the hair from her mouth, and dangled it inside, picking up not one louse this time but many. Next she lifted it and let it hang in front of her, and I could hear her counting under her breath: '*En, två, tre, fyra, fem, sex* . . .' When she had counted off the final louse ('*tjugoen*' or 'twenty-one') and swung the hair up and over her compatriot's pussy, it was hung with lice like a pale strand of kelp hung with albino sea-crabs. She stroked the louse-laden hair over her compatriot's pussy-pelt, and the lice, reacting perhaps to the heat or the moisture of the skin, quickly clambered off the hair and vanished as though into the white surf of a small bay. The Swede encouraged two or three stragglers off the hair by holding it at one end while squeezing the closed tips of her thumb and index finger along it, then lifted it back over to the box for another load. She glanced up at me as she did so, glart eyes wide and candid.

'Ve introduce tirty-two lices, captain. Dat is de tradition. Den dey are hunted on de pussy, using only de mout and teet.'

She looked back at the box, where the hair was collecting lice, then dangled the hair in front of her face again, counting off the lice under her breath: '*Tjugotvå, tjugotre, tjugofyra* . . .' When she had counted the last ('*tjugonio*' or 'twenty-nine'), she swung the hair to her compatriot's pussy and allowed the lice to clamber into their new but, alas, temporary home. None had to be encouraged off the hair this time, and she lifted the hair back into the box.

'Tree more, captain, and ve are done,' she said.

'How many times have you played the game?' I asked.

Again her candid glart eyes fixed on my face.

'Almost all times ve have pedalled de lamps, captain,' she said quietly, then lifted the hair, flicked a supernumerary louse off, and swung the remaining three back to her compatriot's pussy. She watched them clamber free, then announced, 'Ve are ready. I vill eat or you, captain?'

'You,' I said.

She nodded.†

'It is de tradition, captain, dat de hands of de lices-huntress are tied behind her back.'

I looked around my room, then my gaze fell on the first Swede's trousers and knickers, lying discarded on the floor. The Dutch girl was still scrubbing at the carpet, though surely she had removed all possible traces of piss some time before.

'You,' I said to her. 'Enough of that: tie her hands with those knickers.'

'Yes, captain,' she said. She dropped her scrubbing-cloth into the bucket, then came forwards on her hands and knees to pick up the discarded knickers. The second Swede turned her back and put her hands on the swell of her buttocks, wrist over wrist. The Dutch girl twisted the knickers into a thick cord and tied the Swede's hands, tugging hard, then stepped back.

'Let me inspect them,' I said to the Swede. She turned her back towards me, lifting the knicker-tied bundle of her hands. I tested the knot, slipping a finger under the knickers then pulling upwards.

'Too tight,' I told the Dutch girl. 'You will cut off her circulation.'

I let go and the Swede turned so that her hands were presented to the Dutch girl again, who untied the knot with some difficulty, then retied it. I inspected it again, was satisfied and nodded for the louse-hunt to begin. The shadow of a smile that flickered for a moment over the Swede's face was perhaps my last chance to guess I was being tricked, but I barely noted it, assuming she was smiling at the prospect of the hunt, not at the final success of her lies. She walked back to the girl sitting with thighs splayed on my desk and kneeled carefully in front of her. I gestured the Dutch girl to my side, so that she too could have a good view of the hunt. The Swede was puffing air over her compatriot's pussy. Now she turned her head.

'If you vill time me please, captain. Vid your votch. My record is tirty-two lices in five minutes tventy-eight seconds.'

I pulled my watch out and waited for the second hand to reach twelve. The Dutch girl had reached my side and I could sense her trembling with excitement as she watched the blonde pussy and the blonde head poised in front of it.

'Go,' I said.

The kneeling Swede put her head forwards and began to probe through the pussy-pelt with her nose, swinging her head back every couple of seconds or so to squint along her nose at the patch of hair she had just pushed open. Suddenly she jerked her head forwards, pressing her mouth home, and I heard the tiny crack of a louse-killing, almost as though a true hunt were under way and the first Swede's pussy-pelt were a forest in which a rifle had cracked, bringing down a squirrel or jay. I glanced at my watch and even as I did so there was another tiny crack. Sixteen seconds, and two down. The Dutch girl was trembling hard now and on an impulse I put my hand around her waist and drew her close to me, slipping my watch back into its pocket so my hand was free to slide under her shirt and test her nipples for arousal. Another tiny crack sounded, and the Dutch girl jerked to it, for my fingers had closed on one of her nipples and squeezed. It was hard and swollen, rolling like an unripe berry under my fingers. Another louse-crack, then another, and I slid my hand across to her other breast, testing the nipple there for arousal. It rolled under my fingers too, unripe-berrylike. I began to squeeze it just out of time with the cracks of lice dying between the incisors of the Swedish pussy-maid, so that the Dutch girl tensed with anticipation each time a crack sounded, knowing that a second later her nipple would be squeezed hard.

But I was counting the cracks too, and as they reached *tjugofem*, *tjugosex*, *tjugosju*, I released the

168

nipple, slipped my hand free from under her shirt and tugged out my watch again. I raised my eyebrows as I saw that three-and-a-half minutes had elapsed: the Swede seemed to be well within reach of a new record. Had I been more experienced in louse-hunting I would have seen my error, though I should have noted that the intervals between cracks were gradually lengthening. The final lice are hardest to find, as one might expect, for some of them have already been overlooked because of their small size or a colour too well-suited to the pussy on which they find themselves. I might have kept my hand under the Dutch-girl's shirt squeezing those stiff nipples for three minutes to come, because that is how long it took before the final crack – *trettiotvå* – reached my ears from the blonde pussy and strong white teeth. Panting a little, the huntress withdrew from the pussy and looked towards me. I shook my head sadly.

'Six minutes eighteen seconds,' I said.

She shrugged.

'I tought it so, captain. It is alvays best –' and her eyes flicked to the Dutch girl, and widened for a moment '– to hunt dem on a dark pussy.'

The Dutch girl stiffened (looking back now, I realise that the widened eyes may have been a signal to her precisely so to do), and I smiled.

'Then you shall try again,' I said. 'And this time, on a dark pussy.'

24 July. I meant tonight to complete my description of the louse-game with a description of the hunt on the Dutch girl's dark pussy, but what I have learned tonight throws all thought of that from my head. They were lying to me yesternight: the two Swedes and, complicit with them, the Dutch girl. I have read through my narrative of the louse-hunt and obelised the points at which, I now realise, my suspicions should have flared stronger, or flared back to life:

†That whispered word *Löss*, meaning 'Lice'. That had been the point at which one told the other what the tale would be.

†That nervousness when I questioned them about their being discovered unconscious in the hold, lips covered with vomit. I noted that I immediately suspected a lie, but the immediate revelation of beer-drinking lulled my suspicion: this was naturally something to be nervous about, and I did not think they would be concealing something in the very act of apparently unconcealing else. Alas, she was more cunning than I could have suspected.

†That nonsense about the company's time when I asked whether she still had the lice. The readiness with which she answered might even then have put me on my guard, but I had been expecting some excuse for her inability to produce them, not an offer to produce them at once.

†That ready nod when I said she should be the one to hunt the lice. Not suspicious in itself, but part of a pattern of eager co-operation. I should have remembered her customary cabin-girl insolence, but the fascination of watching the louse-hunt had quite distracted me. The nod was, I now realise, but another strand of the web she was weaving around me.

Fool that I was. But fools that they were too, to imagine I had been so comprehensively misled by their tales of beer-drinking and louse-hunts. Oh, I am sure that both were true in so far as both things had been indulged in on the voyage, but neither was the true explanation of their interest in – rather say, their *obsession* with – that translucent glass tank and those lamps they pedalled alight to bathe it in brilliance every midnight. No, the true explanation for that was fouler by far even than beer, and I am still struggling to grasp its full enormity.

My lulled suspicions, snug in the web woven around and under them by those cunning blonde Swedes, remained sleeping till the evening of tonight, when, catching sight of one of the cabin-girls running an errand for the mate or cook, I began idly to muse on the louse-hunt, asking myself whether I should reinvigilate another in the morning. But then I remembered how diminished the first box had been after our two hunts of the night before. The lice would need to be rationed to last out the rest of our voyage. Then a thought struck me: if they had been playing the game regularly in the hold, how many lice had they started with, when we sailed from Llanelli? It must be hundreds, at least. But then they had restocked in Gibraltar, at the Swedish madam's brothel. I decided I would myself pay a visit there on the return voyage, to see the louse-farm pussies of which the girls spoke. How much did the whores earn, to compensate them for the discomfort of the lice feeding regularly on their blood? And was it true that a *connoiseuse* could learn to distinguish the race of the fed-upon from the taste of the feeder?

And there it might have ended, had not the second mate, a notorious whoremonger, happened to seek me out with a star-timing I had asked for. The Swedish madam was still in my thoughts and I questioned the mate anent where she (the madam) traded. The second mate denied that a Swedish madam had traded on Gibraltar, or that any Scandinavian madam, to the best of her knowledge, traded in a brothel on the shores of the far western Mediterranean (and neighbouring Atlantic) since a big-titted Dane had retired the previous year with a fortune earned at Rabat and Ceuta. The best of her knowledge was, I knew, far above the ordinary, and I frowned, wondering how the Swedish girls could have made such a mistake. As I did so, certain features of their behaviour before and during the louse-hunt occurred to me and, turning them idly in my mind, on a sudden I realised the truth and blew a whistle of anger and self-rebuke. The second mate, who had been watching the play of emotions on my face, asked of what I was thinking. I blinked and looked her full in the eye.

'I am thinking,' I said, 'of three white arses and a birch.'

Her lips twitched.

'A merry thought,' she said. 'Am I permitted to share it?'

'You are. You are she who will gather evidence for the prosecution, in fact.'

And I told her to conceal herself again in the hold shortly before the three lamplighters went below to bathe the tank, that she might watch and listen to what occurred. She nodded, saluted and went about her duties. As midnight approached and one of the cabin-girls came to me asking for permission to go below, I found myself able to read clearly the veil of deceit she wore, which slightly stiffened or exaggerated her movements and was wrapped tight around her throat, thickening her voice a little. I had thrown off the tangled web she had woven, practising to deceive, and now she wore it herself, unconsciously. I feigned distraction and gave the permission curtly, and she trotted off eagerly to collect her companions and the goggles. At thought of these goggles I pursed my lips a little. The second mate would not be wearing them, and as before she would not be able to make out all details of their mischief when the lamps were flaring.

In the event, the second mate made out no details at all, or at least remembered none when she was hauled half-conscious from the hold two hours after midnight. Her absence would have been noted far earlier on any ordinary watch, but that was no ordinary watch, for half-an-hour after midnight, shortly after (I later surmised) the three cabin-girls returned from the hold, I lost command of my ship.

172

There was no wrecking, no piracy, no mutiny, but I knew as soon as I heard the *sound* that something was very sadly amiss. The sound began as a low growling, seeming at first to come from all quarters at once, but loudest, it soon became apparent, in the direction of the stern. It rose and fell, as though some great beast couched at the stern had woken from sleep and was stretching its body, but it had settled to a steady roar as I, with two of my officers and handful of seawomen, ran along the deck towards the stern. But as we ran the deck swayed beneath our feet and as I nearly fell I heard others behind me actually do so. The ship had suddenly changed tack and begun to move faster. In a few moments, to my astonishment I felt a light breeze on the back of my head: *blowing from our direction of travel*. The deck was now throbbing faintly beneath my feet and I kneeled on it, laying a hand atop its boards. As I did so, the ship changed tack again, and I heard another seawoman tumble behind me. I turned and met the equally astonished gaze of the mate.

'What is going on, captain?' she asked.

Even as I answered, saying what I believed, I disbelieved it.

'We are now a powered vessel.'

'*Powered*, captain?'

We both swayed as the ship changed tack for yet a third time. We were, it was apparent, being steered back upon our former course. I nodded.

'Powered,' I said, and suddenly remembered the 'repairs' at Gibraltar. A minute later we were in the stern, dazedly confronting what a few blows of a now blunted axe had revealed behind the wood of one of the cabins there: a sheet of shining steel beyond which that giant beast roared, its voice so loud here that I had had to shout my orders at full pitch of my lungs. We soon had to retreat, hands clasped to our ringing ears.

There was now no room for doubt and I repeat the conclusion that then was ineluctably forced upon me:

we are a powered vessel, having been fitted with some unknown class of engine during the fictitious repairs at Gibraltar. The mate swore it was no steam engine and I can only surmise that it is one of the experimental IC (internal combustion) engines, burning a derivative of oil: members of the crew have reported an occasional gout or miasma of foul-smelling smoke from the stern, when the engine is running and the wind is right. It is apparent now that the engine runs whenever the ship does not take the course some unknown helmswoman has determined on, but I have been able to discover no logic to this course, unless it is that merely of keeping the ship well from shore and well from its landfall at Constanţa. I scarcely dare voice the thought that we are being kept at sea by the bursts of power almost as a mouse is kept from safety by the swipes and flicks of a cat's paws. Are we mice in some feline game? Then who is the cat, and what is the game?

I ordered further work to strip the wood from the shining steel bulkhead (the workers are wearing ear-plugs), but perhaps the second mate will be able to give some clue, when she awakes from the drugs the doctor has given her. Her absence was, as I have said, discovered belatedly, and my first thought was that she had been thrown off her feet when the engine began to work, and now lay unconscious in her cabin. She did lie unconscious, but not in her cabin: in the hold. I was brought the news ten minutes after I ordered the search for her to begin, and hurried to the hold to find her being tended by the ship's doctor. Smelling salts had been administered and she was half-conscious, moaning through vomit-streaked lips and complaining of pain in her backside.

I sensed some unspeakable tragedy even then and ordered the five or six crew-members who were clustered around the doctor and her patient back about their business. They departed, leaving me with the doctor and second mate in a hold that echoed with the growl of the engine. The doctor had turned the second mate on to her side and was running a finger over her back and buttocks. Suddenly the second mate cried out and the doctor looked up at me with concern, lifting a hand whose fingertips I could see were glistened with moisture.

'What is wrong?' I asked.

'She seems to be *leaking*, captain.'

'Blood?' I asked.

'No.'

She raised her fingers to her nose and sniffed, grimacing.

'No, captain. I cannot identify it. But it seems to be leaking from her backside.'

'Then get her trousers down. But gently.'

'Aye, captain. But they've been down recently: look.'

I looked and saw that the second mate's belt had been loosened. As the doctor took hold of the waistband and began to ease the trousers down, the growl of the engine suddenly ceased. The doctor's eyes raised to mine again.

'Ignore it,' I said. 'This is more important.'

She nodded, turned back to the trousers and pulled them down carefully. The second mate cried out several times as she did so, as though the mere movement of cloth against her buttocks were causing her pain. The doctor pulled her body further over and turned her knicker-clad buttocks towards me, and my eyes widened as I saw the dark stain that soaked through the centre of them. Then I sniffed.

'It's stronger,' I said. 'That smell.'

The doctor nodded.

'Yes, captain.'

She was carefully slipping the second mate's knickers down now, to further groans of pain from her patient. I waited, a pulse beating anxiously in my throat. What would be revealed? But the pearly buttocks that were

175

exposed inch by inch gleamed up at me unmarked. Where was the wound? The doctor suddenly gasped with horror.

'Wh–?' I started to ask, then gasped with horror myself. I had seen it too. The wound was in her arsehole. The wound *was* her arsehole. It gaped up at us, glistening with some thick fluid, its rim sowled and inflamed. The doctor, hardened though she was (she served some years on the notorious Faerose fishing fleet), gagged with nausea.

'What is wrong?' I asked. 'What has happened?'

The doctor looked up at me, face slack with disgust and horror.

'She has been . . . penetrated, captain. By – by some blunt instrument.'

My own stomach rolled now too.

'Penetrated?'

'Yes, captain. Penetrated up – up the arse.'

I saw the doctor's eyes clench shut, as though she was driving back stinging warm tears. What fiend could have done such a thing? The doctor knuckled brutally at her eyes, then slipped her bag open and reached inside. She lifted something clear, holding it up for me to see. A blunt glass rod. She slipped it into her mouth, sucking, then withdrew it, bending back over the wounded arse. She looked over her shoulder at me.

'If you could help, captain. Hold her buttocks apart for me. But gently now.'

I kneeled beside the second mate too, carefully following the doctor's instructions, folding the cool heavy hemispheres of the second mate's buttocks apart so that her arsehole lay fully exposed, glistening up at us like a sowl starfish oozing mucus.

'Why did you suck it?' I asked.

She glanced at me, her eyes moist.

'The rod?'

I nodded.

176

'To lubricate it,' she said. 'I will have to introduce it. To probe for damage. To see how deep this stuff extends.'

'Very well.'

My stomach was rolling with genuine nausea now at the thought of the rod sinking into the second mate's arse. Repenetrating her. The doctor lifted the rod forwards and slowly lowered it towards the glistening starfish of the second mate's arsehole. I saw the end quiver as the doctor's hand shook, then she mastered her nerves and slipped the rod slowly home. It sank between the buttock-cheeks and the second mate moaned uneasily, as though her abused anal nerves were so tender that even a thin glass rod pained them. Then the doctor slipped it free and raised it. The whole inserted length was glistening with the thick fluid, but there seemed, very fortunately, to be no blood.

'What is it?' I asked. The doctor put the rod under her nose, drawing in a cautious breath, then lifted the rod to me. I put my nose over it and drew in my own cautious breath.

'It's almost . . . herbal,' I said. 'But briny too. Like some kind of mayonnaise. Is it a disease, some kind of dysentery? Is this diarrhoea?'

The doctor lifted the rod away from me and sniffed at it again herself. She shook her head.

'No. My guess is that it has been introduced into her arse, not been generated there or in her gut. Whoever penetrated her squirted this in at the same time. A lot of it too. Just look. Your eyes can tell you that.'

I looked and saw again that she was right: the second mate's arsehole was positively running with the stuff.

'But what to do?' I asked.

'Get her into bed, on the double, while I have a look at this – this stuff under the microscope.'

As she spoke she was reaching inside her bag again, taking out a slide, smearing the rod over it, then handing the rod to me to hold while she slipped a cover-glass on. I took the rod by the clean end, keeping my fingers as far as possible from the end that had been inserted in the second mate's arse. She then slipped the readied slide into a holding box, put the box into her bag, took out a cloth, took the rod back from me, wrapped the rod in the cloth and stowed that away too.

'I'll pull her knickers and trousers back up, captain,' she said. 'We don't want news of this getting out.'

I nodded, pushing myself off my knees then standing up.

'I'll send some reliable crew-women,' I said. 'But is there anything you can give her for the pain?'

'I'll mix something now, captain.'

She reached inside her bag just as I heard footsteps descending hurriedly into the hold and a voice crying, 'Captain! Captain!'

I left the doctor mixing the pain-killing draught and proceeded to the new discovery that awaited me: the wood covering the steel bulkhead in the stern had been half-stripped now, and a secret *door* had been exposed. When I arrived, the ship's carpenter was working on the lock, but plainly having little success: the floor at her feet was littered with discarded tools.

'It's steel,' she told me, 'but far tougher than anything I've ever come across before.'

I stared at the door, wondering what – or *who* – was on the far side.

'Leave it,' I told the carpenter. 'And you –' to an ordinary seawoman '– I want those cabin-girls in my cabin on the double. The youngest two Swedes and that Dutch bint.'

'Aye, aye, captain,' the seawoman replied.

I strode to my cabin myself. To fill the few minutes before the girls were ushered in I began to fill in my journal for tonight, but I had far more time than I anticipated, for they have not yet been found and I do

178

not believe they will be. Now I know who is on the other side of the door, or at least, I know three of those on the other side of the door. I wonder how their ears are feeling now, for the engine has been running these past fifteen minutes, setting us a new course that seems to confirm the conjecture I have recorded above. Depression and fear overcome me now, as I strain to pene– ah, my stomach rolls with nausea again at the mere mention of the word – to penetrate the web of mystery now woven thicker than ever around me, my ship, and my crew.

Later. The doctor has made her report on the fluid found leaking from the second mate's arse and had I ever known her to show symptoms, however slight, of mental imbalance, I should be ready now to dismiss her words as a sign of incipient insanity. Perhaps that is what they are: that alternative seems less fantastic by far than what she told me, namely, that the fluid is *alive*, containing (at her estimate) millions of '*caudate animalcules*' (as, in her shock, she expressed it, seeking, no doubt, to distance herself from her shock by recourse to Latinity). The animalcules were larger than bacteria and corresponded to no protozoic class the doctor had ever come across before. And there we have it: a living fluid injected into the second mate's arse. Even as I write the words, a sense of unreality overwhelms me and I wonder whether I, too, am going mad.

25 July. Horror now stalks the ship. I left a guard of two ordinary seawomen on the steel door in the stern and was wakened in the early afternoon with the news that that they had been discovered lying unconscious on the floor, faces stained with vomit. This time their trousers and knickers were left down and their stripped arses, with deliberate malice, turned upwards, so that the truth was immediately obvious: they too, like the second

179

mate, had been anally penetrated, their tight arses flooded with that unspeakable thick fluid. It is now impossible to keep the news from the crew and in the absence of solid facts the wildest rumours are sweeping the ship. The second mate has recovered consciousness but she could give no coherent account of how she came to be found penetrated and leaking in the hold, and the three cabin-girls remain missing. Either they are over-board or they are behind the steel door in the stern.

A fantastic vision floats before my mind's eye and I see the door open and the three girls creep out upon the neglectfully sleeping guards, armed with a giant syringe charged with that unspeakable fluid. One of the guards is held down and her arse is stripped bare before the nozzle of the syringe is inserted into her arsehole and the plunger depressed, driving the fluid home with a thick squelch. Perhaps the guard's arsehole was licked a little beforehand, to ease the passage of the syringe's nozzle. Then the second guard is treated in the same way, her screams stifled by a cabin-girl's cool palm. Is this the way it was? Are the three girls victims of some sea-psychosis? Did the pussy-lice carry some mind-warping disease or have they cudgelled their brains to madness with 'beer'? I do not know, but I have ordered a heavier watch on the door tonight, with strict orders that sleep is to be avoided at all costs and with a primitive but effective alarm rigged over the door by the ship's carpenter. If the door opens this afternoon, the guards will know of it and at least one, I hope, will escape with news of what it is that emerges from the door to carry out these unspeakable anal violations. I have just been brought the news that one of yester-night's guards is awake and I will go and question her with the ship's doctor. Perhaps she, unlike the second mate, retains some memory of the beginnings of her ordeal.

Later. No use: suffering and shock seem to have wiped her mind clean, as though a moistened sponge has passed over a scribbled slate. Our hopes now rest on the second guard and on the guards placed tonight.

26 July. The guards were useless: two of them are now missing, presumed vanished beyond the steel door, and the other two were discovered unconscious and naked, arses raised to the overhead and leaking that unspeakable fluid on the deck before the door itself. The doctor, who is beginning to show signs of the strain, took samples again and later confirmed the presence of the 'caudate animalcules', though they were apparently dead: the fluid was not so fresh as it had been in the second mate's arse. She tells me she believes the fluid must be generated afresh on each occasion of its squirting into an arse, or else drawn fresh from whatever vessel it is fermented in.

Later. One of the guards first anally penetrated has disappeared from her bed. I ordered a shipwide search and she has not been found. Either these disappeared women are going overboard or they are finding their way behind that sinister steel door in the stern. The first alternative seems almost the preferable, when I consider what horrors might be being enacted in the stern under cover of that throbbing engine. Are cries of pain sounding unheard, as some monstrous pervert, and the foolish young cabin-girls she has coerced into her perversion, conduct anal tortures on her captives, pumping living arses full of that unspeakable living fluid? My gorge rises more than ever now I think on it, for the doctor tells me that she believes it has also been squirted down the throats of some of the victims, thus explaining why they have been discovered with vomit on their lips. I have ordered extra vigilance by all remaining members of the crew, and sealed the stern off from the rest of the ship as best I can, though I fear that my precautions may avail little against the cunning and cleverness of whoever is behind these strange and sickening events. Nevertheless, I pray that I may be able to stem the depredations on my crew.

27 July. My precautions seem to be working: no crew-member was lost in the last twenfer.

29 July. Three of the disappeared women have returned, among them one of the Swedish cabin-girls, but I might almost have wished that they had not done so, so pitiful is their condition and so demoralising an effect is it having on the rest of the crew. They were found naked on the deck near the entrance to the hold, bound and gagged, and when their gags were released they could babble only incoherently of an imprisonment with some tall, dark stranger. One – the Swede – insists that the stranger's skin is glart, like that of a plant, but this I dismiss as a symptom of her madness.

Their buttocks were heavily bruised, as though they had been subjected to cruel whipping or caning over several nights, and the doctor, who examined them privately, has told them that their arseholes have plainly been penetrated repeatedly. Worse than this, however (and my pen, as can be seen, trembles in my hand as I prepare to write the words), their pussies show signs of molestation too, as though some fiend, in defiance of all that is holy and pure, has sought to gain entrance to them with some blunt instrument. The doctor tells me that she found, caked into the pussy-hair of the Swede and one of the other girls, traces of the unspeakable fluid, which hardens almost like a glue when allowed to dry. When she examined the pussy-hair of the third girl, one of the guards who disappeared on that second night, she found that a patch of hair had been plucked, as though the girl had had traces of the fluid dried in her pussy-hair too and picked it out with her fingers to – and now the pen almost drops from my fingers with nausea and disgust – to eat it: the doctor found a pussy-hair caught in her teeth.

Later. One of the returned women has disappeared again, taking with her two crew-members, whom I discover to have been special confidantes of hers. I have ordered the two remaining women placed under close guard, for I am now confident that their return is some tactical feint by the fiend hiding behind the steel door in the stern: she is sending her agents among my crew to work her bidding and bring her fresh victims. I wonder that her agents obey, with the marks of her cruelty and perversion so fresh on their arses – and their orifices.

30 July. I rise from my knees, where I have been praying for the past hour and more, to record that I too have seen the fiend. I was woken last day by screams for help from the direction of one of the cabins where one of the returnees was under guard. After throwing on my daygown, I hastened to the spot with two of my officers, to discover the cabin in a state of hellish confusion: the returned girl was disappeared again, and two of the guards were sobbing hysterically on the floor, fragments of their clothing lying strewn on the floor and vomit shining on their lips. However, one of them, a tough Finn whom I had never thought to see in such condition, recovered sufficiently in a few minutes to describe in a low and broken voice a little of what had happened: they had been attacked by a huge woman whom she had never seen before and who entered, it appeared, through a secret door in one of the cabin's bulkheads. I ordered the bulkhead searched while the Finn continued her tale, describing how the returned girl joined the giant newcomer in overpowering the guards before the Finn was forced to swallow the nozzle of a giant rubbery syringe concealed by the unknown woman in her trousers. The Finn wiped repeatedly at her lips, shuddering with horror, as she described how the syringe squirted a warm and sticky fluid into her mouth, which she was then forced to swallow. Then, after she had been released to vomit in disgust, her companion was subjected to the same. But her tale was interrupted by the uncovering of the secret door, which swung open in the bulkhead on the triggering of some catch. There was a sudden loud commotion from beyond it, and one of my officers, who had put her head inside, cried out that she could see an escaping figure. I ran to the door myself, ordering my officer out of the way, and stepped through into the hidden passage, down which fleeing footsteps were echoing. There was no time for hesitation: pursuit in the hope of capture was my only thought and, crying an order for my companions to follow me, I plunged into the hidden world now revealed, my brain hammering with the knowledge that such hidden doors and passages might exist all over the ship.

In a few strides I rounded a corner and saw at the end of the short passage ahead of me a tall and broad-shouldered figure working at the lock of another door. Those broad shoulders were shaking with what I thought for an instant was fear and confusion but, as I cried out and ran towards the figure, I heard laughter. Before I was within three yards, however, the door swung open and the figure slipped through it, still shaking with laughter. The door then slammed shut and I arrived in time only to beat my hands futilely upon it. The ship's carpenter is now working to open it, but there is little hope of success. I have the crew searching the ship for other hidden doors and shudder at the thought of what there is still to discover about this hell-ship. The woman was obviously listening to what was taking place in the cabin whose occupants she had just violated so foully, doubtless having sent her minion on ahead of her, back to the stern.

31 July. Two more disappearances. The search for hidden doors has proved fruitless, as I suspected it might. We knew almost exactly where to search in that cabin yesternight and even then, I believe, triggered the mechanism of the door more by luck than design.

1 August. Three more disappearances, and four more women discovered lying naked and anally penetrated upon the deck in one or another part of the ship. The disappearances seem to take place almost exclusively among the ranks of those who have been anally penetrated (e.g. the cabin-girls) or have been in discussion with those who have been anally penetrated (e.g. friends of the cabin-girls). My stomach rolls at my voicing the thought, but it is almost as though they have acquired a *taste* for anal penetration, and go seeking her who imposed it upon them: that tall and broad-shouldered, syringe-wielding fiend who may even now be creeping down one of those hidden passages – whose fingers may even now be pressing some mechanism that triggers a secret door, perhaps granting her and her minions access to my own cabin. My heart beats faster at the thought of it and my arsehole puckers with fright.

Later. Two of the disappeared women have reappeared. My intuition combines with my reason to demand that they be isolated entirely from the rest of the crew, lest their tales infect new victims with the desire to seek out this anally violating fiend. Alas, alas, this is impossible: to be isolated they must be placed under guard, but to be guarded they cannot be in isolation. The doctor has examined them and tells me that their buttocks too show clear signs of having been beaten vigorously in the last few twenfers, their pussies clear signs of molestation

185

and their arseholes clear signs of repeated penetration and fluid-squirting, which has caused an anal rash and inflammation in one of them. I have questioned them myself and am convinced from their tone that they are concealing the truth from me, which will be revealed only to companions whom they seek to lure away.

2 August. My suspicions have been confirmed. One of the disappeared women is redisappeared and has taken with her two women with whom she was seen last night in close conversation. There is a contagion of madness raging through the ship and my calculations reveal that more than half the crew has now either disappeared or been discovered lying on the deck anally penetrated. The engine continues to work sporadically, keeping us far from land. The chief mate has asked me to allow a party to attempt to flee the ship by boat and make for a port where naval help might be sought, but I have refused. If the attempt were spotted, as I have little doubt it would be, the fiend controlling the ship might easily run the boat down. Our only recourse now is prayer.

Later. Four more disappearances.

3 August. I little thought the word should ever be penned in the log of a ship overseen by a captain such as I have ever striven to be, but there is nothing else for it. There has been a mutiny and I am a prisoner in my cabin, waiting, so the mutineers tell me, to be initiated into the hellish pleasures of what they tell me is called 'bugray' (or 'bugry'). Time is too short to tell all, for I mean to conceal this log beneath a floorboard, but I believe that I will hear the fiend coming and have time to perform the task of concealment. At last I will see and speak to the bitch face to face, and I hope I will not quail when I too, like so many of my poor crew, am stripped and penetrated orally and anally and perhaps (my pen again trembles in my fingers) vaginally by the fluid-squirting syringe she bears. I believe I might face the prospect with less trepidation if I might have some explanation of *why* all this has taken place – of *what* she has sought to gain by it. *Why* has she so assiduously undermined my crew, initiating them first in careful ones and twos, then in greedy threes and fours into her anal perversions, which are apparently so pleasurable that she has been able to turn the whole crew against me? *What* has she hop–

Letter, from Sister Agatha, Hospital of SS Josephina and Mary, London, to Miss Willhelmina Harker

12 August.
Dear Madam.
   I write by desire of Miss Joanna Harker, who is herself not strong enough to write, though progressing well, thanks to God and Saints Josephina and Mary. She has been under our care for nearly six weeks, having been brought to us in the throes of one of the worst bouts of brain-fever I have ever seen. The crisis is long past now, however, and you need have no fears for her continued welfare, which continues to be our most careful concern. She asks that you convey her regards to your shared mistress and tell her that all her work here is done, though she has exhausted all supplies of cash and wishes that some be despatched *poste restante* before the end of the month, if that be possible. In a few weeks I believe that she will be sufficiently recovered to make her way home to you.

Yours, with sympathy and all blessings,
Sister Agatha.
P.S. My patient being asleep, I open this to let you know something more. She has told me all about you,

and mention of your name and 'sweet face' (as she expressed it) seemed to soothe her even in the worst of her delirium. According to our doctor here, she has suffered some fearful shock that temporarily unbalanced her mind, and she has raved of things I will not commit to paper, though I have no doubt that she will tell you of them herself, when she has recovered and is able to write to you herself. She repeats that she has some fearful news for you, and begs that you brace yourself for it. To myself she will say nothing of what it is she has to tell you, hinting only that it has some connection with her 'employer' – and my heart sinks within me, I must confess, to see how her lips are reluctant to utter even these innocent syllables and the fear that fills her eyes. But all now is safe, and if our prayers can extend protection over her, and happiness to you both, all shall remain safe. My blessings with you again.

Letter from Mina Harker to Caliginia Vestenra

Paris, 24 August.
My dearest Caliginia,
   The excitement of the journey was quite submerged in my anxiety for Joanna, and I could not describe a fraction of what has whirled before my eyes as I have travelled north to be at my darling's side. On the return journey, perhaps, I might make better notes for you, but I fear that I may be even more distracted then, for in place of flying *to* my darling's side I shall be *at* her side, and you will forgive me, I am sure, if I have eyes more for her than for the passing scene. Ah, I am rambling, but I almost fear to set down what I discovered when I reached the dear hospital where the twice-dear sisters have been caring for my thrice-dear Joanna. How drawn and pale she looked, Cali! Sister Agatha had plainly not exaggerated the

slightest in what she said of the shock that my darling has undergone, and I have hesitated to question her (J) on what has happened, for fear of recalling scenes and experiences to her mind that were better left for the while buried. That they recur to her without my prompting is apparent from the way she talks in her sleep, and I have striven – little though I needed encouragement! – to make our lovemaking as strenuous as possible, that she might find peace in a deeper sleep after each bout. Indeed, I am myself beginning to suffer a little from our lovemaking, for Joanna has become strangely crueller in her attentions, and might almost at times be a match for your own dear A in the ingenuity of the erotic pains she inflicts upon me. But there is one curious thing: she now almost entirely neglects my breasts, when in the past she might, by some, have been thought almost *fixated* on them. I am proud of my breasts (as who knows better than you?) and was beginning to feel a little hurt when she neglected to shower them with her customary kisses and caresses on our first climbing into bed together, after so long apart. My darling, as sensitive to the moods of my heart as she is to the moistness of my pussy, guessed what was in my mind and told me that she meant no offence by neglecting my 'splends' (her nickname for them – short for 'splendiferous globes', have I told you?) and that she would more than do them justice in the near future. Just now, for reasons she was as yet unable to disclose, their very size and solidity induced a curiously strong attraction in her that she was afraid to swell by lingual or manual contact, lest she treat my breasts too roughly. I laughed at this, of course, and told her that she was welcome to treat my breasts as she liked, but her evident sincerity soon convinced me that she had good reasons for her refusal, and my breasts have been practically 'off-limits' ever since.

Not that I am complaining, for she has devoted herself, as though in compensation, more passionately than ever to my pussy and bottom, and I have already lost count of the number of orgasms I have enjoyed from her tongue, which seems to have grown even more skilful in the time we have been apart. I have teased her that she has been practising too freely on the Transmarynian girls, and she has denied it with laughter on her lips but no laughter, as yet, in her eyes or heart. I hope to awake it there before long, and know that you will be hoping the same.

Your ever-loving,
Mina Harker.

Letter from Caliginia Vestenra to Mina Harker

Constanţa, 30 August.
My dearest Mina,
Oceans of love and millions of kisses to you, my darling. We have swum in the former and exchanged the latter in the past, and I hope – I *know* – we will swim in and exchange them again in the future. Tonight I am strangely tired and have spent some time speculating idly on these things (my bottom tingles at the confession of *idleness*, which Art would so gleefully have seized upon, but she is away from me, alas, and a tingle is all my bottom will experience, unless I minister to it myself). So, yes, I have been speculating on these things. Have you and I spilled an ocean of love between us? No, but it must be several cupfuls. I imagine them ranged before me, their contents still warm from our aching pussies. But no, not cups, elegant crystal glasses, in a semi-circle, on that small carved table of my mother's (you know, the one in her sitting-room), with moonlight slanting through them. I raise one to my lips and smell it,

drawing in the scent slowly before releasing it with a nipple-hardening shudder. Then I put it back on the table untasted and raise another to my nostrils. I smell it, hold it away from me, twist it slightly to see the play of moonlight through its depths, smell it again, my tongue swollen and thirsty in my mouth, before placing it back on the table and raising another to my nostrils. How many of these glasses do you think we could have filled in our time together, darling Mina? Four or five? Six or seven? Eight? Maybe nine, ten, eleven? When Artemisia returns I am going to introduce the conceit to her and see whether we can fill one from our conjoint pussies.

You may be wondering why my mind is running on these lines – you may have wondered why I am strangely tired tonight. The one and the other – both, in short – are explained in the same way: by the strangest of dreams I had yesterday, when I retired a little melancholy, after seeing Art off in the evening and knowing I shall not see her again for several nights. I confess I cried a little before I slept, but you taught me the remedy for that, and, after I had moistened my pussy with my tears (the brine stung a little on my pussy-lips, for Art had said goodbye to me with even more than her usual vigour) and frotted myself to orgasm twice, I drifted off happily enough. How long I slept before I woke – no, before I *dreamed* I woke, though it seemed then (and seems still) as though I were as wide awake as I am now, sitting at my writing table – I do not know, but from the angle of sunlight that was slanting into my room – that I *dreamed* was slanting into my room – it must have been approaching midday. A little shudder of disgust ran through me, for I know how I hate sunlight even more particularly than most, and I realised that my sun-shutters must have loosened. I was wrong: they had – I dreamed they had – swung open entirely, and my room was exposed to the full light of day. I was struggling to sit up, thinking to climb out of bed and close them, when I seemed to hear a deep voice, commanding me to be still, and a tall shape was outlined against the sunlight, stepping forwards through the windows into my room. I could not see the face, but the broad shoulders and the deep voice convinced me for the space of a pussy-throb that Art had returned early, and had come to console me for her brief absence.

I opened my arms with a smile, calling her unto me, but my joy was suddenly quenched as the figure stepped closer and I smelled a strong feral *sweat*, as though of some great beast, which enveloped me in a cloud, making me gag with nausea mixed, though I know not why, with a curiously pleasurable anticipation, and driving all thought of Art's presence from me. This was not she – and how could it have been, I might have thought had sleep not still befuddled my brain, when the figure had entered as it did, through the windows of my room in full day?

In the next instant, the figure was at my side and the wrist of one of the arms I had raised in welcome and not yet let fall was seized in a burning grip. If I had known before this was not Artemisia, I knew it doubly now: that hand was stronger even than hers, and so hot that I might have cried out with pain from that alone and not, as in fact I did, from the strength of the grip. Then another hand, burning like the first, closed over my mouth and I was plucked bodily from the bed, helpless as a doll in a grip that I verily believe was superhuman. This is part of what convinces me I dreamed: no human creature ever possessed such strength in life, as opposed to fable.

Then I was stripped, dear Mina, stripped utterly naked, and, though I have little doubt that you smile to read of it, thinking this but wish-fulfilment, in the absence of my dear Artemisia, the stripping fulfilled no wish I have ever had, greedy as you know I am for a brutal and domineering lover. Those hands burned as they touched my flesh, and my garments positively *tore* as they were dragged from me. Could I have wished that, wearing a favourite daygown as I was? (That tearing, at least, was no dream, for I awoke to find my daygown flapping open over my breasts, and I can only guess that I somehow rolled on it in the night and did the damage myself.)

And then, once I had been str–

But, as you see, my pen stutters as it comes to record what I dreamed next. Courage, Cali. Courage.

And then, once I had been stripped, the creature dragged down its trousers (looking back, I see I have not mentioned that it seemed to wear nautical clothing) and knickers and forced my head down over its massive thighs, whose coiled strength and power I could sense even without contact. And, Mina: there was thick *hair* upon those thighs! My eyes were weeping freely in the sunlight that bathed us both, but I could catch the glitter of light on glossy dark hairs that paved the massive slabs of the thighs, running upwards to the dense bush of the thighfork. You will see how that last word stutters midway through, for I almost fainted as I wrote it. 'Why?' I hear you ask (and your imagined voice makes me somehow calmer, and better able to continue). Because of what jutted between that pubic bush: a pussy-rooted ~~dildo~~. Oh, I have struck out the word: it seems to sully the page it sits upon, but I think you will still be able to read it. I could feel my eyes bulge with horror as they fell upon this monstrous device and I realised the creature meant to force it between my lips. I struggled, of course, but the horror of my situation seemed, paradoxically, to undermine itself, for I realised now that I could only be dreaming.

A creature of superhuman strength, with hair upon its massive thighs, and bearing a giant d*ld* beneath its pubic bush? What else could this be but a dream? Or rather, what but a nightmare? I held this knowledge safe in my breast, like a talisman, as the foulness proceeded, knowing that my own brain – unbalanced by Artemisia's departure and worry over your absence and dear Joanna's health – was weaving what I experienced. Had I not held this knowledge there, had I thought for a moment that my experiences smacked for a moment of *reality*, I believe I could have been driven out of my wits by what followed, when the creature (my *invented* creature) succeeded in forcing my lips apart and inserted that great swollen *thing* into my mouth.

I begin this section on a separate sheet, dear Mina, and trust you, as my oldest and dearest friend, to consign the sheet to the fire as soon as you have read it, for it will contain a confession at the merest thought of which blood goes pulsing through my face. Here it comes. I have had experience of dildos, dearest Mina. You remember, Hannah, of course, and her 'Freudianism' – that theory of hers about the Tunnel (representing a vagina) and the trains (representing a series of dildos)? I recall how horrified you were by it, though (and forgive me for this, my darling), there was a spark of excitement too, was there not, in your eyes. None perhaps but I could have read it, for I was even then stained with the secret knowledge of my own participation in dildonic perversions. I have used them on other women and once (but only once, I swear!) another woman has used one on me. I will not reveal her name (it is not Artemisia, I swear again). I say this so you know that I am familiar with the things, so that when I say that this dildo in my dream was like no true dildo, you will know I speak the truth. I will resume my story on another sheet, and know that this one will be curling into ash on the fire before you resume your reading.

'Swollen' is *mot juste*, my darling, for the thing seemed veritably to have been pumped full of fluid, like a giant bladder or balloon. Indeed, it seemed (more proof that I dreamed) to have been pumped full of *blood*, for thick veins snaked along its length, and I could feel its searing heat as it slid into my mouth. Then that deep voice (too deep – far too deep – for Artemisia's, I had now realised) was rumbling in my ears, ordering me to *suck* and *lick*, as though the thing were a giant finger that my tongue and mouth could pleasure. I obeyed dazedly, and the deep voice thanked me, already tremulous with oncoming orgasm. Then, like a torrent, a thick and salty fluid, hot almost to boiling, was bursting inside my mouth, pulsing into me like the spurting venom of a basilisk or cockatrice. I had to swallow it or choke, and felt it sear my throat and fill my nostrils with its briny reek as I did so.

Then the great thing (I fancied it had begun to soften fractionally) slid out of my mouth and I was retching, for the salty fluid had settled in my stomach and I could feel it glowing there like poison. One of the creature's burning hands held my neck while the other stroked my forehead and that deep voice rumbled words of comfort in a language I could not recognise.

I remember nothing more till I awoke to find myself back in bed, my torn daygown again on my body and my mouth and throat still seeming to retain traces of what I realised now had to be a dream. But my torn daygown was not the only evidence that it had not been entirely a dream, for there was a crusted patch of vomit on the floor too, dear Mina, in just the spot I might have expected to find it, had I indeed been pumped full of fluid from a giant d*ld* and then been allowed to vomit it up.

I am half-convinced now that a smile touched my face as I looked at the spot, as though something inside were pleased at the memory, or at the confirmation that the dream – the *nightmare* – was not wholly spun of mindstuff, but corresponded in two particulars to reality. I think now that it was the meal of seafood I ate after Art left me: my stomach was disturbed and I vomited in my sleep, contriving to lift myself half out of bed to direct the stream on to the floor and somehow tearing my daygown in the process. Yes, that is it, I am sure. It must be so. But *you* may be sure, my darling, that I will check and double-check my sun-shutters today, and that I am counting the hours – and even the minutes! – more anxiously than ever till my love's return. And yours too, my darling! I long to have you with me again, my darling, for I know nothing ill can happen to me when you are near, and that my gloom and depression will lift.

Give Joanna a kiss and a tweak of the pussy-lips from me. I am praying I will see no reproach in your eyes when next we meet, for the revelation I have vouchsafed you in this letter and that is now, I am sure, wholly burned to ash.

Your ever-loving,
Caliginia.

Caliginia Vestenra's Diary

Hilingama, 24 August. I must imitate Mina, and keep writing things down. Then I will have an exact record of what it is I have experienced since we parted, and be able to tell her all when we meet again. Ah, how I long for that! Then perhaps the sunlight I seem to feel falling

196

all around me will dim and I will be left in safe darkness again. Last night I dreamed again as I did twice (or was it three times?) at Constanţa, and what sickens me most is that now the dream is not so sickening to me. Can I deny it? No, or at least, if I do so with the lips in my face, the lips between my thighs will bear another tale. A silent one, a tale that glistens and oozes. For that is the state in which I found my pussy, when I awoke from my dream, and the moisture on my fingertips confirmed what I remembered feeling in the dream: that what had once been so hateful to me was now a source of pleasure: the hairiness and appalling strength of the creature, the size and turgidity of her d*ld* – no, I will have no hypocrisy here, and will write the thing in full – the size and turgidity of her DILDO, the smoothness and heat of the dildo's blunt, bald end, so roughly inserted between my lips, and the warm thick fluid that spurts from it after I have ministered to it with my tongue and lips for so few seconds. All these make my pussy moisten and my nipples harden, and the deepness of that remembered voice, brittle with gratified pleasure, as she praises me after my tongue-servicing, is almost sufficient to bring me to orgasm. By dint of repetition I know the words she is saying now: they are in Transmarynian, and she is calling me a 'good girl' (*fată buna*) and also a 'good slat'. I can guess that some of this – 'good girl' – lodged unawares in my memory when I listened to Mina practising her Transmarynian vocabulary for Joanna, but where has 'slat' come from and why should I be called it? I looked it up yesternight in a Transmarynian dictionary in a bookshop (having called there to buy a present for Art's return) and discover it means '*şipcă*'. Does the creature mean I am sturdy, that I keep a metaphorical rain of unhappiness or depression from her?

25 August. Reading over my entry for yesternight, I realise I finished on a foolish note. The question I posed is nonsensical: the *creature* means nothing, it is my own – what is the term? – yes, my own *subconscious* that seeks to convey some meaning to my conscious self. This repeated dream is a message from me to myself, and I shall find the key in time. Perhaps I should have found it already, if I did not feel so confoundedly sleepy all the time or, at least, all the time during the night. But by day, once I know the sun has risen, my lassitude seems to fall from me and it is almost an effort to retire to bed. Once I am there, however, I sleep easily enough, as though I am eager for the dream. And I *am*. Yes, I confess it now. I am disappointed when I do not experience the dream, or at least I am disappointed when I wake and do not remember having experienced it. But twice now the sun-shutters have been open when I awoke with no memories of the dream, though I clearly remembered having shut them (perhaps not so firmly as I might once have done) the previous morning. Today I am inclined not to shut them at all, but rather to see whether that will conjure the dream clearly for me, with clear memories to relate to Artemisia, who returns on the morrow. What will she say to me? Will she rebuke me for my perversity, or laughingly incorporate elements of my dream into our love-play? Will she be jealous that I am dreaming of a lover bed-companion even stronger and more brutal than she, or take it as a tribute to her own prowess, that my poor brain must invent such a phantom in her absence? I shall know soon enough.

Letter from Artemisia Rustavic to Mina Harker

Albemarla Hotel, 2 September.
My dear Mina,
   I am at my wits' end and write to you almost in despair, knowing that you will respond if you can out of the love you bear for Caliginia and, through her

(might I hope?), for myself. The help I request is this: can you shed any light on the strange illness (if illness it be) that Caliginia is now suffering? I believe, from hints she has let fall, that she wrote to you of it in recent nights, before it seized such hold of her mind and actions. Yes, you will see from that how she will not speak of it to me – not even to me, from whom I once thought she could and would conceal nothing of what was in her heart.

But to write of that brings tears afresh to my eyes, so I shall instead sketch the illness and see what you can make of it. I may tell you that I have had an old Georgian friend, a Dr Helsingvili, across from Tblisi to examine her, and she professed herself baffled, or at least professed herself unable to comment before she had returned across the Black Sea to consult her library. Perhaps I am reading too much into her demeanour, but I believe she knows more of what is taking place than she has yet revealed, out of fear for Caliginia and consideration for myself. But at least she left me with a long list of precautions to take, and my mind is relieved a little that Caliginia seems to have rallied under their influence. But to business: here are her symptoms:

Her pattern of sleeping is seriously disturbed and for choice she will rest during the night and rise by day.

I have twice discovered her bathing naked in sunlight in her room, and her skin has acquired a faint but unmistakable 'tan' (this, Dr Helsingvili tells me, is the technical term). She has lost all concern for elementary sun-discipline and seems careless whether or not the sun-shutters in her (or any other room) are well-secured before sunrise.

She has lost almost all interest in lovemaking (yes, it is Caliginia I am writing of!) and has striven, in the brief sessions she has permitted me, to introduce certain love-plays that smack to me (and I am a broad-minded woman, as you know) of morbidity and almost – though I hesitate to write it – of perversion. I will not go into details, but say merely that these love-plays revolve principally around her bottom.

Though she will not make love to me save on rare, bittersweet occasions (sweet in themselves, bitter in their infrequency), she has increased the number and vigour of her solitary masturbations, and seems to have acquired a new fetish for fur or hair. Yesternight, for example, I found her frotting herself with a fur-wrap of her mother's, which she was dragging repeatedly up between her thighs while whipping her inflamed nipples with one end. Normally I should have been delighted at her inventiveness, but she refuses to share the fetish with me, and on the two (!) occasions she has performed cunnilinctus on me since my return (and I have been back a week!), I have distinctly heard her sigh with disappointment as she pressed her head between my thighs, as though they lacked something she was accustomed, and excited, to find there.

These symptoms have remained, though lessening, since I took up the precautions Dr Helsingvili recommended (strict sun-discipline, with locked and bolted sun-shutters), while the strange whitish diarrhoea she was suffering, and the inflammation and soreness of her dear bottomhole, are rapidly easing. I confess I can make neither head nor tail of any of this, as though I am staring out with smarting eyes over a sun-blasted landscape, and I hope (I *pray*) that you may be able to cast shadow over the scene, that I might pick out true causes and, by removing them, restore my love (and yours) to her true self.

With fondest affection,
Artemisia.

Letter from Mina Harker to Artemisia Rustavic

Paris, 4 September.

My dearest Artemisia!

Hope is yours, my darling, though you may have to pass through strong light to achieve what it holds out to you. As you surmised from the hints she dropped, Caliginia did indeed write to me of her 'illness' and of the strange 'dream' that accompanied it, or rather engendered it, and that I now know can have been no dream. I cannot claim credit for this knowledge myself, however, and you will owe your relief to one whom you have not yet met but who already loves you for the love you bear for Caliginia, a dear friend and past lover of hers. I speak of my butchwife*, Joanna, who has been able from her own experience to supply the shadow you sought for the glaring scene presented to you by Cali's behaviour. I had not shown her Cali's letters, for, as you may know yourself, my Joanna is but recently recovered, or rather say half- or third-recovered, from a severe and brain-taxing 'illness', and I had not wished to burden her with worry for one for whom, as I do, she has the strongest and purest affection. Your letter, however, I did show, for she insisted on it after I had accidentally let fall some hint of its contents. My fears about worrying her unnecessarily seemed confirmed when I gave her the letter as she lay in bed, for I watched her face brighten with horror as she read, till she reached some passage that overtaxed her nerves. A faint cry escaped her lips and a moment later her head slumped unconscious to the pillow. (I guessed then, and have confirmed it since, that the passage in question was that in which you spoke of Caliginia's morbid interest in love-plays revolving around the bottom.)

When my darling recovered consciousness a minute or so later, her face was drawn and anxious, and the

201

first words on her lips were 'The Countess!' Gnomic, you think? You will not think so when you have read the enclosed transcription of Joanna's journal, for you will know precisely what – precisely *who* – is responsible for your darling's suffering and I am sure that your resolve will match ours. I do not believe myself that Joanna is yet strong enough to travel, but she insists on returning to Romania to root up an evil for which (despite all my arguments to the contrary) she holds herself partly responsible. But you will be impatient now, I am sure, to read what Joanna has written, so I will end things here. The two of us will be with you within the week, I promise, and we can make our plans then.

Please, if you can, ask Dr Helsingvili back from Georgia to assist her: Joanna says that the precautions she recommended reveal that she knows a great deal of the peril we face. Give my love to Caliginia, and have no fear that the slightest trace of blame for this 'illness' attaches to her!

All my love,

Mina.

Enc. Joanna Harker's Journal

6 September. I thought never to write in this diary again, but the time has come and what Mina has told me forces me to lay my own feelings aside, in order to prevent others from enduring what I have endured. No, that is wrong: for others *have* already endured what I have endured, and to a greater extent and longer. The poor crew of *The Demeter*, if what Mina tells me is true (no, it *is* true: I cannot shield myself from that by equivocation), they too have fallen prey to the fiend. I do not yet feel able to write her name again, though I must steel myself to it in a few minutes. 'Her' name I should rather write, and I cannot call 'her' a Hell-spawned bitch for, though of a surety 'she' *is* Hell spawned, 'she' is no bitch. I will call on the technique I employed before, when imprisoned in 'her' castle, and breathe deeply and slowly for a minute, to calm myself before I resume my narrative of what happened there.

I have done it, and am ready. Let me set her name down first. The Countess. The Countess. The Countess. There. Now that I have set the word down, I can speak it aloud, I think. Yes. I can. It tastes bitter in my mouth, like the –

I have just returned from retching in the bathroom – I was not so calm over this matter as I thought. The memories lie in wait for me, ready to seize control of my heart and guts, squeezing the one like dough and twisting the other like a rag. It is good that I have sent Mina away for the evening, for I fear that I should have broken down completely in her presence, knowing that comfort awaited me in her arms. Alone I can steel myself to the task, I hope. Yes. I am calmer. I will begin, and hope that things that seem at first mysterious to my readers will become clearer on a second and third reading.

So, to begin: I left off my diary at the point at which I was to climb again to the roof and the Countess's glass coffin, not knowing whether she slept or lay awake and ready for me. I needed the keys for Mary and the remainder of the milk-slaves. Having added that final entry to my diary and hidden the book on a high shelf of the Countess's library, I undertook the lonely task that awaited me, climbing those three sets of stairs and stepping once more on to the roof. The eastern sky was tinged sowl with coming dawn, I saw, but the Countess seemed to lie motionless, gorged with milk in her glass coffin, and I believed that I had come in time. I crept to the coffin, using all my skills of quietness and stealth, and attempted to raise the lid. No use! I thought at first: there seemed no purchase for my fingers on the smooth glass, till I noticed the slight depressions halfway along the lid and, slipping my fingertips there, I found I could gain sufficient leverage to accomplish my task. The lid was heavy and I knew that if it slipped the Countess would be awake in an instant, but I poured out all my strength and managed to get the thing safely open. So far I had not dared lower my eyes to the keys where they lay at the Countess's hip, for fear of a glimpse of the massive member she bore between her thighs; now I dared, and saw, to my unutterable relief, that the member was quiescent, lolling beneath its bush of pubic hair like a flaccid serpent or sausage. The thought of reaching in for the keys while the thing was in full erection was almost intolerable to me, but it was asleep. Better by far that it had been awake while its mistress slept. Instead, *it* slept while its 'mistress' lay awake – I use the word (mistress, I mean) *faute de mieux*. I learned this as I reached inside the coffin for the keys and sensed suddenly that a powerful gaze had fallen on my face. I looked up at the Countess's face and gasped with horror when I saw that her eyes had opened and were glaring at me in the twilight of pre-dawn. Without conscious thought I snatched the keys up, turned and began to run for the door, hoping that I might somehow evade her pursuit inside the castle and reach the dungeon levels with time to release sufficient milk-slaves for the uprising we (Mary and I) had purposed.

All hope of this was wiped brutally from my brain as from that door stepped another naked figure: one of the Countess's 'twaughters' (again I use the term *faute de mieux*). She too was naked and her body was identical in all important respects to the Countess's: hard, flat, and angular, with a coating of dense hair on thighs, chest and arms, no breasts to speak of, the skin a sallow glart and an obscene snake hanging between her thighs. I heard deep laughter from behind me and spun to see the Countess rising from her coffin, one hand clutching at her lower member and jerking at its head as it rose to turgid and obscene life. Another deep laugh from behind me and I spun back to the door to see the 'twaughter' advance on me with her hand performing the same office for her snake, and two further twaughters were stepping through the door at her shoulders, hands busy in the same way. I shrieked and am not ashamed to confess that I fainted: the dashing of all my hopes and the appearance not just of the horror I had feared but of that horror four times multiplied were too much for my overburdened nerves.

I awoke downstairs, stripped naked and tied breast-down on the great table in the library, with a pillow propped under my chin. A voice murmured in front of me, apparently announcing my revival, and I opened my eyes to see four armchairs drawn up in front of me in bright sunlight. Three were occupied, one empty. The whereabouts of its occupant (the Countess) I realised a moment later, when a heavy palm landed on my upraised buttocks, though it did not create pain there so much as re-create it, and I realised that a buttock-slap had been what had brought me out of my swoon.

'Ah,' said a familiar voice, and the Countess stepped from beside my buttocks into my line of vision. 'My dear Joanna, you are awake. Awake and ready to . . . *service* us.'

I could not restrain a shudder at the manner in which her tongue and lips caressed that word 'service', or at the shuffle of eagerness that ran through the occupants of the armchairs: the Countess's three 'twaughters', all naked and all armed with a fully erect thigh-member. The Countess too was naked and as she walked in front of me and turned to face me I saw that her thigh-member too was fully erect, straining towards me. She chuckled as my eyes fixed on it, widening with horror.

'Does my cock not please you, my dear?' she said in Transmarynian, no longer troubling to disguise her arrogance and contempt.

I struggled to master the fear that filled me.

'Release me,' I said. 'This is a wicked violation of all laws of hospitality.'

Laughter from all four greeted my words, and the Countess was still richly amused as she replied.

'We are wicked men, my dear, and violation, as you will shortly learn, is our way of life. But for once I am inclined to pay for what I take, and offer you a bargain. Before you suck our cocks – indeed, *while* you suck our cocks – you may ask any questions you please, and have full and honest answers. But perhaps your first question is, naturally enough, what a cock is. This, my dear, *this* is a cock.'

And she seized her thigh-member by the root and waved it at me, the pressure of her closed hand making it swell more than ever, its thick and snaking veins bulging obscenely along its cylindrical length. Against my will a question was forced out of me and I spat it at her now, careless of the consequences.

'What are you, you monster?'

More laughter greeted this, but it was not shared by the Countess, who released hold of her thigh-member – her *cock* – and shook her head sadly.

'Such an insult, for your humble host. I, a monster? We, monsters?'

And she stepped aside to allow me full sight of her three twaughters again, whose voices I now recognised as those of the three 'women' who had molested me outside the glarthouse.

'No, my dear Joanna, we are not monsters, we are *men*. We are of your kind, of your flesh and blood, we are simply . . . equipped differently, and possess different – shall we say? – different *tastes*.'

My head was spinning with fear and exhaustion, but a small core of defiance was hardening somewhere inside me too.

'You are monsters,' I said. 'I know everything. I know of the wretched milk-slaves you keep imprisoned below the castle. I know of your cruelty and wicked-ness.'

I trailed off; the Countess had raised her hand and was shaking her head sadly again.

'You know a little,' she said. 'The full truth you have barely guessed. So I think we shall tell you more of the truth, to pay you for the services you are about to perform for us – the *sexual* services, my dear.'

I felt my pussy, exposed between my tied-apart legs, crawl with anticipation at these words. The Countess turned, motioning one of her 'twaughters' forwards.

'Paul, place your cock at my disposal for a brief lesson, if you will.'

Paul rose from the armchair grinning, her rigid thigh-member jutting out insolently before her. The Countess took her by the shoulder and guided her forwards until she was standing with her thigh-member nearly in my face. I could smell a feral reek rising from it, and noted the way it ticked gently to her heartbeat. The Countess took hold of it, drawing back a hood of skin that covered its bulbous end.

'This, my dear,' she said, 'is a cock. A wonder of creation, is it not?'

She pushed it left and right, then up and down, allowing me to see that bulbous end from all angles. It was coloured dark vace and shaped like a firewoman's helmet, its brim studded with tiny warts. On its very top was a slit, for urine, I guessed (half-right, as it turned out).

'And a cock, my dear, is the mark of a man. Or rather – that is the phrase you use constantly in your diary, is it not? – a cock and *balls* are the mark of a man. These are balls.'

She released the cock and hefted what hung below it: a leathery wrinkled sack in which I noted, as her fingers prodded and pressed, two large oval glands (her twaughter winced a little as she manipulated the sack and its contents, and I half-consciously stored the fact for future reference). The Countess released the sack and took hold of the cock again, tugging back the hood, which had ridden up over the head a little again.

'A cock and balls, my dear. The mark of a man. I am a man. Paul here, he is a man. Joseph, he too is a man, and Richud, he too. We four, we are men. Each of us bears a cock and balls and, for that, you call us monsters. No, my dear, my very dearest, we are not monsters: we are of your kind and are designed along the same general lines, merely to different ... specifications. For proof, I evince Paul's body. Note that, like you, he has breasts.'

Her hands rose, tweaking the shrunken nipples of her obscene twaughter, one after the other.

'And even this –' her hand dropped back to the cock, lifting it then letting it fall '– Paul's fine cock, this too corresponds to something in your own body. This cock is Paul's clitoris. And these, his balls –' her hand lifted the sack again '– these are his ovaries, encased –' her left hand joined her right at work on the sack '– in a *scrotum* formed from his pussy-lips. Do you see the seam?'

And I could: a seam divided the sack in two. Her hands released her twaughter's cock and she continued.

'We men are based on the body-plan of you women, and perhaps you could say we have evolved from you. Once, indeed, we dwelled in company with you. Once, indeed, we were necessary for your very existence, as you were for ours. For we gave you children. With our cocks and balls. Ah, I see the incredulity in your face. For a moment it almost mastered the horror and disgust. But here, ready to hand, is the proof of my claim. Paul's fine cock.' Her hands returned to it. 'Note the slit in the cockhead. What do you think it is there for, my dear?'

'She pisses through it,' I said.

'A brief word on vocabulary, my dear. You are employing the wrong pronoun. *She* does not piss through it: *he* does. He pisses through *his* cock, the cock that belongs to *him*. He: nominative. His: genitive. Him: accusative. Himself: reflexive. Can you try and remember that? Good girl. Now, that is half-right: piss can be discharged through this fine cock too, but not only piss. Also seed. Seed from his fine big balls. Seed for the seeding of . . . children. But I see incredulity in your face again, my dear. Disbelief. Perhaps you wonder whether you are dreaming? Ah, this is no dream, as you will shortly learn. Today you will begin the first stage of the process that will, in a few months at most, see you seeded by one of us. Next year you will bear a child to one of us.'

Defiance flared up in me again.

'Nonsense,' I croaked. 'I am two years from child-bearing.'

'No. You are four years, at least, into child-bearing. For many months past you have been ripe for us. For me and for my suns. Ah, you do not recognise the word, I see. These, my dear –' and she – he – pushed Paul back from me, back towards the armchair she – *he* – had vacated '– these are my suns. My "twaughters", if you prefer.'

'Nonsense,' I croaked again. 'They are nothing like you.'

The Countess chuckled.

'Suns, my dear, do not necessarily resemble their father. They may take after their mother much more. Joseph here is the spit of his, are you not? Though I think he has my nose, and my spirit, of course, like both of his bruthers. Ah, now I see that you are confused. I am pushing too much on you too quickly. All this talk of "fathers" and "mothers" – I forget how confusing it must be for you. Because for you, of course, there is only the mother, giving birth only to the twaughter, who resembles her in every respect. Is that not so?'

I nodded.

'And that is the only way it can be, is it not?'

I nodded, but with less certainty.

'Among the *higher* animals, that is, though perhaps you have heard rumours of recent scientific discoveries among lower genera?'

I nodded.

'Where there may be two mothers?'

I nodded.

'Good. Then you are not wholly ignorant. Two mothers. Or, at least, those are the terms in which these discoveries have been transmitted to you. Your government does not choose, as yet, to reveal the truth. But in fact, it is not two mothers that some lower creatures possess, but two *parents*: a mother and a *father*. That is what my three suns possess: a father, who is I, and a mother, who is different for each of them. I planted my seed – oh, I see it is no use using words. You require a practical demonstration. Boys, on your feet. Your cocks have been stiff for long enough without discharge: it is time to show our honoured guest what you are made of.'

My eyes were streaming with tears from the uninter-rupted sunlight now, but I would have heard the three creatures whom the Countess called her 'suns' (ha!) spring eagerly to their feet even if I had not been able to see them at all.

'But draw the curtains first, Jo,' the Countess ordered, 'or the poor dear won't be able to see what's going on in the fine detail she requires, and deserves.'

Feet ran across the floor and I heard curtains sliding across the windows. I sighed with relief as the sunlight was cut off and I could see almost clearly again, then choked with horror at what I could see: Paul and Richud advancing on me, hands busy on the heads of their cocks, with 'Jo' running to join them, hand poised to begin work on his cock too.

210

'Do you see, my dear?' said the Countess. 'They are now *wanking*, as we say in Transmarynian, that is, stimulating themselves to orgasm. The head of an erect cock is sensitive to friction, and when it receives sufficient friction for a sufficient length of time, the cock – or, rather, the conjoint system of cock and balls – will discharge. *Ejaculate* is the technical term. You will observe this very shortly: seed will come spraying from their cocks and you will receive it, if I guess their intentions right, full in the face.'

The three creatures were beginning to pant now and I noted that their dwarfish nipples were peaked as though from pleasure. Their hands cycled on the heads of their cocks, getting faster and faster, then suddenly almost blurring, for the Countess had said, 'He who comes first can have the first blow-job.'

Paul, who was standing in the middle of the masturbating line, switched hands from right to left, frowning with concentration, and I thought he was going to be first to achieve whatever the Countess had meant by 'spraying seed', but Joseph was tweaking at his own nipples with his free hand, then moistening his fingertips with spittle and rubbing it well in, then starting to groan.

'Careful for your eyes, my dear,' said the Countess, but before I could work out what he meant Joseph was 'coming': his hand suddenly stopped working at the head of his cock and he took a pace forwards, pointing his cock at my face almost like a pistol. In the next instant, something flashed in the cockslit, and a jet of white fluid had shot across the four or five feet separating us to splatter full on my face. I cried out with surprise and pain, realising now what the Countess had meant, for a droplet of the fluid had landed in one of my eyes and was stinging there furiously. I heard Paul begin to groan now too and, though my eyes were clamped shut now as further jets of Joseph's cock-fluid splattered on my face, a moment later I felt a fresh series of jets landing there, as Paul achieved orgasm. The fluid was warm and heavy, like an overcooked paste or sauce, and filled my nostrils with a salty, feral reek as it slid down my cheeks and chin. Then the jets had ceased to land and, eyes still tight-shut, I could hear Richud working away at his cock, then beginning to groan like her twinsters (no, *his bruthers*).

'Slow but sure,' said the Countess, 'and I think you will find his come the most copious of all.'

So it proved: I counted eight distinct jets against my face as Richud stepped forwards and came from a distance of no more than two or three feet all over my face. The seed splattered my forehead and hair this time too, and trickled down over my eyebrows. Then it was over and I heard Richud step back, his panting slowly beginning to slow and subside.

'Marvellous, boys,' said the Countess's voice. 'You have made an old man very happy, and I could only wish that you had made a young woman very happy too, with three helpings of warm spunk trickling down her face. But she is not sufficiently sluttified for that yet. In a week or two, perhaps. Now, my dear, are you convinced? Your face has just been flooded with seed. If your womb had had the fortune to receive the same it is possible that you would be shortly about to conceive.'

I shook my head, eyes still shut, feeling the trickling 'spunk' on my face change direction on my skin as my head moved.

'Ah, you are still incredulous, still disbelieving. So tell me, my dear, tell me what you know of pregnancy. Describe the only possible means to me while your own lips bear witness against you, for even now they are dripping with a second possible means. Come. Describe pregnancy to me, my dear.'

I blew air through my lips, trying to get as much 'spunk' off them as possible, so that no trace could enter my mouth.

'Begin, my dear. Do not trouble yourself to clean your lips: your mouth will be full of spunk soon enough, I promise, and you might as well get used to the taste.'

'Fiend,' I muttered.

'What was that, my dear?'

'Fiend!' I said clearly, eyes still shut as 'spunk' trickled over my eyelids.

Laughter greeted this. The three creatures were back in their armchairs, I could hear, and the Countess still stood to one side, ~~her~~ his cruel eyes searching (I could sense) my splattered and humiliated face. He stopped laughing, and I trembled a little at the tone of command that had crept into her – his – voice.

'Enough of that. Describe pregnancy to me.'

'It begins at the tweth,' I began hesitantly.

'And when is that?' the Countess rumbled.

'Twenty-three. Twenty-three years of age. If a woman is fertile, one or more of her eggs will seed and implant in her womb. Then nine mo–'

'And how does an egg seed?'

I frowned a little, puzzled at the question.

'It seeds itself.'

'And that is the only possible way?'

'Yes.'

'Do you mean "Yes, of course"?'

'Yes. Of course.'

'Ah, you have not quite lost your spirit, I see. But other things you will lose, I promise, and soon. First, you will lose this illusion of yours that eggs may only self-seed. That is untrue. An egg may also *be* seeded. By sperm. By the substance now trickling down your delectable face, my dear. That is sperm. And if it had been squirted into your womb and a suitable egg had been waiting, that egg might have been seeded by it. But, my dear, you look puzzled again. What is troubling you?'

'Squirted into my womb, Countess?'

'Count. I am a Count, not a Countess. Count Caradul, at your service.'

I heard her click her heels ironically, then continue, 'But this sperm-squirting into your womb. You wonder how it might be achieved?'

I nodded silently, my eyes half-open now, so that I could see how the Countess – the *Count* – licked her – his – lips, as though with relish, before she – he – replied to the question he had himself posed.

'By insertion of a cock into your cunt.'

My head swam with horror, my now bulging eyes fixed on the array of cocks before me, jutting up arrogantly between the thighs of the Count's 'suns' as they lolled in their armchairs. I could feel my cunt squirming between my splayed thighs, as though trying to burrow itself deeper, to conceal itself within my body, safe from the fleshy threat of those obscene and swollen members. The Count chuckled, richly amused by my horror.

'But my dearest, my poppet, why the stricken face? Cock in cunt was once the most natural thing in the world. Many centuries ago, before the coming of a curious plague whose details have been passed down from father to father, women once gave birth only after cock-insertion and sperm-squirting, and could do so at any age between the menarche and the menopause. None of this *tweth* nonsense then, when we men ruled the world and you women lay at our feet in awe-stricken admiration and service. Then came that curious plague, and you women somehow acquired the ability to give birth without cock-insertion, without sperm-squirting and, though these did not lose all their potency, they lost almost all of it. In five generations, we men were reduced to a handful, for a man can be born only from sperm-squirting. Parthenogenesis, virgin-birth, a self-seeded egg – that produces only women. Thereafter, year on year, sperm-squirting lost more and more of

214

what little power it had left. In many regions it lost its power entirely and we men were confined to a solitary stronghold, Transmarynia, where women retained something of their old fertility. Even that in time disappeared, until only I remained of the once proud race of men, searching without rest, without even hope, for a cure to the malady, for a way to reawaken the womb to the sperm that boiled continually in my balls. Tell me, my dear, how old you think I am?'

I managed to take my eyes from the threatening row of erect 'cocks' and look at him.

'Forty-five,' I said. 'Perhaps fifty.'

He laughed again, shaking his head.

'No, my dear. Double that, and double it again, and again, and you are still short of my true age. I approach this year my five-hundred-and-eighteenth birthday. We men, you see, like you women, are practically immortal. You give birth to identical copies of yourselves, and achieve immortality that way. We men achieve immortality in our own persons. Tell me, my dear, what colour is our skin?'

I frowned.

'Glart,' I said. 'That is why you wore powder on your face, to disguise it from me.'

He nodded.

'Yes. But our skin is not glart, it is *green*. If you could truly see that, you would find my skin even more unnatural than presently you do. You women, you see, in retreating from the cock, also retreated from that great celestial symbol of the cock: the giant glowing glans in the sky. The furnace-faced fuck-father, my dear. The *sun*. You became nocturnal and took to eating insects and, as your hearing and smell sharpened, so your sight dulled. Like bats, my dear. We men remained in the light of father sun, and we retained colour vision. True colour vision. We do not see in your blacks and whites and greys, we see in colour. That is why I say our skin is green. The green of plants, for we carry the same photophilic chemical in our skin as plants do, and may harvest the sun's bounty with it in the same way. We do not need to eat as you do, though when faced with vigorous exertion we choose to do so. It is also true that drink, of a special mineral-rich kind –' I shuddered, knowing of what he spoke '– is necessary to us, as it is to plants. Thus it is we have the life-span of a tree, or rather I and my suns do. I was the last, but also the greatest of my race, for I discovered a means of *enhancing* this ability to eat light, and so extended my own life while I searched for a means to replace those of my bruthers whom I had lost one by one over the centuries. As you see, I succeeded.'

His hand jerked at his twaughters – his *suns*.

'My three fine suns. The first men born in nearly five hundred years. But not the last. Oh, by no means the last. Not now I have discovered the secret. The secret, my dear. Which I will now reveal to you. Which I will now have *enacted* on you.'

Grins had appeared on the faces of his three suns as he was speaking these final words; now, as though he had uttered a cue, they pushed themselves out of their armchairs again and advanced on me, idly jerking on the heads of their erect cocks.

'The secret of womb-awakening, my dear. For I discovered that a woman's body must be *accustomed* to the presence of sperm before it is squirted into the womb. The woman must first swallow it and receive it in her arse, so that her body grows used to its presence and does not reject it when finally the cock is inserted in the cunt and sperm squirts home into the womb. This is what I did to each of the three women who had the privilege of being mother to one of my suns. Her body was thoroughly accustomed to sperm by mouth and arse before I inserted my eager member in her tight cunt and sent my sperm squirting into it to seed her womb.'

My head was swimming again. Must receive it in her *arse*? Thoroughly accustomed to sperm by mouth and *arse*? What did the fiend mean? Was I to have those members inserted – my Goddess! Consciousness almost left me at the mere thought.

'First, therefore, comes the ingestion. My suns will one by one insert their cocks into your cool and welcoming mouth, where you will suck and lick them to orgasm. You will then swallow the resultant sperm. At first, perhaps, your stomach will reject this bounty, but shortly, I promise you, your natural instincts, suppressed for centuries, will reassert themselves and you will thirst for this salty milk. Or could I perhaps call it a yoghurt? Joseph, you may have first suck, as I promised.'

I almost fainted as Joseph stepped forwards to me, lifting the head of his cock towards my mouth. It reeked hotly of its previous discharge and I could hear the blood pulsing through it.

'Open your mouth, my dear,' said the Count. 'Or I will abuse your delightful buttocks until you do.'

Groaning, I opened my mouth and allowed the eager cockhead to enter, glowing on my tongue like a coal.

'Now suck, my dear. And lick. And when he ejaculates, you must swallow every drop. If you then vomit it up, no matter, for Paul and Richud will replace what your stomach has rejected. Tomorrow your mouth-training will recommence, and by the end of the week I promise that you will be opening your mouth very willingly. Sperm is an acquired taste, I admit, but I have found that you women acquire that taste very quickly.'

I will not describe in detail the obscenities that followed: how first Joseph, then Paul and Richud inserted their cocks into my mouth and were sucked and licked by me to copious orgasm, whose salty liquor I swallowed to the last drop. As the Count had predicted, I vomited after the first sperm-swallowing, my stomach rejecting Joseph's warm ball-juice, but I retained the second and third loads delivered into my mouth and swallowed by me. They lay thick and foul on my stomach as I was untied from the table and taken to my room for sleep before the second day of my sperm-training commenced. In my room I forced myself to be sick again, not wanting to retain any of their sperm, and my chamberpot was a third full of vomitus and sperm as I took it to the waste-pipe in the wall where – so long ago it now seemed – the Countess had tipped the contents of my bath on the first night of my imprisonment in the castle. I tipped the chamberpot and its obscene contents down the pipe, distractedly noting the distant murmur of the river and wondering briefly whether I should beg forgiveness of its tutelary spirit, for befouling its waters with such filth.

It was as I turned away from the pipe to return my chamberpot to its accustomed spot beneath my bed that the thought struck me, though it seemed at that moment a literal pipe-dream. If only there were some means by which I could descend the pipe to the river! The river might flow too swiftly for safety, and I might drown once I had trusted myself to its waters, but better that, surely, than continued imprisonment and continued sperm-training. For next, after the mouth-training – and not the least of my fears was the Count's promise should be proved true, and I should come to rejoice in the taste of the sperm pumped into my mouth – next, I say, would come the arse-training, when one by one those enormous cocks would be inserted into my tender bottom, to fill my rectal chamber with warm and sticky sperm. The thought of it sickened me, and my heart fluttered above my rolling guts. So it was that, though convinced the exercise was useless, I turned back to the waste-pipe to examine it more closely. The mouth was obviously too small for more than an arm or leg to enter, but by speaking a few words into it I discovered from the echoes that it widened considerably a few feet in and down. But what if the walls were smooth and afforded no purchase for hand and foot? I could hardly let myself fall the many feet to the river that murmured far below.

By now, however, the exercise of examining the pipe did not seem so futile as at first: the mouth, I saw, could easily be broken wider if I had some tool to work at the plaster; and a tool readily suggested itself in a coat hanger from my wardrobe (though all my clothing had, I noted, been removed, so that I would now be forced to remain naked). I dug at the plaster experimentally with the coat hanger and noted with satisfaction that it crumbled easily – and more easily still, when I squatted atop my chamberpot, filled it with piss, and splashed the contents on to the plaster as I worked. In reaction to the despair that had formerly filled me I found myself positively trembling with hope, and three times at least I had to stop work and breathe myself back to calmness.

In an hour, or perhaps a little less, I had broken away enough of the plaster to insert my head and neck fully into the pipe, and by careful whistles I was able to perceive that the interior of the pipe was rough surfaced enough to admit of finger- and toe-holds by which I could descend to the river – though what length of fall awaited me at the last I did not care to conjecture. Another half-hour of work was sufficient to grant my whole upper body access to the pipe, and in under two hours, my chamberpot long since emptied of piss, I was crawling into it and lowering myself to begin my long descent. Two thoughts filled my overtaxed brain: the hope of final freedom and the certainty of rebellion. Whatever awaited me below, I should have escaped the clutches of that abhuman fiend and ~~her~~ his suns, and the thought of their anger and frustrated lust filled me with delight me as I climbed downwards, feeling the air grow cooler and moister around me.

I cannot describe much of the hours and nights that followed, for the final drop I had to make into the river was enough almost to knock me senseless, and I retain only fragmentary memories of struggling to keep afloat as the river rushed me through its subterranean domain to deposit me at last on a stony bank in the open air, beneath the cool and friendly light of the moon.

Finally, after lying I know not how long in a semi-delirium, I was spurred to my feet by the approach of day and the thought that perhaps a pursuit was already under way, and I staggered away from the river for help. It was provided on that first night, I believe, by a peasant mother and twaughter whom I have vowed I shall track down and reward; and thereafter by a succession of Transmarynian women who gave the lie to the fear I had half-entertained that the Count's writ might run too well in that region for me to evade his vengeance.

To tell the truth, however, I soon began to doubt my own memories of the monster, his three equally monstrous 'suns' and his tormented milk-slaves, and by the time I reached the Hospital of SS Josephina and Mary in London I was more than half-convinced that I had dreamed most or all of what had taken place in the castle. Perhaps some protective mechanism was at work in my mind, shielding me from full realisation until such time as I should have recovered sufficiently from my physical privations to face the truth. If so, that protective mechanism yielded to the claims of love when my dearest Mina reached my side and I learned of Caliginia's 'illness'. From the details given by her lover Artemisia there can be only one conclusion: the Count has reached my homeland, and one of my dearest and oldest friends is plainly being subjected to the sperm-training of which he spoke, with the intention of forcing a pregnancy on her. She must – and *will* – be rescued before the Count's scheme comes to fruition, and we

220

must learn once and for all what fell purpose the Count has in transferring the scene of his operations from Transmarynia to Romania.

Mina tells me that she will write to Artemisia and request her help in organising a search of the Count's castle by the Transmarynian authorities. We may discover documents there that will guide us in our quest and may even, if one yet remains, arrest and interrogate one of her suns. It goes without saying, I hope, that the milk-slaves concern me almost more than the peril that threatens poor Caliginia, though I suspect that the Count may have liberated them before his departure for Romania aboard that ill-fated vessel the *Demeter*, of whose melancholy fate Mina has apprised me. I must write to the chief medical officer in Constanţa and ask her to watch those poor seawomen for signs of pregnancy, for it is all too apparent that they too were subject to sperm-training on that artificially prolonged voyage. This, I am sure, is part of the Count's monstrous scheme: to impregnate the women of Europe with his foul sperm, and somehow re-establish the dominion of *men* of which he so proudly spoke. I am praying that he be frustrated in all his endeavours.

Joanna Harker.

Letter from Artemisia Rustavic to Mina Harker

10 September.
My dearest Mina,

I thank you a thousand times for your letter, and Joanna a further thousand times for the extract from her journal. The cloud begins to thicken on the brightness of my perplexity and distress, and much that was formerly blinding now becomes plainly visible. I may tell you that Dr Helsingvili has concurred fully with Joanna's diagnosis, and she now says she might have arrived at the truth herself from her researches, though she believes she may have been too late to save Cali from suffering the third stage of this unspeakable 'sperm-training'; that is, the vaginal penetration. Ah, my thighs clench and quiver even to think of it, and I misdoubt that the Count's 'thigh-member' could be half so appalling in the literal flesh as it is in my imaginings – though doubtless it is, and more. But my own fear and distaste are submerged in the anger – nay, the rage – I experience every time I consider what this fiend has been subjecting my poor darling to! Not content with violating the sanctity of her mouth, he (I am glad I can mark the monster out with such an uncouth pronoun as *that*) has made himself sovereign of her bottom. My teeth grind as I imagine how he forced himself home into her exquisite velvet sheath, and I experience in my own breast something of the pain and bewilderment she must have suffered. Worse still is the thought that she has been permanently perverted by her experiences, and will be for ever striving to introduce anal play into our lovemaking. But Dr Helsingvili tells me that the young are resilient, and will spring back from experiences that would permanently warp and corrupt the old.

I will trust that my old friend speaks sooth – in fact, I must do so, for Cali must endure one further bout of anal atrocity, if the good doctor is to have her way. She has prepared a scheme of entrapment for the fiend, arguing that if we denied him all further access to Cali and her bottom he would be forced to pastures new, where we might occupy many further weeks in tracking him down or, worse, fail to do entirely, leaving him free to rampage through our womanfolk, sperm-training them by mouth and bottom before forcing his way into their pussies and impregnating them with his male-spawning seed. And so it is that today we have left Cali barely protected, trusting that he will return to her as he has so often before. The sun-shutters of her room are closed but unbolted, and his unspeakable lust for the ripe hemispheres of Cali's bottom will, Dr Helsingvili assures me, quite remove all thought of a *trap* from his mind. A trap awaits him nonetheless, and where he least expects it: buried in Cali's bottom itself. Dr Helsingvili has prepared a special glue or plaster that even now lies waiting beyond Cali's bottom-mouth for the fiend's 'cock' (another uncouth vocable for an uncouth thing). The greater heat of his metabolism, so the doctor tells me, will cause a chemical reaction in the plaster that will set it solid in seconds, and the fiend will find himself trapped by the cock in his own paradise. Dr Helsingvili sits waiting in an adjacent room, and is confident that the monster's predicament will be plainly audible, as he struggles to release himself. Thereupon she will give a blast on her whistle, and every woman in the house will descend upon the intruder.

I was worried, of course, that the plaster would bind Beauty and Beast together too long, but the doctor assures me that the heat of the monster's cock will have the opposite effect after a few minutes, loosening the plaster and allowing us to slide him free of that which he should never have invaded – and never will again. I have taken twice as long to write this letter as normally I might, for I am constantly listening out for the whistle (foolishly, for it will be audible along half the street) and as constantly tilting my head to stare at the ceiling in the direction of my darling's bedroom. If the whistle sounds soon, you will find my narrative interrupted by a blot of ink, for I shall have sprung to my feet and raced for the stairs. Ah, I thought for a moment that it had come then, but it was only the creak of a stair – my ears are supersensitised and the slightest noise makes me quiver and jump. I shall lay down my pen now, and complete the letter when the trap has been sprung and the fiend is tied and waiting for the police.

Later. No! No! No! I have sacrificed my darling's bottom for nothing, for the fiend is escaped, and I could swear, though my ears were still ringing from the force with which Dr Helsingvili had blown on her whistle, that I heard his laughter echoing beyond the swinging sun-shutters as I burst into Cali's room almost on the doctor's heels. What can have alerted the monster Dr Helsingvili is at a loss to say, but she believes he may have probed Cali's bottom with a finger first, and so discovered the presence of something out of the ordinary there. At that, one might have expected him to flee the scene, having realised that his atrocities were detected and a trap laid, but his audacity – his *courage*, I grudgingly concede – is, like his cunning, of no common order, and he paused to express his contempt for us in signal fashion. Brace yourself for what follows, my dear Mina – and Joanna too, for I know you will read this too, my darling, and that Cali is as dear to you as she is to Mina or me.

Well then: Dr Helsingvili heard a sudden uproar from the room, as of the monster trapped by the cock in Cali's bottom and struggling in his blind rage to free himself. She snatched up her whistle and blew, then raced to enter Cali's room and be the first to hurl herself on the fiend. Fast as she was, however, I was faster and, though I had the stairs to climb and a corridor to negotiate, the good doctor was in the room only two or three seconds before me. She tells me that if the gap had been greater she might have tried to shield me from the sight that awaited me, and she was already moving to snuff out the candle when I entered. Perhaps my saying that allows you to guess what the fiend had done. If so, I am sure your horror echoes mine across all those miles between Bucharest and London. Yes, on discovering that a trap had been laid beyond the portal of Cali's bottom, the fiend took one of the candles in the room and inserted it deep where we had hoped his cock would go instead. He then lit it, so that Dr Helsingvili's first sight on entering the room, and mine, of Cali naked and face down on the bed, bottom raised by a pillow beneath her hips, candle protruding thence and burning. The uproar was factitious, designed to spring the trap when the prey ran no danger of being caught in it, for the sun-shutters, as I have said, were still swinging from the speed with which he had thrown himself through them.

You may be sure that they are closed and locked now, sealing the room in darkness as Cali lies sleeping off her ordeal, gently drugged by one of Dr Helsingvili's herbal preparations. My own ordeal I prefer to endure awake, for I have a semi-mystical sense that I can bear myself the pain and humiliation Cali will otherwise have to suffer in her own person. My eyes, I freely confess, are still sowled and moist with the tears I shed as we manoeuvred the snuffed candle from Cali's bottom, and not the least of the pangs I suffered came when I heard her positively murmur with pleasure at the movement of the thick wax within her snug bottom-chamber. For a moment, such was my love for her even in such perversity, I was tempted to suggest to the doctor that we pleasure her a little with the candle before removing it, sweetening the bitter sting of her 'buggery' (this, the doctor tells me, is the technical term).

My pen trembles a little in my hand at what I am about to write now, but I will not shrink from it, for if the impulse exists in *me* that is further proof that no shadow of blame attaches to Cali for the pleasure she has experienced. Perhaps all of us dominants harbour this repulsive impulse: to penetrate the bottoms of our beloveds, for I confess that my mouth dries and nipples throb a little at the thought of pushing the candle deeper into its socket of bottom-flesh. Perhaps rotating it, pressing it first left then right, so that its hidden end, buried deep in the darkness of her bottom, swung first right then left, dinting that velvet rectal wall.

But I said nothing of this to the doctor, and believe, and hope, she guessed nothing of it as I assisted her to slide the candle free. I was concerned, of course, about the plaster-trap that plugged Cali's bottom still, but the doctor has assured me that it remains semi-liquid, not having been subject to the heat of the escaped fiend's cock, and will slide forth easily when next she moves her bowels. The doctor asked to be allowed to take the candle away for further examination, saying that her pocket-lens may discover hidden clues along its length, and it is on this examination that she is now engaged, I trust, in the room next to my sleeping beloved's. I mys–

Later. I predicted a blot if I had to break off the letter on hearing the doctor's whistle for the springing of the trap, but did not supply that blot. In the previous line you see that I have repaired the omission, for the doctor's whistle has sounded twice this night, and summoned me again to Cali's room but an hour past. I will have to be careful that the tears falling freely from my eyes do not add further blots to the page. From which you will guess that some fresh calamity has befallen us. Aye, it is so: a fresh calamity, and a worse one.

I wrote before, did I not, that I grudgingly conceded the fiend a courage and cunning of no common order. I must grudge again, and raise my estimation perhaps of both, certainly of the latter. Something whispers within me that I seek to evade my own responsibility in this – that by praise of my enemy I avoid blame of myself, but I cannot see that this is truly so. No one could have guessed the truth of the matter from what met our eyes as we entered Cali's room that first time: the victim deserted on the bed with bottom raised and candle burning, and those sun-shutters swinging beyond her. Dr Helsingvili, like I, leaped to the obvious conclusion, and leaped so easily that she, like I, almost forgot that she leaped. There perhaps, if anywhere, our fault may lie. We knew our opponent was cunning, and had just had further proof of it in the ease with which, to all appearances, he had evaded the trap we had laid for him. Nay, not merely evaded it, but mocked it even as he sprang it. Perhaps our chagrin at this contributed to the ease with which we accepted things at face value: the brutalised one deserted, candle-buggered on the bed; the brutaliser fled, having candle-buggered.

And there is a further consideration (yes, I know I am postponing the news I must give you, but you will understand when you have it): the speed with which he must have worked to achieve what he did. I have been in Cali's room pacing out distances, but even now I can scarce believe it. Dr Helsingvili tells me now the greater activity of his metabolism, accounting, *inter alia*, for the heat of his cock, grants him also greater strength and speed and allowed him to do on this occasion what he did. If you have not begun to guess, my dear Mina, my dear Joanna, do not be afraid to confess it, for it will reassure me in my own guilt. If you *have* begun to guess, or have guessed all, I congratulate you and heartily wish that you had been here instead of me, that your perspicacity might have shielded Cali from the worse harm that was to befall her at the hands – nay, at the *cock* – of the fiend. Yes, brace yourself, for here the news is now of our fresh and worse calamity. The news is – even now I can scarce bring myself to write it – that the fiend returned and had his way with her again. Or rather, he did *not* return and he did not have his way with her *again*, for he had not succeeded in having his way at all with her previously, save by proxy of the candle, and he had *not* in truth fled the scene. No, all the while the good doctor and I were removing the candle from Cali's bottom, *he lay hidden beneath her bed,* having created the uproar, leaped across the room to set the sun-shutters swinging, and then leaped back to dive under the bed in what must have been a positive blur of motion. Thereafter he had only to wait while the candle was removed, the victim comforted and dosed with the sleeping draught, the sun-shutters locked and bolted and the victim left to sleep off her ordeal. Then he emerged and set about his worst work of all.

My pen trembles in my fingers as I write, but your horrified love for Caliginia will decipher the words however illegible, I know. Yes, he had already trained her to accept sperm by mouth and bottom; now the third orifice beckoned. Dr Helsingvili has reconstructed the scene and it re-enacts against the darkness of my eyelids whenever I close my eyes. He lit a candle (the smoke of its final guttering is what brought Dr Helsingvili belatedly into the room) and laid Cali naked and innocently sleeping on the bed, thighs wide apart, to begin the preparatory work on her pussy. The doctor believes he worked at it first with his tongue, checking its state of arousal closely with the candle from time to time (there are splatters of wax on her thighs and in her pubic hair), before commencing work with his fingers, slowly inserting them to begin stretching her pussy-lips in preparation for the insertion of his cock. This stage would normally, the doctor suggests, have been extended over nights (though less to reduce the suffering of the victim than to prolong the pleasure of the fiend). Thanks to our interference, and to our belief that we could use Caliginia's body as a trap, he now had only minutes to prepare her for the trauma of cock-insertion in this last and most sacred of her orifices. 'And what of her maidenhead?' I hear you ask (with tears running, I need not be informed, down your horror-flushed cheeks). Well, it was stretched but not broken as the fiend slid his throbbing member into her, though I believe the pain and soreness are scarcely lessened by the care he apparently took to leave her *intacta sed violata*.

The doctor believes that she must have cried out at this stage, even in drugged sleep, but the fiend must have had a hand across her mouth, smothering her cries of pain as he inserted himself fully into her pussy and released the boiling torrent of his sperm. Alas that the insertion and the release of sperm could not have succeeded each other as narrowly as I have just written them, but the sowlness and soreness of Cali's pussy are such that the doctor reconstructs some minutes of thrusting and partial withdrawal, as the fiend gathered sufficient pleasure in his cock to cause his balls to overflow in tribute to the slickness and softness of Cali's sacred sheath. Not least of the horror that occurs to me in all this is that a cock exceeds a pussyhorn as much in its capacity for pleasure as in its size, but Dr Helsingvili has assured me that this cannot be so. If one imagined a pussyhorn expanded to such a size, surely there would be pleasure in such excess as to be painful in its insertion into an orifice as beautiful as Cali's mouth, or as tight as her bottom, or as slick and soft as her pussy. No, the head of his cock must be coarsened to endure such insertion, which conclusion is strengthened by the necessity for thrusting and friction before he could spill the loathsome load of his balls. Ugh, it makes me shiver with disgust to imagine them swinging between Cali's thighs from the root of his cock, though I shall say nothing of this to Cali for the time being, nor of the state in which we found her pussy. When the doctor's whistle summoned me (she had, as I said, smelled the guttering of the candle by which the fiend had guided his pussy-sucking, and been moved to investigate), I rushed up the stairs again and found the doctor stooped between Cali's thighs, splashing their pearly skin with her tears as she probed at the glistening lips of her pussy. Sperm was spilling from it plentifully, but I could smell that the doctor's fingers were releasing pussy-juice too.

I cannot believe that Cali had taken pleasure in her penetration, however, and it is apparent to me that this juicing is an involuntary reaction – perhaps an ancient defensive mechanism, to expel an intruder. That makes my chest tighten anew: to think of that poor, defenceless pussy leaking its futile juice in the face of the size and strength of its oppressor.

Dr Helsingvili reconstructed the fiend's cunning as she checked Caliginia's pussy for injury: telling me that it was apparent he had remained hidden under the bed and crept forth to complete his mockery of us when, in all innocence, we left Cali drugged and sun-shuttered to sleep off the candle-buggering. When she had completed her examination, the doctor wiped her fingers on the bedclothes and told me that my darling appeared to be have suffered no immediate injury but was surely in some danger from the sperm that now filled and overflowed from her pussy. The manner in which she spoke of this, and the determination that glinted in her eye, half-prepared me for what she said next: that she herself – holding herself responsible for what had happened – would have to suck out the sperm with her mouth, as the surest and most delicate means of simultaneously removing the sperm, soothing the pussy and provoking the cleansing production of further pussy-juice.

I objected at once, of course, laying claim to the blame and the task myself, and after a minute or two of argument the doctor had nodded sadly and moved aside for me to set to work. If your stomach rolls at the thought of it, do not, I beg you, contemplate the state of mine as I bent between my beloved's thighs and extended my tongue to begin. I will not describe the taste and texture of what I lapped up from that sacred chalice, but I steeled myself to swallow every drop with the thought that my darling had already done the same in more disgusting fashion yet: direct from the cock that spurted it. My sperm-sucking and swallowing was at second hand and, if there could be a choice in horrors, it must be best to drink sperm from the pussy of one's beloved, knowing that one benefits her thereby and makes amend for one's fault.

However it may be, I licked and lapped with a will, and soon had the overflow swallowed and was probing deeper for what remained within. There was (I will confess it here, but beg that it go no further) a strange pleasure in this, despite the foulness of the task on which I was engaged, for never before had my tongue passed between her pussy-lips so deep. A taboo was broken in service to my beloved, and I can but half-regret that this was so. Soon her pussy began to leak fresh juice and her accustomed scent filled my nostrils and mouth, gladdening my heart, for I knew that she was cleansing herself of the poison that had been squirted into her. When the scent reached the doctor's nostrils she clapped me on the back and urged me to greater efforts, and I willingly obliged. Little did I imagine when Cali first made herself mistress of my heart that I should perform such a service for her! When I finished I stood aside and let the doctor treat her with a mild saline douche, and I was pleased to see that the sowlness of her pussy-lips was greatly reduced, though the doctor reports that even now they are sore and tender to the touch.

I suspect that by now, however, your eyes are too blurred with tears to easily decipher what my fingers are too tremulous to clearly write, and I will close my letter here with all love and an unshakeable promise to supply further news of Cali's progress soon. Please, if you are able, hurry back to her and to us, for she has need of your loving comfort as I and the good doctor have need of your assistance in tracking down and extirpating once and for all the menace posed by the Count to all that is holy and pure. The doctor tells me that Joanna's personal knowledge of his methods may tip a balance that, I fear, is already tilting against us. I can hope that the consideration compensates her a little for the painful way in which she acquired this knowledge.

With my fondest love to you both,
Artemisia.

Joanna Harker's Journal.

21 September. I have lived ten years since last my feet touched the soil of my motherland, though it was but May that I left her borders. The marks of my suffering show on my face, I am sure, for though they are fading I see them for myself in the mirror and I read them reflected in the face of dear, dear Caliginia on our reunion. Alas that she may have read the reflection of *her* suffering in *my* face, for she too has passed through bright air and horror since our last meeting, and come within a cock's spurt – no, closer – of an ultimate abomination: impregnation by the Count. The thought that one so dear to me could have borne a child to that fiend fills my bowels with heat, and the thought that the child could have been in his own image (a *male*) redoubles it. But she is safe – in my relief, I will write it again: she is safe safe safe. Dr Helsingvili has examined her daily since her pussy was so nefandously penetrated, and inundated, by the Count's cock, and has staked her professional reputation in the presence of all of us that she is unimpregnated. For me, now that I have met the doctor and seen her wisdom and skill, that staking of professional reputation would more than suffice, but the doctor has also staked her love for Caliginia, against which, so she assures us, and I readily believe, her professional reputation is but a feather. So Caliginia's worst suffering is all ~~behind her~~ in her past, we may hope, and it is those of us who love her, and who blame ourselves (I too) for what she has endured, who prepare to endure suffering in the future. We must track down the fiend and uproot the menace he poses to all that is good and pure. Those words have been on Artemisia's lips since the night of our arrival, and ring more urgent with every repetition. Cali is safe from him now, but Dr Helsingvili is convinced that he will already be at work sperm-training some other victim or victims, whose wombs will in time be ready to receive his sperm.

But perhaps I had better place that in its correct place, in a transcription of the doctor's words on our reunion, when Mina and I arrived in Artemisia's house in Ploeşti. Tears of joy flowed freely, for three of us – Mina, Caliginia, and I – had been separated for many months, and it was a first meeting between Artemisia and me, and between Dr Helsingvili and the two of us (that is to say, me and Mina). I loved the doctor at first sight: a slim, petite woman in her early forties, her glossy black hair touched elegantly with grey, her face innocent of make-up and her tits firm and high despite her years (I longed to test, and several times since have had the satisfaction of testing, their resilience and weight in my own hands). Her accent (for she is a Georgian) made my pussy tingle with pleasure, but I did not, despite my immediate lust (which Mina shared, and shares), fail to mistake the authority and intelligence with which she spoke. Artemisia chose wisely in summoning this paragon to our aid, and it was an evil night for the Count when she enlisted in the ranks ranged against him. I truly believe that she could have *penetrated* his designs (I offend against modesty with deliberate irony) even without my help, though she assured me that my ear-witness account of his boasting was of the greatest help in her own researches, the fruits of which she unveiled to us after the first minutes of joyful reunion were over. For a moment, as she called us to order, I felt resentment glow within me; then I recalled that our joy was premature: there can be no true rejoicing, and no true happiness for any of us, until we know that the Count is banished for ever and can never again lay cock to an innocent woman's orifices. The doctor read all this in my face and smiled sadly.

'Ah, Madam Joanna,' she said. 'I see that you forgive me for raising the business of the Count very soon at the beginning of your so joyful homecoming. Yes, I wish that I must not do it, but how can it be otherwise? We must track him down – we must extirpate him – and every night, every hour, every moment is vital. Even now perhaps he is sliding that foul *membrum* of his into the innocent mouth or bottom – ah, Madam Caliginia, forgive me for raising the memory, but I must speak truth – into the innocent mouth or bottom of a sleeping girl. If we give him let and leave, he will be ready to flood another pussy with his sperm before the end of the month has come. But we cannot – we *will* not give him this! The face of the starry heavens would come bright in very horror should we so to do. So, therefore, what to do? First, we must discuss and dissect. We must know

234

this monster: every hair on his chest and thigh, every wrinkle of his sack of balls, every vein of his – I shudder, for I know what I speak of next, as you will shudder when I speak of it – every vein of his cock. Your help, Madam Joanna, have been of the most valuable. It was a shame of the greatest that you could not retrieve your journal yet from the Count's castle, but you have reconstructed it with skill and your letters of the past week have never left my side. I have pored over them; I have put them to heart and I have pickled the Count in a jar of my imaginings and examined him from all angle. Now, we must discuss my thoughts. You must say – you especially, Madam Joanna, but all of you – where you agree and, most important of all, where you disagree. We must decide on our course of action and follow it to the last letter. That is not so? Ah, good. Then, to proceed.

'It is all true, every word of it, what the Count boasted to you in his castle. He is a monster, it is true, but truer to say a *man*ster, for a man is what he is. A creature of fable in the very flesh, with that hair upon his body and no breasts and that cock of his between his hairy thighs. That cock of his which Madam Caliginia here knows only too well. Which he has inserted into her mouth and bottom, not to mention her pussy. Of which the spendings she has tasted. That is not so? Yes, it is so, and I could wish a thousand times a thousand that it is not so. But it is. And it is so even now for some other girl, or girls. Whom we must rescue. So, I have studied the Count. What know we of him? Of his purposes? Of for why he has travelled here, to the shores of the Black Sea, to Romania? Plainly, there is some evil he has to work here that he cannot work, or not work so well, as he can at home, in Transmarynia. Therefore what is it that calls him here? I suggest: prey. Prey in numbers he cannot dream of in his homeland. The greatest city in the world, Bucharest. Many millions of

235

young womans for him to work his way upon, with his foul, his retchable sperm-training. To raise up more like himself. More men. And in this way he means to re-establish the empire of which he spoke to Madam Joanna. But why, I ask, has he paused here, to have his way with Madam Caliginia? Why wait here, when Bucharest beckons? I suggest it is for arrogance' sake. He has learned of Madam Caliginia from Madam Joanna – no, please, I know you have not spoke of her to him, but consider, did you not write of her in your journal, at your departure from Romania? Yes, I thought it. And this is why he has paused here: he knew of Madam Caliginia from the journal of Madam Joanna, which he has read without her permissions, and it seem a great jest to him to pause a time here and work his way with her, to sperm-train her, to if possible impregnate her and leave her to bear his child before he went his way to Bucharest. You, Madam Joanna, you have defied him. Yes, is it not so? You have escaped from his castle! For the first time, a prisoner has fled his net! And in his anger, and his arrogance, he turns on your friend and your love, Madam Caliginia. In his anger, that he be defied; in his arrogance, that he knows your efforts against him will be unavailing. Yes, is it not so?

'But now, I think, he has gone on his way to Bucharest. There awaits him the academy, is it not? That for which you have travelled to Transmarynia, Madam Joanna. How go its terms? "For the underprivileged young womans of the lower classes", is it not so? With scholarships, overseen by the Count himself? Plainly, this is a part of his scheme, but I feel we will find no academy "up and running" when we enquire again in Bucharest, as we have enquired for some nights now. He does not feel safe to emerge from hiding, as yet, for he knows we will be at work against him. But consider: he has his agents here. Foolish womans, deluded by his wealth, for we know this of him also, that he be very rich. Look at how his castle in Transmarynia remains unviolable, though Madam Mina and Madam Joanna try for the very hardest to rouse the authorities there. He has bought influence there, and doubtless the fear of him runs very deep in that country. Here that fear is not, but his silver is, and the incredulity of the people. In Transmarynia, the people fear and speak not; here, the people fear not, and so we may speak not. Who could believe this tale we have to tell? That such a creature could be, in this nineteenth century? With his hair, and his cock, and his love for the sun and the day? We could speak, but we would not be believed. We gain at most laughter. I hear it now. And how I wish laughter were strong enough to send him whence he surely came: evil myth and ill fable.

'But though he be of myth, he is not mythical, and though he be fabled, he is not fabulous. He is real! And he, being real, explains our own taboo against *penetration*. Though centuries have passed since we received that cock of his in our tender orifices, we fear to receive it by instinct. Why else is "dildo" such an obscenity upon our lips? Why does it give so much of horror to all true gentlewomans? Our own instincts prove the truth of him, and the experiences for some of us here give the double proof. Have not Madam Caliginia felt his cock in her own body, and Madam Joanna the cocks of his suns? Have not I and Madam Artemisia seen the glistening slime of his sperm? Has not Madam Joanna with her own eyes seen and spoken to the milk-slaves of his castle? And to the milkmaids of the inn which she visited in Transmarynia? And not one of them at the tweth? Not one of them nursing or with child? This is something I know of his kind from my books: his ability to bring the milk in young womans before their time. It comes from a bite he delivers to their breast. This explains the garbled tale of the *vampire*, of which he is a kind, it is true, but not with the supernatural powers.

237

He has no power over the wind nor mist, nor the lower creatures, and no power to change his shape and pass through the solid walls. No, he is natural, though monstrous, and he is only like a vampire in that he drinks a fluid of the body, namely milk, and also that milk is vital for his existence, and also for his pleasure. You remember, Madam Joanna, the milk-slave to whom you conversed beneath his castle? The soreness of her breast, the bites thereupon? Yes, you remember. You remember how I asked you of it before you spoke of it. I knew it would be there. There is something in his bite that brings the milk to young breasts, for he feeds on milk. This is what keeps him strong, but he must have light too, monster that he be. But in his strength there is his weakness, thank the Goddess. This *glart* skin of his, that drinks the light like the plant, he cannot let darkness lie upon it for long. That is why he has that glass coffin of which Madam Joanna spoke. When sleep overcomes him he must lie there beneath the stars and moon, naked, and I think he must – argh, monster that he be – bathe in sun too, for his health. Is this not so? For has he not brought glass coffins with him to Romania, aboard the ship *Demeter*? Those tanks, for the private aquarium in Bucharest, of which the newspaper spoke. Which is a lie, though the newspaper knew it not, but close enough to the truth for us to see what is there. Yes, he has brought his glass coffins here, and so he has shown his weakness. These coffins of his must be placed beneath the sky, or they are useless to him. If we find them and smash them, I do not believe he can replace them. Else why did he not buy them in Romania, or have them made for himself with a glassmaker of Bucharest? No, they are of special glass, that has some special property for him, essential to his health. So there is our purpose, and our hope. To find his coffins and smash them, till he has only one left and must come to it to fall into our trap. Is it not so?'

We agreed, of course, for each step of her logic was secure, like the sections of a pipe carrying water downhill, picking up speed and force, till it bursts forth in the symmetrical spray of a fountain. Dr Helsingvili smiled and nodded at our murmurs of agreement and continued.

'Therefore this now is our problem: to find these coffins of his. How? Perhaps you are thinking that it will be easy, for they must be in the open air, beneath the heavens. But consider: he will not have them placed at the level of ground for any passer-by to stumble upon – smash! like so – but high up, on towers and roofs. And how will we, stumbling at the level of the ground, see them where they are? Eh? Ah, yes, Madam Rustavic, the answer, I see it in your eyes.'

She chuckled then, and nodded for Artemisia to take the floor, though it was apparent that the doctor could have solved the problem herself, and had already done so, long before she raised it.

'A balloon, Doctor,' Artemisia said. 'By day, when the city sleeps, we can scan the city from above, and the glass coffins will betray themselves with flashes of reflected sunlight.'

The doctor nodded.

'Yes, yes, it is so. With his own symbol of his power he will be betrayed.'

Mina now asked where we could obtain a balloon at such short notice, and the doctor nodded again towards Artemisia.

'I can have one waiting for us on our arrival,' Artemisia said. 'From AO stores. Artillery observation,' she added. 'And,' she went on, as the doctor made as though to speak, 'I will be careful to go through unofficial channels. We will keep everything off the record.'

The doctor nodded with satisfaction.

'A wise thought, Madam Artemisia. Very wise. There

239

are greatly shining forces against us, but with precaution of the sufficient, we shall overcome them, is it not so?'

Artemisia then wanted to discuss who would go aloft and how they should signal to the ground, but the doctor persuaded her to wait until we reached Bucharest. It was then, her round face breaking into a beam like a child's conjurer reaching the climax of her trick, that she reached into a pocket of her dress and drew out a fan of tickets.

'But that will not, my dear Madam Artemisia,' she said, 'be delayed for very long.'

She handed the tickets out one by one, and I saw that they were dated for that very morning, though when we compared tickets we discovered that we would all be sitting apart, in separate carriages.

'A wise thought of my own,' the doctor said. 'We do not travel as a party, for that may attract attention, of which we want to attract nothing. He perhaps has his spies at the station here and also there. But they will be watching for four womans, or perhaps three, as a party, is it not so? Therefore we travel individually, and arrive individually, and his spies see nothing.'

I burst out in congratulation of yet another example of her foresight, and found that Mina had chosen the same moment and almost the same words to express her own congratulation, which made us all laugh and sent us happily to our packing for the journey to Bucharest. Artemisia made a swift visit to the local telegraph office to wire the friend of hers who would arrange the balloon.

Soon two of us will hang above Bucharest in it, waiting for the flashes of sunlight that signal the presence of his coffins. The task would be impossible in a city populated by *his* kind, for glass would be naked to the open sky everywhere; but not in our cities, where, like all wholesome creatures, we hide sedulously from the sun.

Joanna Harker's Journal.

22 September. Late morning. I write this half-an-hour before Mina and I go aloft in the balloon to begin the first stage of the search. The five of us argued for some time about how the search would be conducted, but it was decided that no signals should be flashed to the ground, in case unfriendly eyes caught them. Instead, one of the women in the balloon will scan the ground through a sun-adapted telescope, calling out any sighting to the other, who will note them on a map of the city. Artemisia was the obvious choice to go aloft first, but the doctor pointed out that she was an even more obvious choice to remain on the ground with the winching gear, in case official notice were taken of our search. Her authoritative bearing and familiarity with the jargon of police and military would be best to obviate suspicion, and her friend who supplied the balloon will be with her in uniform. They have a plausible tale prepared, but we are all praying that the search will go entirely unremarked and the tale go unused. We ascend at one in the afternoon, when the city should be in its deepest sleep, and even those few who are on the streets are scarcely likely to be scanning the sun-blasted heavens. I am to take first turn at the telescope, and Mina at the note-taking. Now that a chance has finally come to strike back at the Count I am filled with an exhilaration that matches, or rather say surpasses, the exhilaration I felt on beginning my escape from his castle. The escape, though, was a blow of *his* evaded, not a blow of *ours* struck, as this search from the sky will be. I seem to hear the tinkle of smashed glass already – it makes strange music in my ears, and I hope this proves a good omen. Ah, I hear the wheels of the cab that is to carry us to the park where the balloon will be inflated. I have already seen it uninflated and might have doubted that such a heavy roll of cloth could take to the air in the fifteen minutes Artemisia promises; but she connected the gas bottle and twisted the tap on for a few moments, and the balloon began to expand fast enough. Caliginia's scream cut the experiment shorter than Artemisia had intended, for she said the swelling sausage of cloth brought back unhappy memories, but she could laugh about it a minute later, and I am inclined to read that as a good omen too. If we are to turn the sun against him, why not a cock-symbol too?

Mina has just knocked. The time has come.

Glossary

Ban (plural *bani*): (Romanian) n. an everyday unit of Romanian currency, equalling one hundredth of a *leu* (plural *lei*).

Butchwife (pronounced *'butch-uff*): n. the dominant partner in a lesbian marriage. Cf. femwife.

Circumcingulum: n. a metal band around the waist of a menstruating woman designed to catch stray blood when she is inverted for a diner to drink menstrual blood from her vulva.

Chelce: adj. pink, esp. as applied to the cunt.

Coléoptères frits au beurre de lait Parisienne: n. beetles fried in butter made from the milk of Parisians.

Dolomètre/dolometer: n. an instrument for measuring units of pain.

Femwife (pronounced *'fem-uff*): n. the submissive partner in a lesbian marriage. Cf. butchwife.

Fortday: n. fortnight, period of fourteen days.

Glart: adj. greens and blues.

Glartbottle: n. the bluebottle fly, *Calliphora vomitoria*.

Glarthouse (pronounced *glart-house*): n. a greenhouse.

Menopote: n. a drinker of menstrual blood.

Muscă: (Romanian) n. insect of the class *Diptera*; fly.

Pussyhorn: n. the clitoris.

Sanguicunnilinctus: n. the drinking of menstrual blood from the vulva.

Sowl: (rhyming with 'howl') 1. adj. yellows and light reds. 2. vb. to make sowl.

Sowlhead: 1. n. a woman with red hair. 2. *–ed* adj. redheaded.

Treadle: n. a lever worked with the foot.

Twaughter: n. (tw(in)+(d)aughter) a daughter born by parthenogenesis as an identical clone of her mother. In the Europe of *Vamp*'s universe, women give birth to their twaughters at the tweth (qv).

Twenfer: n. a period of twenty-four hours.

Tweth (also tweth-year): n. 1. the twenty-fourth year of life, during which twenty-three-year-old women in *Vamp*'s universe give birth to their twaughters (qv). 2. a period of twenty-three years.

Twinster: n. a twin sister.

Vace: adj. browns and dark reds.

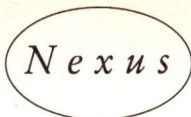

Nexus

NEXUS BACKLIST

This information is correct at time of printing. For up-to-date information, please visit our website at www.nexus-books.co.uk

All books are priced at £5.99 unless another price is given.

Nexus books with a contemporary setting

ACCIDENTS WILL HAPPEN	Lucy Golden ISBN 0 352 33596 3	☐
ANGEL	Lindsay Gordon ISBN 0 352 33590 4	☐
BARE BEHIND £6.99	Penny Birch ISBN 0 352 33721 4	☐
BEAST	Wendy Swanscombe ISBN 0 352 33649 8	☐
THE BLACK FLAME	Lisette Ashton ISBN 0 352 33668 4	☐
BROUGHT TO HEEL	Arabella Knight ISBN 0 352 33508 4	☐
CAGED!	Yolanda Celbridge ISBN 0 352 33650 1	☐
CANDY IN CAPTIVITY	Arabella Knight ISBN 0 352 33495 9	☐
CAPTIVES OF THE PRIVATE HOUSE	Esme Ombreux ISBN 0 352 33619 6	☐
CHERI CHASTISED £6.99	Yolanda Celbridge ISBN 0 352 33707 9	☐
DANCE OF SUBMISSION	Lisette Ashton ISBN 0 352 33450 9	☐
DIRTY LAUNDRY £6.99	Penny Birch ISBN 0 352 33680 3	☐
DISCIPLINED SKIN	Wendy Swanscombe ISBN 0 352 33541 6	☐

------- ✂ ----------------------------------

Please send me the books I have ticked above.

Name ....

Address ....

....

....

.... Post code...................

Send to: **Cash Sales, Nexus Books, Thames Wharf Studios, Rainville Road, London W6 9HA**

US customers: for prices and details of how to order books for delivery by mail, call 1-800-343-4499.

Please enclose a cheque or postal order, made payable to **Nexus Books Ltd**, to the value of the books you have ordered plus postage and packing costs as follows:

UK and BFPO – £1.00 for the first book, 50p for each subsequent book.

Overseas (including Republic of Ireland) – £2.00 for the first book, £1.00 for each subsequent book.

If you would prefer to pay by VISA, ACCESS/MASTERCARD, AMEX, DINERS CLUB or SWITCH, please write your card number and expiry date here:

....

Please allow up to 28 days for delivery.

Signature ....

Our privacy policy

We will not disclose information you supply us to any other parties. We will not disclose any information which identifies you personally to any person without your express consent.

From time to time we may send out information about Nexus books and special offers. Please tick here if you do *not* wish to receive Nexus information.   ☐

------- ✂ ----------------------------------

FOLIO POLICIER